PRINCE OF CONTROL

A Bratva Arranged Marriage Romance

BRATVA HEIRS

RENEE ROSE

 Formatted with Vellum

WANT FREE RENEE ROSE BOOKS?

Go to http://subscribepage.com/alphastemp to sign up for Renee Rose's newsletter and receive a free copy of *Alpha's Temptation, Theirs to Protect, Owned by the Marine, Theirs to Punish, The Alpha's Punishment, Disobedience at the Dressmaker's* and *Her Billionaire Boss*. In addition to the free stories, you will also get bonus epilogues, special pricing, exclusive previews and news of new releases.

FAMILY CONNECTIONS

Author's Note:

Bratva Heirs features the now adult children of the Chicago Bratva series. You do not have to read that series to enjoy this one. If you have read the Chicago Bratva series, please do not try to do the math on any of the ages for anyone featured in this series. Liberties were taken. Think of it as soap opera aging. :-)

For fans of my Chicago Bratva series, this map shows the family connections between the Bratva Heirs and the Chicago Bratva characters. Readers new to my bratva men, you can skip this section. I didn't want to bore or confuse you with too much info-dumping in the book, so I made this section instead.

The Bratva Heirs

Ben "Baron" Baranov - Son of Lucy and Ravil (*The Director*)

Liliya "Lili" Baranov - Daughter of Lucy and Ravil (*The Director*)

Lennox Taylor - Son of Oleg and Story (*The Enforcer*)

Jude Taylor - Son of Oleg and Story (*The Enforcer*)

Tuesday Taylor - Daughter of Oleg and Story (*The Enforcer*)

Leonid "Leo" Popov - Son of Maxim and Sasha (*The Fixer*)

Mila - Daughter of Pavel and Kayla (*The Soldier*)

Zoya "Zoe" Novikova - Daughter of Dima and Natasha (*The Hacker*)

Anya Novikova - Daughter of Dima and Natasha (*The Hacker*)

Lara Turgeneva - Daughter of Adrian and Kat (*The Cleaner*)

Darya Taylor - Daughter of Flynn and Nadia (*The Player*)

Rustik Taylor - Son of Flynn and Nadia (*The Player*)

Alexei "Alex" Petrov - Son of Kira and Maykl (*The Gatekeeper*)

Feliks Petrov - Son of Kira Koslova and Maykl (*The Gatekeeper*)

PROLOGUE

Author's note: This first chapter was originally written as a bonus epilogue to the Chicago Bratva series for my Kickstarter supporters, but I realized it was too important to the Bratva Heirs to leave out, so I'm including it here. This will be the only section in Ravil's point of view in this book.

Ravil Baranov

My eyes burn as my wife, Lucy, and I walk out of Thornecroft University's freshman dorm.

"Our nest is officially empty." I squeeze her hand.

Ben, our oldest, is a senior at Thornecroft, and we just helped our youngest child, Liliya–Lili, for short–move in. I hung her bulletin boards and lifted furniture to place her rug where she wanted it, and then there was nothing else to do but leave. Our presence in the one-room dorm was no longer helpful. Lili couldn't get to know her new roommate with the two of us hovering.

Still, leaving my precious daughter here sends a pang through my heart. It's an unexpected emotion. I didn't have it with Ben, but he's always seemed older than his years. Lili is my well-protected *printsessa*. Our baby.

But Thornecroft, known as the "Harvard of the Midwest," is the safest university in the world. Tucked in the outskirts of Whisper, Illinois, the rich, elite, and, like me, most dangerous people of the world have sent their offspring to study here for over two hundred years. Senators' sons, ambassadors' daughters, and the world's royalty sit in classes with the children of uber-rich movie stars, cartel leaders, and mafia.

Security is tight, and Chancellor Ogden, a dangerous man in his own right, somehow manages to keep wars, assassinations, or paparazzi from penetrating the bubble of safety he keeps around the campus. There are rumors that he's part of a dangerous cabal that runs the world. There are rumors he is former CIA. It's possible both stories have some truth built in.

Lucy drags in a long, terraced breath like she's holding back her tears, and I turn to wrap my arms around her. We stop in the middle of the sidewalk, creating an obstacle for the parents and students pushing carts filled with dorm decor from their cars to the freshman dorm buildings.

I kiss the top of my wife's head.

There's a hollowness in being empty nesters I didn't expect. I thought today would be more of a celebration. A finish line. We raised two bright, capable children into adulthood and now have time to focus on our reconnection. But it feels like an appendage is missing.

"I'll miss her so much," Lucy chokes.

"I know. Me too." I slide my arm around her waist to guide her to our Lucid Gravity SUV. "We will say goodbye to Ben, and then I'm stealing you away for a spa weekend."

Lucy looks over, her brown eyes bright with tears but her expression warm and soft. "You are?"

I stop again to cradle her cheek with my hand. "Yes, *koty-onok*. I thought we might need a place to find each other before we get back to Chicago."

"That sounds perfect." Lucy's voice is still clogged with tears. It makes me want to draw a sword and slay every monster around my wife. But of course, there are no monsters to slay.

This is exactly how it should be. Children grow up and move out. Their adult lives are just beginning as we face middle age. It's not like our lives will be dull without the kids at home.

I'm *pakhan* of a bratva dynasty that now spans two continents. Lucy pulls the strings of our political empire—managing the campaigns of our handpicked state senators, governor, and representatives. Because when you're head of an underworld dynasty, it helps to have friends in high places.

We pull around to Baranov House, a sprawling Victorian on the outskirts of campus. Yes, it's named after me. Ben asked me to donate five million to the school to buy it just to have a fortress even more secure than the dorms where he could protect his friends. Most young men rush a fraternity or seek entrance to one of the elite Thornecroft Society Houses. Mine saw a way to create his own. He came to me with a proposal in the middle of his freshman year, explaining why having his own Thornecroft House, which would join the invitation-only society houses on campus, as a haven for those under his protection was important.

Thornecroft has fraternities and sororities, but what the school is really known for is their society houses. These houses used to be single-sex, but now some are coed. They're very exclusive and selective invite-only societies that go beyond frats. These societies aren't just about brotherhoods and building connections. Thornecroft's society houses are about culminating the type of power and influence that decides elections around the world.

Ben promised to repay me every penny of the donation.

I told him it wasn't necessary—that I expected him to enjoy his college experience with his friends. That I didn't care if they turned the place into an "Animal House," like the old American movie.

Instead, they impressed me by turning it into an enterprise. Inside Baranov House, or what the students on campus call *the Gulag*, for reasons I probably don't want to know, Ben and his band of brothers—*and* sisters, since times and gender roles have changed—run a variety of legal and illegal money-making activities. They wire me a payment every month, as if they were one of my bratva cells.

I tried to keep Ben out of the bratva business, but despite it all, he molded himself exactly in my image. He essentially created his own bratva, though they don't call themselves that.

I double-park behind Ben's Range Rover in the driveway, and we get out and walk to the door. The house is a four-story, 20-bedroom behemoth, with wide-open common areas Ben and his crew convert into a dance floor and party space on weekends.

I'd insisted on an alarm system and bullet-proof windows when they bought it, but it looks like they've added new security measures since I was last here. Thumbprint-activated door locks. Cameras hang from every eave, probably some I also can't spot, viewing and recording every inch of the property.

I press the buzzer because the security is too tight to allow walk-ins. Inside, young men and a few young women lounge on couches, easy chairs, and barstools. In the past, Ben's given me the rundown on all the residents. Their varied skills are impressive.

Anders, Ben's best friend, an Asian-Norwegian who plays social director for the house and front man for most of their activities, opens the door.

"Hei Hei!" he calls out in his country's greeting. "Baron is right here."

Baron is Ben's nickname, short for Baranov, and fitting for bratva royalty. My understanding is that Phoenix, Ben's roommate freshman year, gave him the nickname.

Ben turns from where he's giving instructions to Zoya—who goes by the Americanized Zoe—one of my hacker's auburn-haired twins. She and her sister are sophomores this year. Both of them started in freshman dorms like Lili to make friends but ended up moving into Baranov House within the first month at Ben's urging. He compulsively needs to protect his family, and it seems bratva ties are thicker than blood, even for the next generation.

"I'm on it," she says to Ben and waves to us with a smile. Her twin, Anya, sits on the couch with a laptop on her thighs. Her repose reminds me of the way her father, Dima, used to lounge in my penthouse, his fingers clicking away on the keys as he hacked some governmental agency while watching an action flick with his brother. Our kids grew up together, along with my fixer's son, Leo, and my gatekeeper's sons, Alexei and Feliks, who are just sixteen months apart and both built like refrigerators. They now play football for Thornecroft University and will probably be picked up by the NFL.

The rest of our friends from our original bratva cell live in Los Angeles now. Dima's twin, Nicholai, moved there because his wife is the public relations manager for the Grammy-winning band The Storytellers, who are friends of ours. He and my former enforcer and soldier run a legitimate real estate empire for me in Hollywood. Their children grew up in the limelight of fame and fortune through The Storytellers.

My former soldier Pavel's wife and 19-year-old daughter, Mila, are both famous actors now.

Anya and Zoe both come over to hug and kiss us.

The entire crew of our older children stayed in Whisper this summer to continue running their enterprises.

"Hey Ravil—hey Lucy." Leo flashes me a grin as he walks over and hugs Lucy. He's eighteen months younger than Ben, but the two are just as close in college as they were growing up.

I shake his hand.

"Are you guys taking off?" Ben asks. We had dinner with the entire gang last night, so we've already had time to visit him on this trip.

Lucy goes in for a hug from Ben, and he wraps her up in his arms. He's taller than I am now, broad-shouldered with sandy blond hair and Lucy's brown eyes. He kisses the top of her head, much like I do, and my chest tightens with pride.

I regret the seriousness of his gaze—the way his eyes look far older than his years. The watchful, controlled way he carries himself, ever-vigilant for anything in his world slipping out of his control.

It's my fault. I tried to keep my family sheltered from the violence of my profession, but it still seeped through. Ben got blood on his hands at a young age under dire circumstances.

In order to control his world and avoid another incident, he became a leader. He learned to always know where people are coming from. To consider all angles to protect those around him.

I shake his hand, then pull him in for a man hug. "Watch out for your sister." I thump him on the back, but there's gravity in my voice.

Ben matches my tone. "I will." His gaze is intense and serious. "I wish she would move in here."

"I know, but she wants her freedom. I checked her dorm, and the security is tight. She'll be okay if she stays vigilant."

"I have her schedule, so I know where she is at all times and where the potential threats might be." Ben glances at Anders. "I already took care of the one professor on campus known for preying on female students."

I flick my eyebrows. This is the first I've heard of it. I suppress the sense of alarm that I should've known what happened and advised him on his course of action. I taught him a lot, but he may not know how to avoid all legal repercussions. Or where to dump a body in Whisper.

But he probably didn't handle it that way. He can handle business on his own, in his own way. As much as I want to swoop in and help, I have to let him fly.

Still, I can't help but remind him, "You know if you ever need help with *anything at all*, I can send someone out here or come myself. All it takes is one call." I can't say in front of Lucy what I mean—that I'll send a fixer. Or an enforcer. A cleaner. Whatever he needs.

"I know." Ben's voice carries the authority of a leader. I see the weight of responsibility for his entire crew—everyone who lives in that house with him—and possibly the entire campus resting on his broad shoulders.

I know the event that made him this way. It haunts me as much as it still haunts him.

But he wears the mantle like a king. He has the strength and fortitude to hold up the leaden crown that rests on his head.

The young prince is all grown up.

My phone buzzes with an incoming text, and I glance at the screen. It's my Moscow *Pakhan* Adrian Tergenov, with our code for an emergency.

"Excuse me," I say to Lucy and Ben. "I need to make a call." I walk through the house and out the French doors to the enormous, landscaped garden the Baranov House uses for its frequent campus parties.

I hit the call button for Adrian.

At one time, he was my best cleaner. Eighteen years ago, I sent him and his wife Kat to Moscow to take over and run our arm of the bratva there.

"What is it?"

"I have a problem. A big problem." I hear tightly coiled violence in Adrian's voice that I haven't heard since the years when he came to me to seek help in finding his sister and the sex traffickers who had kidnapped her.

"Tell me."

"It's about Lara."

I go still. Lara is Adrian and Kat's only child, who goes to college in Paris.

Business is business, but anything involving our children is a grave matter. We violated bratva code when we took wives and had children. I did it first and allowed the rest of my cell to follow. The reason marriage is outside of the bratva code is because women and children can be used as pawns against us.

That's why I doubled down on building an empire and gaining influence. Everything I've done has been to keep our families protected.

"Anatoli Rostov's son, Abrasha, is after her. Now he's calling me, asking for an alliance in marriage."

Anatoli Rostov is one of the richest and most dangerous members of the Russian oligarchy. He has homes in Turkey, the Arab Emirates, and the French Riviera. He controls much of the political world in Russia. Ben had a run-in with his son the year he went to boarding school in Switzerland.

We've had to battle to accumulate enough power to remain separate from Rostov's dirty dealings. To build our empire without infringing on his. I had to prove we had enough power–both political and guns–that we weren't worth messing with.

I thought we had managed to surpass them in terms of power held in Russia, but if Rostov is trying to flip Adrian, we have trouble on our hands.

Rostov is known for sadistic torture and gruesome murders. He uses fear to gain power. Ben reported that his son was a full-fledged psychopath.

"Has he kidnapped her? Is he holding her as leverage?"

"No. It seems they've had a few dates. When I asked Lara about Abrasha, she sounded indifferent. But according to Rostov, they're already a couple. He's looking to unite our houses in marriage."

I clench my molars. "What did you tell him?"

"I told him I could not because my daughter had a long-arranged marriage to your son."

I go quiet, absorbing this.

"It was the only thing I could think of to keep her free of his clutches. He won't pick a fight with you, especially not if it's a marriage arranged from birth."

I turn to look back through the French doors, where my son still stands with his mother. Ben sees me looking and takes it as a summons. He nods and walks toward the doors.

Blyad'. He would do it. Ben has the same protective instincts I do. He shelters the weak and vulnerable. It's the reason Thornecroft was the only college I felt comfortable sending Lili to. I know he'll keep tabs on her and eliminate any dangers.

If I asked him, he would go along with the lie Adrian told, marrying Lara to keep her safe.

But it would end his chosen life. He's already far older than his years. Do I really want him married at age twenty-two?

Then again, it could be a marriage in name only. He could

still have his own life, as long as he keeps Lara safe here at this house and pretends she's his wife.

Lucy will kill me, though. She never wanted her children wrapped up in the business. Then again, she wouldn't want to see Kat and Adrian's daughter trapped in a marriage to the man who tortured everyone weaker than him as a boy.

My mind spins. It might not be forever. Five years, maybe, until Rostov forgets about using Lara as a pawn in his game.

I blow out my breath. "Put her on the next plane to Whisper."

Adrian's exhale of relief is audible through the phone. "*Spasiba, Pakhan.* You honor me."

"You're my brother. I would never let harm come to one of yours."

I end the call and put the phone in my pocket, staring at the manicured hedges as if they might reveal the perfect way to tell my son that I just locked up what could be the rest of his life.

The French doors open, and Ben walks out. "Did you need something?"

"Yes." I scrub a hand over my face. "Ben, there's something I have to ask of you."

CHAPTER ONE

Three days later

Baron

I'm not a man of "big feels," but I always thought I'd feel *something* on my wedding day.

I also imagined I would actually know the woman I was marrying. And be out of college already.

I'm in my Range Rover on the tarmac of the private airfield, tapping my fingers on the wheel as I wait for the jet to arrive with my bride.

The woman my father told me three days ago I could protect by putting a ring on her finger.

Lara Turgeneva has no social media for me to troll. Probably because she's a bratva princess and, like the rest of us, was taught to keep a low profile.

I had Anya scour the internet, but she came up dry until she hacked the Russian government to uncover a passport and driver's license photo. It's hard to tell much from them. She might be pretty; she might not.

No one looks good in those pictures.

Supposedly, we knew each other as toddlers before her family moved from Chicago back to Moscow. I remember nothing. I wish I knew something about her. She's probably scared. I don't have any plans to get into a genuine romantic relationship with her, but I'll do my best to make things comfortable. This is awkward for both of us. I'll make sure she understands that I don't expect her to consummate the marriage or share my bed.

She can even date whomever she likes, if she's careful and keeps it a secret.

The roar of jet engines makes me peer up through the windshield. A small jet glides in and makes an elegant touchdown. I wait until they've opened the door and attached the gangplank before I climb out of the Range Rover.

I wore a suit. Not to impress my bride but as a show of good faith. To show her I don't want this, but I will make it work. I will follow my father's instructions: pick her up, marry her, and install her in Baranov House, where I can protect her. Except we can't get married until twenty-four hours after we've picked up the marriage license.

I'm not doing it because my father asked it of me although I would've done it for him. While I'm certain he's a ruthless killer, and I know he's the head of an international crime organization, he commands nothing but my love and respect.

Like I said, I would've done this without his request. When I heard who was trying to marry Lara and why she needed my protection, I couldn't refuse.

Brash Rostov is a psychopath. I went to prep school in Switzerland with him for one miserable year. He's the son of the notorious Russian oligarch, Anatoli Rostov. If he were simply arrogant and full of himself like the rest of the rich assholes I had to suffer space with that year, I'd leave Lara to her chances with him. But there's no one—not even a woman I don't remember—that I'd let marry that sadistic beast when all I had to do to save her was give her my name.

I got thrown out of that school because I beat the shit out of Brash.

He is everything that is wicked and wrong about the Russian oligarchy—a hateful sadist who I heard had tortured teachers, animals, and younger boys.

The girls found him charming, as I recall, because he was good at hiding that side of himself with them. But I caught him choking the librarian's daughter, and that was the end of private prep school for me.

If I'd known getting kicked out would be so easy, I would've picked a fight with him sooner. I hated living with those arrogant old-moneyed *svolochs* although that year prepared me for success at Thornecroft.

If Brash and his father are after Lara, I'm happy to step in and be the roadblock he can't get around. As far as Brash knows, Lara's dad promised her hand to me at birth, and he couldn't get out of the arrangement without risking a war with mine.

I approach the stairs as a slender figure appears in the doorway.

Lara wears black loungewear, like she's mourning our upcoming nuptials. She piled her dark hair on top of her head in a messy bun. A large purse is slung over one shoulder, and when her gaze lands on me, her arm tightens down on it, like she's scared I'll steal it.

I puzzle over that gesture as we approach each other.

She carries herself with authority, shoulders square, chin lifted. Good. She's not some frightened mouse I'll have to comfort. The less emotionally involved we become, the better. That will make it easier to divorce when the marriage is no longer necessary.

As she draws closer, I can study her face. She's gorgeous. Dark, messy hair that's thick and wild. Her skin is pale, her wide-set eyes bright blue. A dusting of dark freckles covers her nose. She wears little or no makeup–her beauty is natural. She studies me back from under thick, natural lashes. Her lips are full, but they're set in a tight line like she's pissed.

That's when I start to teeter off my white steed. I was thinking of myself as the knight in shining armor–here to save the damsel in distress.

But the damsel looks like she wants to throat-punch me.

I stop approaching and let her come to me. I'd planned on a cheek kiss. Maybe a quick embrace if she's a hugger. Since she looks more like a crotch-kicker, I abort any plans of touching her.

"Lara."

There's something familiar about her, even though I have no memories of her from childhood. We were just preschoolers when she moved away.

Her big blue eyes narrow, and she stops in front of me, still keeping that purse of hers held tightly to her side. "*Da.*" Her tone is cutting. She lifts her chin, spreading her free hand and gesturing down her body. "Here I am–as summoned by your family to be your wife," she says in Russian. "I hope I'm what you expected."

I blink, careful to keep my expression blank as my brain scrambles to catch up.

Then I put it together. *She was told the lie.*

For whatever reason, her father didn't trust her with the truth. Either he doesn't think she's capable of playing pretend, or she was actually in love with Brash.

If it's the latter, I'm out. She can have him. I don't need to suffer the disdain of a woman who thinks my family would control her future like she's chattel.

Except even as I think of throwing her back to him, something in me rebels. Not just my protective side although I still would defend her against any man who tried to hurt her. Not just the most competitive part of me that needs to win any contest against Brash. Beyond that, a possessiveness rises up in me that I've never felt before.

As I look at the fiery woman glaring at me, I abandon my previous plan to keep this marriage a sham. She belongs to me. We belong together. I'm not sure why I believe that, but it's something about the way she seems familiar. But not like I knew her before—more like I've been waiting my whole life to meet her. I'm turned on by everything about her. Not the least, that she presents a challenge.

The fact is, Lara is mine.

She was fake-promised to me, but we'll be legally wed, and that means I'm the guy—the *only* guy—who gets to have her.

Is she what I expected? I reply in English, my tone dry. "Not really."

Her pale skin flushes pink. At least I know she speaks English.

I hold out my hand. "Come. We have a marriage license to pick up."

———

Lara

Benjamin Baranov doesn't look as menacing as my father and most of his associates, but I get the feeling he's deceptively dangerous. Blond hair falls across his forehead in a casual, beachy style, but his eyes, framed by thick, dark brows, appear ancient in his young face.

Dressed in an expensive suit, he doesn't look like a college student playing dress-up. He wears it with casual elegance. There's no outward aggression in his posture, just quiet power in the carriage of his shoulders. Like he rules his kingdom with control and cool, calculated decisions.

I clutch my purse closer to me as the flight attendants follow us to Benjamin's shiny black SUV with the five giant suitcases that contain all the belongings I could pack in the hour my father gave me before bundling me into the private jet.

Just yesterday, I'd come home, exhausted from a day of classes at Académie Internationale des Langues de Paris followed by a three-hour shift for my new internship. The one I spent the first two years of college setting myself up to get. I opened the door to find my father sitting at my kitchen table with a deep frown between his brows.

He hadn't told me he'd left Moscow to fly to Paris. When I asked if he brought my mom, he said she was too angry with him.

Stupid me.

I'd thought he'd come to tell me they were getting a divorce.

Never in a million years could I have predicted this.

"Pack your things, Lara. I'm sending you to Illinois."

I blink. My brain stops computing. "What?"

He nods with a grave look. "There's something I should have told you a long, long time ago."

My heart slams against my ribs wildly. "What do you mean? What are you talking about?"

"I entered a contract with Ravil Baranov when you were a baby ."

I stare at him. None of this makes sense. Ravil Baranov is the powerful pakhan of the Chicago Bratva, where my father entered into the brotherhood. They are close associates. Friends.

"You're to marry his son, Benjamin."

I sway on my feet, suddenly light-headed. "That...that's absurd."

"It was a long time ago, and I didn't know he intended to hold me to it. Certainly not so soon, while you both are still in school."

I back away from my dad. "No." My head shakes on its own

accord. *"I won't. I can't. I just started my internship. I have one more year of school. This is crazy. Why would I marry a stranger?"*

"It has to be now. Ravil demanded it, and he's far too dangerous a man to cross."

"But...why?"

It just doesn't make sense. We don't live in medieval times. The patriarchy is dying. I shouldn't be chattel in some bratva machination.

"I don't know why now, only that he has his reasons. I've made arrangements for you to transfer to Thornecroft where Benjamin attends school, so you can finish your degree. It's one of the most prestigious colleges in the world."

My nose burns. Angry tears flood my eyes. This is insane!

"And if I refuse?" My voice trembles even though I try to keep the words even.

My dad's expression turns even more grim. "Then none of us are safe."

How can that be? My father, one of the most powerful men in Russia, can't keep his wife and daughter safe from the bratva on another continent?

This is worse than my parents divorcing. This is my entire world crumbling to my feet.

No wonder my mom is mad at him.

A tear slides down my face, and I see a flicker of distress on my dad's face.

He reaches for me, but I pull away.

"I'm sorry, but marrying Benjamin Baranov is the only way to keep you safe."

Safe from what?

I have no idea what the Baranovs or the Chicago Bratva want with me. I still can't believe my father sent me here—

alone. I could be walking into a trap. Maybe they intend to hold me hostage to make Papa do what they say.

Maybe it *is* for marriage, and I'll be a hostage for the rest of my life. After all, marriage is one of the oldest methods of ensuring an alliance with other kingdoms.

I steal a glance at the bratva prince walking beside me. Will he expect me to share a bed? Consummate this marriage? Bear his heirs?

My stomach, which has been in a tight knot since I found my father in my flat, feels queasy.

Benjamin takes my luggage from the attendants, easily handing the heavy bulk into the trunk of his vehicle. I catch sight of tattoos marking the backs of his hands and wrists. So he's part of it all. I wondered, because he's in college, if he was already a member of the brotherhood.

Of course, he is.

I wish I'd learned the meanings of the tattoos. Has my groom killed before? Tortured?

My mouth goes dry. *Raped?*

Will he force himself on me?

My palms emit cold sweat. These people are so dangerous that they struck fear into *my father—*and he's a monster in his own right. He wouldn't have uprooted me from college in Paris unless he absolutely had no other choice. My mom wouldn't have let him. The decision had to be completely out of his control.

Benjamin escorts me to the passenger side of the SUV and opens the door.

Oh good. It's nice to know that the killer I was promised to has nice manners.

He waits until I get in, like a chauffeur. I refuse to look at him until I realize he's leaned his forearm against the top of the car and is peering down at me.

"Is there a gun in your purse, Lara?" His voice has a teasing quality.

My knuckles whiten on the purse, and my gaze snaps up to where he looms over me. I see amusement in his brown eyes, and the slight curve of his lips.

Cold washes through me. He's so confident, he's not afraid of a loaded gun.

No answer comes to mind. My jaw clenches as I glare up at him.

"You planning on shooting me?" Again, he's completely relaxed. Seemingly amused by me.

Oh, look at my cute bride who showed up with a gun to kill me.

I try and fail to swallow. My face burns. My legs tremble, ready to run like a gazelle away from the lion chasing me.

He holds his palm out. "Give me the gun, *printsessa*. We're not going to hurt each other in that way."

In what way are we going to hurt each other, Benjamin?

That thought has me imagining a measured hurt. The pain-for-pleasure type.

Wait, no.

I am *not* imagining Benjamin Baranov tying me up and whipping me with a riding crop.

That's...nuts. I'm not interested in that.

I eye his tattooed knuckles, wondering what it would be like to have them closed around my throat while we have sex.

Will he force me?

Why am I picturing him forcing me?

I don't want that. Of course, I don't.

I don't move, so he makes a beckoning gesture with his fingers. "The gun, Lara." The teasing quality drops away from his voice. I hear cold authority.

I sit there and debate what would happen if I said no. Or if I pulled it out and pointed it at him.

I realize that despite his relaxed pose, his gaze is intense.

Focused. If I pointed the gun at him, I'd have to be willing to pull the trigger.

As if he reads my thoughts, he shakes his head. "You're not a killer, *printsessa*. And you're safe with me. Or you will be if you behave."

Something about his gentle coaxing breaks me. Tears burn behind my eyes.

I don't want him to see them, so I thrust the whole purse his way and look away as he opens it and removes the pistol, tucking it into his waistband like a pro.

When he slides into the seat beside me, I ask, "Are you a killer, Benjamin?"

He turns to study me. I hold my breath under the intensity of his gaze.

"I've killed."

I can't breathe.

He starts the SUV and puts it in drive. "And I'd kill again—for you."

The breath leaves me in a whoosh. I'm suddenly light-headed. Shocked and slightly turned on.

"Why?" I demand.

A slight tension radiates from his shoulders. When he answers, the words are flat and emotionless. "You're my wife."

CHAPTER TWO

Baron

After stopping at the courthouse to get our marriage license, I take my bride to Baranov House, or the Gulag as it's known on campus. Lara gave me the cold shoulder for most of the trip, and I didn't try to warm her up.

I'm not the charming guy—that's Anders or Leo.

I'm the one who strategizes and keeps his mouth shut. The guy who stays five steps ahead of everyone else, so I can control the outcomes around me. My mom calls it PTSD. I call it being a leader.

Right now, I have a lot of mental plans to reconfigure. I need to figure out how to protect an unwilling bride. I'll have to control her to keep her safe, but I have a feeling she'll fight me tooth and nail.

My brain flashes to installing her permanently in the house dungeon.

Yes, we have a dungeon downstairs. It's why Baranov House is known on campus as the Gulag. Rumors about it are wild, and I encourage all of them. Some say it's a bratva torture chamber—the place we bring our enemies to exact revenge.

Others know—it's a sex club.

We almost never allow outsiders to enter it, which raises the mystique of the house to epic levels. Nearly every party-goer here spends the entire time trying to get invited down-stairs. That's what enables me to charge exorbitant amounts of money to people on the nights we decide to allow invite-only entry.

Those who are invited sign NDAs and then are sworn to secrecy with veiled threats.

I find people's imaginations work far better to control behavior than any threat or promise I could make.

I imagine stripping Lara out of her clothes and fastening her wrists and ankles to the St. Andrew's cross. Teasing her with the perfect application of intermittent pleasure until she goes mad and begs me for a release.

Or even better, a genuine relationship.

But I'd settle for her orgasm.

It's a delectable thought.

But of course, locking her up against her will won't work. I'll have to tempt Lara into the dungeon the same way I do the rest of the world—by denying her entry.

In the meantime, I'll keep her close, so I can watch over her. My original plan was to bring a contractor in to divide my large bedroom in two. But I'm glad I didn't have time to make the call.

My bride isn't sleeping anywhere but in my bed.

If her father thinks she's in so much danger he sent her here within days of my agreement, I need to take her protection seriously. That means keeping her close.

Making the marriage appear real to anyone who observes us.

I don't examine the more personal reasons I have for wanting her in my bed.

I park in the driveway next to Leo. "This is our place."

She sends a wary look at the house, as if it might suddenly animate and attack her. "*Our* place?"

"Not just for us. There are twenty members of the house. Twenty-one now, with you. Come in. I'll introduce you."

I take two of her suitcases and carry them to the front door, using my thumbprint to open the lock.

Half of the house members loiter in the living room. This is my version of the communal brotherhood my father cultivated in the Chicago high-rise where many of us grew up.

We're the bratva heirs. The generation born into my father's kingdom. A band of brothers and sisters with our own set of rules: Stay sharp. Protect each other and what is ours at all costs. Defend the weak from bullies. Wrest power from the campus autocrats. Leech money from the trust fund babies to pay for our enterprise.

They all stare as we come in, taking in the suitcases. The way my hand lightly rests on Lara's back. My subtle declaration that she belongs to me. She's under my protection, and they will accept her in, like they accept anyone I bring into our fold.

Zoe sits cross-legged on the couch next to Phoenix and her twin, Anya, who sprawls across the "L" of the couch with a laptop in her lap. Their father, Dima, is a hacker for my dad's cell. There's no firewall he can't get through, and last year, when she moved into Baranov House, Anya honed her skills not only in hacking but in complex money laundering.

It is one of the many services we offer for an enormous fee. Along with several other illegal ventures.

My dad tried to keep me out of the bratva—even going so far as sending me to boarding school when I got obsessed with joining, but he allowed me to observe. After I had blood on my hands at too young an age, he let me train in every form of self-defense—from mixed martial arts to sharp shooting. I absorbed the lifestyle in every way I could. You could say the apple didn't fall far from the tree.

"Hey, everyone." It occurs to me I should've given them a heads-up about the whole arranged marriage thing before I brought Lara in. I guess I was in denial about the massive effect her presence will have on our house dynamics and activities.

Then again, if I'd given them a heads-up, one of them might say something about the marriage being a sham, which Lara can't know.

"This is Lara Turgeneva, my fiancée."

"Your...what now?" Phoenix puts down the game controller and stares from the sofa where he was playing with Zoe.

I tip my head toward the door. "There are two more suitcases in the trunk."

He jumps to his feet. "On it."

As he passes by Lara, he shakes her hand. "I'm Phoenix. It's nice to meet you." He sends me a *what-the-fuck?* look as he steps out.

Anders and Leo give me similar looks, but Anders goes to help Phoenix, stopping to shake Lara's hand and introduce himself.

Phoenix was my roommate freshman year. A transgender student from North Carolina, he found some haters that first week of school until I straightened them out. His safety was the impetus for me securing this house. I needed a place I could build the sort of community I grew up in and protect my friends.

"You have a fiancée?" Anya asks, climbing to her feet.

"When did this happen?" Zoe demands, also standing. "I'm so confused."

I glance at Lara, who stands stiffly beside me, refusing to look my way. I clear my throat. "Our parents arranged our marriage at birth."

"*Your* parents," Anya repeats in disbelief.

"Yes."

"Wow. Okay." She and Zoe come over, and Zoe throws her arms around Lara. "Welcome to Thornecroft."

Lara stiffens and doesn't hug her back, but something in her softens. I send Zoe a grateful look when she pulls back.

"This is Anya and Zoya. But she goes by Zoe." I introduce them in Russian, so Lara will know she'll have friends here who speak it, not that her English isn't perfect. Of course, it would be. She lived her first few years here, plus she has an aunt and uncle and cousins in Los Angeles she probably visits.

"Nice to meet you," Lara says.

"Leonid. Call me Leo." Leo introduces himself in Russian and goes in for a cheek-kiss, which Lara accepts.

One part of me is grateful to Leo for his easy charm, but most of me wants to deck him for touching her.

"My parents had an arranged marriage," Leo offers.

"Wait—what?" Zoe looks from Leo to Anya. "Aunt Sasha and Uncle Maxim had an arranged marriage?" Zoe is the house's social media/publicity manager. She announces the parties we host and in exchange gets a cut of the door charge.

Leo nods. "My grandfather was on his deathbed, and my mom was about to inherit all the interest in his oil wells. He needed to keep her safe, and my dad was the only man he trusted."

Anya turns her gaze on me. "Why was your marriage arranged?"

Damn her.

"That's between my father and hers." My tone says *fuck off*.

Anya lets it go. "*Pozdravleniya.*" She offers congratulations in Russian.

"Leo, you'll need to code her thumbprint to the door." I start handing out orders, as is my way. "Anya, hack into the registrar and see if they have a schedule for her yet." Classes start tomorrow.

Anders and Phoenix appear with the other two suitcases. I switch to English because they don't speak Russian. "My room," I direct them. Anders picks up one suitcase I brought in and carries one in each hand up the stairs. Phoenix follows with the third.

"Are you hungry?" I ask Lara.

She shakes her head. She appears shellshocked. I get it. Baranov House and its occupants are a lot to take in, even to those who haven't been abruptly uprooted and sent off to marry a stranger. "Let's get you to bed—you've had a long day."

Lara digs her heels in when I try to steer her toward the stairs and sends me a furious look.

I look back at her, keeping my expression mild.

Her mouth thins to a mutinous line, but she squares her shoulders toward the stairs and marches up them.

I pick up the final suitcases, drinking in the delectable sway of her ass as I ascend behind her.

Fume all you want, printsessa. You belong to me now.

———

Lara

I don't know where I'm going, which makes my dramatic exit far less dramatic. All I know is that I don't appreciate being controlled by the twenty-two year old gangster who has more swagger than half my dad's men.

What...*was* all that?

My brain is having a hard time assimilating everything that's going on around here.

At first glance, this seems like a normal college living situation with normal college students. Of course, I've never been to an American college before, but I've seen movies. Since we moved to Russia I've returned to visit the United States many times over the years. My aunt Nadia and Uncle Flynn live in Los Angeles.

I take it all in. It's a big house—like the fraternity or sorority houses in the American comedies filled with friendly, good-looking young people. But the old Victorian-era house is in perfect condition, like it's been newly renovated. A *lot* of money went into this place. And the thumbprint security? Why is that necessary? The furniture is high-quality, and the house is spotlessly clean—other factors that don't go with student housing in my mind. And the weirdest thing is the way the students obeyed Benjamin's orders like he's their *pakhan*. One look from him, and they jump to comply. But several of them speak Russian, which means they could be born into it. Like him. Like me.

A shiver runs through me.

I'm in danger here. I can feel it.

I still don't understand anything that's happening. There's a bigger picture I can't see, and the undercurrent of secrecy and violence scares me.

I pass the Asian guy with a Norwegian name and accent—Anders, I think—and the slight-figured Phoenix, who might be trans, on the stairs. I must be headed in the right direction. I pause at the second landing.

"Keep going, *malyshka*," Benjamin murmurs behind me.

I flush and whirl. "I am not your baby."

He looks at me with no emotion—just that hint of amusement. Of power. I hate how his fathomless expression unnerves me. He says nothing, just looks at me. It's somehow more intimidating than any reply he could have made.

Suddenly breathless, I turn back to the stairs and continue upward. I pause at the next landing.

"One more."

At the top of the last flight of stairs is an enormous bedroom, clearly the prince's chambers. It's as beautiful as the rest of the house, with hardwood oak floors polished to a sheen and covered in a thick, plush shag orange rug. There are large windows on three of the walls. On the fourth wall is a closet and an en-suite bathroom with a small window.

It's surprisingly cheery for a criminal's lair.

There's a king-size, four-post bed draped in what looks like a fluffy goose-down comforter in a dove grey silk duvet. Like Benjamin, the bedding shows measured control. The bed is made, but the king-sized feather pillows mound in a casual heap at the head.

Benjamin props the suitcase he carried on its side on a footstool and unzips it. "I'll get a second dresser in here for your folded things. For now, there's plenty of room and hangers in the closet."

He walks into the closet, pulling the gun he took from me from his waistband. He opens a safe, and I catch sight of stacks of cash when he deposits it inside.

I'm too tired to unpack. I just want a shower and to go to bed.

"Where do I sleep?"

I'm not sure why I bother asking. It's obvious where he expects me to sleep. In his giant bed.

With him.

As exhausted as I am, my body heats at the thought of being under those covers with him.

"In my bed."

Something about the way he enunciates each word makes

me whirl to see his face. My lips part to draw a breath when I catch the way he's looking at me.

Like a hunter who just caught his prey. Like a hungry lion looking at his next meal.

His gaze sends an electric zing right between my legs. My pussy clenches. Clit throbs.

But I refuse to be turned on by the idea of him claiming me.

"I'm not sleeping in that bed with you." I suspect this battle is already lost, but I'd have no self-respect if I didn't make my resistance clear.

Benjamin shakes his head with mock remorse. "My wife doesn't sleep on the floor."

"*You* could." Maybe not my most forceful argument. Like I said, I don't have high hopes of winning this one.

"Not in my house. Not with my wife in the room."

"I'm not your wife yet," I say stiffly.

His eyes glitter with anticipation. "Tomorrow, *printsessa*."

I stand on trembling legs, staring at him. For some unfathomable reason, my panties are damp, and I can't stop wondering what happens tomorrow when we come back to this bedroom.

"There are towels and washcloths in the bathroom. Do you need anything else?"

"To go back to Paris." My voice wobbles, and I curse myself for showing him my pain.

He closes the distance between us, and I suddenly find myself in his arms.

I push against his chest, but he catches the back of my head and angles my face up to his. "I know you didn't ask for this." He catches my gaze and holds it. "Neither did I. But we're going to make the best of it."

I want to fight him, but tears make his face blurry.

"Together, *malyshka*. We're a team now."

He takes mercy on me and releases me from his gaze, pulling my face against his chest.

I don't want to take comfort from him. I hate the sob that climbs up my throat, but when he kisses the top of my head, it comes out in a huff. I squeeze my eyes closed, and tears soak his shirt.

His thumb massages the base of my skull. It feels wonderful.

No. I will not fall for this nice guy act. I know he's anything but.

"Don't," I choke and push him away, and he allows it.

"We're not a team. I'm your prisoner. And I'll be fighting you every inch of the way." I lurch toward the bathroom. When I turn to shut the door, I see him still standing there, watching me. The tiny smile that plays on his lips tells me my instincts were right.

Benjamin Baranov is *not* a nice guy.

He's the devil.

CHAPTER THREE

Baron

I head downstairs to find everyone waiting for me.

Right. In another quick revision of plans, I decide to bring them all in on this with me.

If I'm keeping a secret from my bride, I'd rather not also keep it from my team. My best friends. I need their support.

"Meeting in half an hour in the dungeon," I say. The dungeon is soundproof and operates with fingerprint locks. People in the rest of the house—mainly, my reluctant bride—can't hear anything we do or say down there. "Are Alex and Feliks back from practice?"

Leo checks the camera monitors on his phone. "They're walking up right now."

"Good. Tell them about the meeting. Oh—also—Melinda Tracy is banned from Baranov House this year. Make sure everyone knows."

Anders' head snaps over at the mention of one of our frequent dungeon visitors. She's a Type A personality who uses pain to relax. I think Anders has a thing for her, but since she usually comes to me to inflict pain, she hasn't noticed yet. "Because of her dad?"

I nod. Her dad was just announced as the running candidate for Vice President. If he wins, Melinda will bring the Secret Service crawling all over campus, and I can't have them anywhere near our business.

I pull my phone out to text Lili, my sister, to join us. She'll need to know, too.

I didn't want Lili to know about or see the dungeon. When I thought she was going to move in here with us, I was going to close it down. If it were up to me, she'd be here in Baranov House where I could protect her, but she somehow talked our parents into her freedom.

I fucking hate it, but I had Leo put a tracking strip in her dorm keycard and her phone and install extra security cameras around her dorm room, so we can make sure she's safe.

Since I didn't shut down the dungeon, her finding out about it was probably inevitable. She'd hear about it around campus eventually and would pester me or the twins—whom she's close to—until we let her in on it, anyway.

I head to the kitchen to eat a quick meal. After we streamlined and broadened our revenue-generating ventures at Baranov House, I hired a cook in addition to the cleaning crew. Emma, a young single mom from Whisper, comes in five days a week to buy groceries and make dinners. She likes the job because she can bring her three-year-old daughter, May, with her.

I like the reminder that everything lying around this house has to appear benign enough to be seen by outsiders, including a three-year-old.

Thirty minutes later, we assemble in the lounge area of the dungeon, where plush leather sofas, love seats, and captain's chairs can be angled to either watch the action or for conversation around some low tables.

Right now, they're grouped for conversation.

"You guys are absolute perverts." Lili walks down the stairs with Zoe, eyes wide.

I wince. She didn't need to know this about me. "You can't tell anyone what you're seeing here tonight," I warn after giving her a quick hug.

"Please," she scoffs. "The Gulag is literally all anyone in the freshman dorm talks about, especially when they hear my last name. Everyone wants to know what's downstairs and why I'm not living here. There's already a rumor that there's some super drama between us, and we hate each other."

I flick my brows. I built the intrigue of The Gulag around campus gossip, so I don't mind it. "Don't disabuse them of any stories. The wild rumors are what bring people through the door."

Lili shakes her head as she looks at me. "You're just like Dad."

"I'll take that as a compliment. I know you're still in orientation, but this week, I need to see you in our gym for self-defense training," I say.

She looks at me blankly, and I realize she doesn't know about the rigorous training I require the house members to maintain. Everyone here has had extensive Krav Maga training, and we spar weekly in the house gym.

"What are you talking about?"

"I'll send you the schedule," Leo says. "You can spar with me."

Lili looks annoyed with me. She thought she'd have more freedom at college than I'm going to give her.

"How was orientation week?" I ask, remembering how a normal brother would act. I already know where she's been and what she's done because I've tracked her every move. It helps with the nightmares to feel like I have control of every possible outcome. Now I have Lara to add to my worry list. "Fun," she says lightly. Lili lived through the same trauma I did, but it hasn't affected her the same way. Maybe she was too little to have that danger impelled into every cell. Or maybe she has too much trust in my being able to protect her from anything.

I believe her because she looks bright. Happy. That's good because I would want to solve any problems she has or kill anyone who hurts her, but she would hate me for it. "I made friends. My roommate's cool. It's good. So what's the big emergency?"

"I'm getting married."

Lili gapes at me the same way the rest of them did when I brought Lara into the house. I explain the situation to everyone, including the part about Lara's father lying to Anatoli Rostov about us being betrothed since birth, and Lara not knowing that was a lie.

"So basically, I have to keep her safe, but she thinks I'm the enemy."

Leo nods as if it all makes perfect sense. Alex and Feliks are like stone men, absorbing it all without expression, awaiting orders. There's no battle I could fight that I wouldn't want them beside me. Anders and Phoenix look doubtful. Based on their frowns, the women clearly don't like it.

"What if you just told her?" Lili asks.

"Yeah. You're not the enemy. She should know that," Zoe says.

"I can't. If her dad didn't tell her, it's because he needs this to look real, or he doesn't trust her not to go running back to Brash Rostov."

"True," Leo says. "You think she's in love with him?"

I shrug, keeping my face blank of the spike of irritation

that notion causes. If she's in love with him, she'll be even harder to protect and in even more danger than her dad suspects.

Thank fuck, Adrian's gut told him to get her away from him as quickly as possible.

"I need to find out. Anya, if I give you her phone tonight, can you set something up, so I can track her and all her calls and messages?"

Lili makes a sputtering noise. "You can't do that. It's an invasion of her privacy."

"I've been charged with keeping her safe. I will do whatever's necessary."

It's not that there's now an ugly jealousy twining its way around my throat at the idea of my lovely bride being in love with another man.

Not at all.

"I just need her phone for twenty minutes," Anya promises.

"Perfect. I'll bring it to you after she goes to sleep." I look at my sister. "Lili, I need you to corroborate the story. Dad arranged my marriage years ago. We both have known it all along."

Lili rolls her eyes and blows out her breath, but nods. "When is the wedding? Seems like I should come since I am your sister. Shouldn't I be a bridesmaid or something?"

"I want to be a bridesmaid!" Zoe perks up. Anya snorts.

"It's just a trip to the courthouse after classes." I glance at Anya. "Speaking of which—"

"Here's the class schedule." Anya hands me a printout with Lara's classes. I take a quick scan of them. They are mostly in the linguistics department. It seems my bride is a modern languages major. I guess that explains why she attended college in Paris.

I take a photo of the schedule and text it to everyone.

"Keep an eye out for her. Let me know if you see her with anyone who looks like trouble. I'll find a photo of Brash and send it to you."

Alex clears his throat like he wants to say something. I raise my brows.

"I don't know if this is the right time, but..."

My control issues snap into place. If there's a leak in my systems, our security, our enterprises, I need to know about it. "Tell me."

"I overheard some of the guys on the team talking before practice. They didn't know Feliks and I were there."

Blyad'. "What'd they say?"

"I didn't catch it all, but I definitely heard, *take Baranov House down this year.*"

Feliks nods his agreement. "We made the Titan House parties look lame last year." Titan House is a male-only society house. Half of the football team are members, and the rest of the members are legacy—their membership insured through bloodlines that go back to the school's origins.

Before Baranov House took over Thornecroft's social landscape, they ruled the school with alpha male-oriented elite parties that attracted the most popular sorority girls.

I nod. I can handle whatever they bring. I expected trouble and have planned for it. "Okay. Try to figure out how they will hit us. I'll grease all the right wheels before our party."

"So back to this wedding. Do you have a ring?" Lili demands.

I wince. A ring. That would be a good plan for a wedding ceremony. Especially one we're trying to make look legit.

I mean, it will be legit. By tomorrow night, Lara Turgeneva will be my wife.

Dark satisfaction floods me at that knowledge, but I tamp it down. Legally binding Lara to me is just the first move in this battle. There are too many unknown variables for me to celebrate my victory just yet.

"I'll get a ring. And I'm going to be at the ceremony," Lili says firmly. "How do I pay for it? Should I use Dad's Amex?"

"No." I reach in my pocket and pull my Gold Card out of my phone case to hand to her.

Lili inspects it and shakes her head. "You have your own Gold Card. I... don't even want to know what's going on over here."

"No, you don't," Leo says, just as protective of my little sister as I am.

"I'll pick you up for the ceremony," I tell her.

"I'm coming too," Leo says.

"Me too," Zoe says.

Anya raises her hand, like we're doing a head count. Phoenix and Anders also raise their hands.

"We'll have football practice," Alex says apologetically, tipping his head toward his younger but even larger brother.

"No worries," I say. "It wasn't really supposed to be a thing."

"Isn't it though?" Lili challenges me. "You're getting *married*. And I know you're doing your stoic, hard-to-read thing, but it seems to me like..." she pauses and raises her eyebrows, letting anticipation build.

"Like what?" I cut in when it drags on too long.

"Like you're into it."

CHAPTER FOUR

Lara

It's still dark when I wake, and for a moment, I don't know where I am. Then it all rushes back to me with a sick feeling.

I'm in the United States. In the bedroom of the man I'm supposed to marry.

My eyes fly open, and I scan the bed. Is he in here—with me? The jetlag made me crash last night, so I slept like the dead until now, when my body decided it was time to be awake. I never heard Benjamin come in, if he did.

I hold my breath and listen, but I can't tell if I'm alone. I reach for where I left my phone plugged in beside the bed. A paper slides beneath it. A paper that wasn't there when I went to bed.

I hit a button on my phone, which shows me it's four in the morning here. No wonder I'm up—it's long past the time I'd be awake in Paris. The paper under my phone is a printout of my class schedule.

Because that's not intrusive. Not at all.

I mean, it is helpful, but there's also something creepy and controlling.

Did Benjamin move my phone, too? Was he trying to check my messages?

Well, good luck with that—I have screen lock.

I use the light of the screen to shine over the bed, and my pulse speeds up the moment I detect the large form on the other end of the bed.

At least he gave me space. I was half-afraid last night that he'd try something.

I look back at my phone. There are a slew of messages. Two phone messages from my mom.

I haven't called her since my dad showed up. I don't know whether or not I'm mad at her. It sounded like this was all my dad's doing. Either way, I'm not ready to talk to her. If she's as upset as I am, that's only going to make me break down.

There's a string of texts from Brash, the Russian guy I had a few dates with before I left Paris. He's the son of a rich oligarch. I found him to be full of himself, but despite his self-absorption, he took an interest in me. I don't know if it's because I'm Russian, and he feels a certain connection with me over French women or what. Anyway, he was a gentleman on our dates—attentive but not too pushy. A kiss at the door but no pressure for sex.

We had a date scheduled for last night that I didn't even remember to cancel.

Oops.

Knowing his ego, he's going to be put out.

Not that it matters. It hits me square in the chest. I'm not going back there. My life in Paris is over. My internship and future job possibilities just died. I'm getting married today.

I open the texts and wince. Apparently, he went to my place, waited a half an hour and left. Then texted a couple more times asking if I was okay.

I text back in Russian:

> I'm very sorry I forgot to cancel our date. I was on a plane to the U.S.

> In a crazy turn of events, I found out I have to marry an American. (I'm not joking).

> I won't be back to Paris, and I can't see you again.

The large form on the other side of the bed jerks awake, and Benjamin sits up, one hand reaching for his bedstand, like he's going for a gun.

My husband is jumpy when he wakes. Good to know.

I flip the phone, screen down, so he won't see the light, but Benjamin turns to look at me, scrubbing a hand across his face.

"Jet lag has you up early, huh?" His voice is a deep, sleepy rumble. It's sexy. Or maybe it's just finding myself in bed with a man that makes my nipples tighten.

I twist to look over my shoulder at him, allowing the light to shine again.

Oh, damn. His sandy blond hair is loosely tousled and hanging over his forehead. He's not wearing a shirt, and the muscles of his chest stand out in glorious relief. Is he naked?

Wait—why am I even wondering that? *Gospodi*, is he, though? Did he come to bed with me last night naked?

Or did he have the decency to wear his underwear? And what kind of underwear does he wear? The small, tight kind? Or boxer shorts?

Gah. Again, why am I picturing him in his underwear right now?

My phone rings.

I glance down. It's Brash calling.

Blin, I swear internally. He's usually more of a texter. I definitely don't want to have a conversation with him right now. Especially not while I'm in bed with my fiancé.

I hit the decline button and catch Benjamin's gaze on the screen of my phone.

"Who was that?" His tone is casual, like we're a long-married couple who shares these kinds of things. Like we know and care about the same people. Like we know each other.

"None of your business."

It's probably too early in the morning to pick fights with my soon-to-be husband, but I need to establish boundaries. I still don't understand why I'm here or what he wants with me, but I know it can't be for any good reason.

In a flash, I find myself pinned on my back with Benjamin rolled on top of me. Turns out, he *is* wearing boxers, but through the fabric, I feel his hardening cock nudge between my legs.

I'm instantly wet, my body responding to his dominance. To his closeness. He smells clean, like soap and his own unique man-scent.

"Oh, *malyshka*," he chides, looking down at me with glittering eyes. His hands manacle my wrists, pinning them to the bed beside my head. "You're my wife." Our gazes lock. His is so intense, I swear he can see into my soul. "Everything about you is my business."

I turn my face to the side to break eye contact as he continues, "...from the kind of birth control you use to how you take your coffee in the morning." He lowers his lips, like he's going to kiss the side of my neck.

My heart pounds. *Birth control I use? Gospodi!* Is he planning on getting me pregnant? Is that what this is about?

And—am I going to let him seduce me like this?

No. No way. I can't. Not even if he does look like a Greek Adonis. Not even if my body responds to him like he owns it.

"Don't."

He instantly freezes, his mouth so close to my skin I feel his warm breath. He hovers there a moment, then eases off me, rolling away and releasing me.

I'm one part relieved, one part disappointed.

I'm happy to know I have agency over my body. That he'll stop when I say no. Or at least he did this time.

But my body mourns the loss of his heat against my skin. The fact that I won't find out how it feels to have his mouth on my flesh. And I'll never know what he planned to do after that kiss.

Not that I think he was following a plan.

His dominance felt instinctual, which would be a huge turn-on if we were dating. If I weren't his prisoner.

"How *do* you take your coffee in the morning?"

I'm stunned at how quickly he switches from intense to casual. Like we didn't just have a moment where our hearts were beating together as his body covered mine.

I force an equally casual tone. "*Cafe au lait.*"

He starts to roll out of bed then pauses to ask, "Are you getting up now, or are you going to try to fall back to sleep?"

I swing my legs over the side of the mattress. "No, I'm up."

I don't look, but I'm intensely aware of him pulling on his pants behind me. The stranger I shared a bed with last night is getting dressed. Every cell in my body is aware of his nearness. The state of half-dress both of us are in.

"I'll make that coffee, and then I can show you around campus before your first class."

It sounds so thoughtful. It *is* thoughtful. I just don't trust him or any of it.

Still, I don't have the slightest clue where to go or how to get around this campus, and I'm not so full of pride to refuse help when it will make my life easier.

"Okay," I agree, stepping into the large walk-in closet and clicking on a light. For a reason I don't care to examine, I don't shut the door behind me to give myself privacy as I dress. As I slip off my sleep shorts, I would swear the sounds of Benjamin getting dressed stop.

Is he watching me?

Do I *want* him to watch me?

I guess I must, or I would've shut the door. That's crazy.

I mean, he *is* attractive. I wouldn't have said he's my type, but I know why I respond to him. He carries the same confidence and edge of danger as my dad. My dad's violence feels closer to the surface, but there's something about both of them that makes people follow their leadership.

But screw that. I'm mad at my dad right now. I'm not going to admire some guy who's as lethal as he is.

I pull on a skirt and turn to look over my shoulder.

Benjamin is staring openly at my ass.

"Like what you see?" I demand as I zip up the back.

"*Malyshka*," he rumbles, scrubbing a hand across his jaw. "You have no idea."

My nipples pucker, tenting the thin pajama top I'm wearing.

Benjamin's gaze drops to them, noticing.

I despise the way we, as women raised in the patriarchy, have this sense of waiting to be chosen by a man, waiting to be found sexy, beautiful, whatever. That's never been me. I know my worth. I've never needed or desired the validation of others, especially men. Still, I flush with satisfaction.

Benjamin wants me.

In fact, judging by the expression on his face, he's downright *hungry* for me.

Well, I don't hate that.

I give him my back again, but a tiny smile plays on my face as I take off my pajama top and put on a bra.

I may be here at the whim of the Baranovs, but I'm not completely powerless. There's always the currency of sex. I don't intend to use it, but it's good to know it's a tool in my pocket.

———

Baron

I hold the front door for Lara to step outside. Dawn breaks across Whisper with the sky changing from black to gunmetal grey. The sweet smell of grass fills the air. Campus is silent, and the air is still. This is the time I usually take a run or go to target practice, but making my new bride comfortable is top priority today.

Lara brushes past me in a rust-colored pleated mini-skirt and a matching pair of soft leather boots that come up to her knees. Her cream square-necked top perfectly frames her cleavage and hugs her tits, making her waist look tiny. She smells of the coffee she just drank and some warm, butterscotch fragrance I want to lick off her.

I'm dying to put my hands on her waist. To lower my face to her neck again and breathe in her scent.

I fucking *loved* having her in my bed last night. The most controlling part of me—probably the same part that makes me masterful in the dungeon—wants to hoard her like a possession. I've had a lot of women but never wanted to make one mine before. Despite the number of young women who throw themselves at me, none have interested me enough. Not even the ones who have bared themselves—both literally and figuratively—to kneel at my feet and accept pain and humiliation. I feel a tenderness for them. I'm protective of them. But I never wanted to conquer and consume anyone like I do Lara.

Is it just the challenge? The fact that she's mine but doesn't want to be?

Or is there something special about her? Like, this was all fated, and some soul-level part of me recognizes that she's my destiny?

"Baranov House sits on the southeast end of campus," I tell her. I sweep a hand to indicate where the rest of the campus lies. "Most of your classes are in that direction." I touch my thumb to the garage keypad, and the door slides up. Lara stays on the porch, watching me doubtfully.

The garage is packed with house member's bikes, scooters and motorcycles–all good for getting around campus. My motorcycle is electric, so nearly silent, which is nice for an early morning. I put on a helmet and grab another for her, then start it up and drive it over.

"It's walkable, but for expediency, let's take my bike, so I can show you the whole campus." I hand her the helmet.

For expediency, and so I can get close to her.

I hold my hand out to her to help her climb on behind me.

She doesn't move.

I wait. I'm not going to insist. Lara is mine whether she chose it or not. I don't have to throw my weight around.

Her jaw clenches, but after a moment, she ignores my hand and puts on the helmet. When she throws her leg over, her mini skirt rides up her thighs and gives me a flash of panties.

My dick gets hard. I can't help myself–I mold my palm to one of her exposed thighs and squeeze.

She freezes, but before she can react, I remove it and accelerate.

She catches her breath, her hands flying out to grab my waist. I love the feel of her hands on me. I glance back as I start down the road. Her dark hair—worn down today in layered waves, blows back. Her full lips part.

Anya set me up to receive the records of all Lara's texts and phone calls. It was Brash who texted her this morning. I was pleasantly surprised she hadn't told him she was leaving town until this morning. That means they can't be that close. If she were in love with him, she would've said goodbye in person. Then again, maybe Adrian prevented it. Still, her text wasn't that personal.

That doesn't mean Brash will stop pursuing her. She's an asset his father decided he wants in his arsenal. Maybe Brash even sees something in her himself although he's a sociopath. I can't believe he could ever care about her.

But maybe he sees the same thing in her I do.

That thought makes me grit my teeth. Even if Lara never accepts me and our marriage remains nothing more than a sham, I will do whatever it takes to keep Brash Rostov from ever touching or even thinking about her again.

I drive the motorcycle through the cool morning air, glorying in having Lara's soft curves molded against me. "This is the Modern Languages building." I pull in front of the hundred-year-old three-story brick building. "Your first and third classes are in here."

She nods but says nothing. I keep going with the tour, showing her where each of her classes will be, pointing out the main library, the food court, and the gym. Sunrise breaks the horizon, warming the sky to a light peach glow as I drive half a mile off campus.

"Where are we going?" Lara asks, no doubt realizing we're away from the old brick structures of the university and heading down toward Whisper's town center.

"I wanted to show you the best bakery." I pull up in front of The Velvet Crumb, a light-filled bakery/cafe that opens at six a.m. "It's not a Parisian cafe, but the scones are incredible." I stop the bike, and Lara immediately tumbles off as if eager to be away from me. She yanks her skirt down as I open the door to the bakery. The scent of freshly baked bread wafts out as we step inside.

The bakery features vaulted ceilings with old Victorian-era ceiling tiles. White tile covers the floors and eighteen-foot walls, giving it a bright and airy feel.

"Are you hungry yet?"

Lara glances at the cases of delectable goodies–braided breads stuffed with herbs and cheese, a large variety of scones, croissants, and tarts–and nods.

I step up to the counter with my hand lightly resting on Lara's lower back. The girl working the counter bustles over. When she looks up and sees my face, she startles and blushes under her white baker's hat. "Um, hi, Baron."

I don't know her, but she must be a Thornecroft student.

Lara turns to look at me quizzically.

"Hey there," I say easily, brushing off the recognition. Most everyone at Thornecroft knows me. That's the benefit of cultivating a bad-ass status.

"Can we get a couple of *cafe au laits* and–"

"Do you mean lattes?" she interrupts.

"Sure." I know they're not exactly the same because I Googled it this morning to make sure I got her coffee right. But close enough. She's not going to find many cafes in this country that serve *cafe au laits*.

"To eat, we'll have–" I turn to look inquiringly at Lara, "what would you like?"

"I'll try the pumpkin chocolate chip muffin," she says.

"And I'll have the maple walnut scone. For here, please."

The cashier bobs her head and rings us up. "I, um, heard there's a back-to-school party at Baranov House Friday," she ventures as I hold my phone up to the device to pay.

Ah. That's why she looks a little nervous-giddy. One of

the ways I turned Baranov House into a cash cow is by making our parties exclusively invite-only. That doesn't mean they are small and intimate or free. Not at all. They're huge.

So huge, the fraternities, long known as the sole source of social activity on campus, have taken a hit.

It just means we created a sense of mystery and exclusion which makes everyone want to attend. Whispers of the dungeon in the basement help boost that reputation.

"There is," I say. "Are you coming?"

She turns a deep shade of red. "Um, no. I don't have an invite."

I reach into my pocket and pull out one of the party invitation cards Zoe had printed. Each has to be signed by a house member in order to allow entry. I pick up a pen. "What's your name?"

"Tori."

I write "Tori +1" and sign on the line, then slide it across the counter. "Consider yourself invited."

Tori takes the card and tucks it into her pocket then opens her mouth but hesitates to speak.

What now? I raise my brows.

"Um, does this invite get me into the dungeon?"

I give her a completely blank look. "What dungeon?" Perpetuating mystery and exclusivity is what drives rumors in Whisper.

She flushes. "Nevermind. I just heard...right. Nevermind." She waves her hands in the air. "I know nothing."

"There's nothing to know. Tori, this is my wife, Lara. She just transferred here from a school in Paris. I want you to take good care of her anytime she comes in here, okay?"

Tori bobs her head. "Of course. Nice to meet you, Lara. Welcome to Thornecroft."

"Thanks." Lara turns her electric blue eyes on me and stares as Tori moves away to make our coffee.

I pull a fat wad of cash out of my pocket and tuck it in her pocket. "You probably don't have any U.S. dollars. This should get you by."

"You are just like my dad," she says. There's condemnation in her tone.

"I'm guessing that's a bad thing?" I usher her to a two-person table by the big picture window and hold her chair for her to sit.

"You act like everyone is under your command."

I sit across from her, keeping my expression neutral. She's right. I *do* believe everyone's under my command. I believe everyone has a leverage point that can be toggled. Tori's was a simple invite to a party. Some people's is feeling included. Some people's is fear.

I'm willing to push all the levers to get my desired outcome.

"I don't do it for shits and giggles," I say mildly.

"Shits and giggles?" she repeats. It's obviously an English phrase she hasn't heard before. Her English is perfect without a trace of an accent, but she hasn't lived in America since she was a tot.

"For fun. For my entertainment."

The way her brows drop tells me she doesn't believe a word I'm saying. "Why do you do it, then?" she demands.

"I do what's necessary to protect what's mine."

She chuffs. I want to kiss her pouty lips. Show her how well I'm going to take care of her. "And I'm yours?"

I hold her gaze steadily. "Yes."

CHAPTER FIVE

Lara

Starting classes at a school I didn't know I'd be attending a week ago is an out-of-body experience. I don't have the energy to return Brash's texts or calls.

He no longer matters. He's not part of this life.

Benjamin—or Baron, as others call him—asked me questions about myself over breakfast. He wanted to know what made me want to study modern languages. How many languages I speak. What I hope to do as a career.

I found him easy enough to talk to. As easy as it was to ride behind him on the back of a motorcycle hanging onto his rock-hard abs. He's appealing—there's no denying it.

But I'm not falling for any of it. I'm some pawn in a game they're playing, and I don't have a choice. I won't forgive him for that, no matter how charming he might be.

I go through the day, just focusing on finding my way around and getting oriented.

I don't have any headspace to think about Benjamin—or "Baron," as the girl at the cafe called him—and his declaration that I'm his. Like a piece of property.

There's a sliver of me that also loves the way he takes care of me, but I want to stomp that piece of my heart into the sidewalk and grind it under the heel of my boot. I can't let myself be attracted to him. I can't allow myself to be seduced by his courtesy.

Although I may be feeling as possessive about him as he is about me because when the girl at the cafe blushed and spoke his name for one brief moment, I thought he'd slept with her, and I wanted to scratch his eyes out.

Is he a player? And what is this party everyone's talking about? What is the dungeon? I meant to ask him about it at breakfast but forgot.

I exit my class and round the bend only to have a short, round young man barrel into me and drop his books.

"*Blyad'.*" He looks up from under a mop of unkempt hair. Then says in accented English, "I'm sorry."

"It's all right," I reassure him in Russian, stooping to help him pick up his books and the papers that went flying everywhere.

His face lights up. "You're Russian?"

I hand him the papers I collected. "*Da. YA iz Moskvy.*"

"I'm Denis," he says as we both stand. He shifts his mess of books and papers to one arm and extends a hand.

I clasp his hand. "Lara. Nice to meet you."

"I just started here. It's a relief to know I'm not the only Russian on campus."

"You're not. I just started here too, actually." I draw in a long breath and sigh it out.

It's been a day. Considering how early I woke up, I'm ready for it to be over. Too bad I still have a marriage ceremony to get through.

"Actually, there are a bunch of Russian-Americans as well," I tell him, thinking of the occupants of Baranov House.

"Not the same." He dismisses them with a wave. "I guess I'm homesick." His apologetic smile is lopsided.

My stomach twists. "So am I."

"I don't mean to be too forward, but I would love to get a drink or coffee with you." He sends me a hopeful puppy look. "—just as friends," he adds quickly. "I know you're out of my league."

Aw, the guy is a dork but totally likeable. I hesitate. What's the harm? Denis is homesick and needs someone he can talk to. I suspect Baron won't like it. But that's his problem, isn't it?

"Sure," I say. "Let's do it."

"Tonight? At Whisper's End?" He names a corner street bar I saw near the bakery this morning.

"Not tonight. How about tomorrow?" I suggest.

He beams at me. "Tomorrow it is. Five o'clock?"

"Sure. See you there."

I round the corner only to find Leo with his back propped against the wall. He's looking at his phone, but a chill washes over me. He must've been standing there listening the whole time.

He sends me a white-toothed smile. "*Privet*, Lara."

I stare back at him. I can't think of anything to say because my mind is churning over the fact that I'm being spied upon.

"How's your first day? Need help finding anything?"

"*Nyet*," I snap and toss my head, walking as quickly away as I can without running.

My eyes burn as I push open the door and stumble outside, dying to be free. Not of the building but of my life.

Of this crazy situation.

Of Benjamin Baranov and whatever his sinister plans are for me.

CHAPTER SIX

Baron

"Here are the rings." Lili holds out two tiny plastic bags, one containing a thin gold band and one with a thicker band.

Lili, Zoe, Anya, Leo, Phoenix, and Anders all gather in the living room of Baranov House where I told everyone who wanted to go to the courthouse to meet. "There are adjustable sizers inside for now until you get them properly sized. Or until you know your bride well enough to buy her something she would actually like. Where is your bride, by the way?"

I check the app on my phone that tracks her phone. "Almost here. Thank you, Lils." I pull her in for a half-hug and kiss the top of her head.

"How was your first day at Thornecroft?" Zoe asks.

"Great. Except I think my math professor hates me for some reason."

"Vasiliev?" I ask even though I already know her schedule and professors. Professor Vasiliev is the bane of my existence at Thornecroft.

She sends me a surprised glance. "Yes. I thought he might be nice to me since he's obviously Russian. Is this your fault?"

I shrug. "No, but you're fucked. I have him again this year for statistics. I think he knows we're bratva and therefore believes we're thugs. Dad doesn't know him personally–I asked when I had him freshman year because I thought maybe they had a beef or something. Watch out–he will look for any excuse to dock points off your tests, so be meticulous."

"Well, that sucks."

"It does."

"Lara made plans to meet some Russian *mudak* for a drink tomorrow at five," Leo says.

I go still. As is my way, I show nothing on my face, while chaos rips my insides to shreds. "Who?"

Leo shows me the screen of his phone. It shows a photo snapped in the Modern Languages building of a short, nerdy guy talking to Lara. "This guy. They were speaking Russian. He says he's a transfer student."

"Send it to Anya," I snap, turning to look at my hacker. "Anya, find out who he is and if he has any links to the Rostovs."

"You got it, *pakhan*."

"Don't call me that," I say reflexively, my mind still chewing on the new transfer student. It sounds like trouble to me. What are the chances that a Russian transfer student shows up right when Lara Turgeneva slips out of Brash Rostov's clutches?

"Why not? We're bratva. We're basically our own cell, and you're the boss."

I ignore the question, frowning, still deep in thought when the door beeps with the electronic lock opening, and Lara walks in. Leo programmed her thumbprint to work this morning before she left for class.

Lara stops in the doorway and stares at us.

I'm sure we look like a mob waiting to attack her. I wish to fuck she wasn't so sure I was the enemy.

I tip my head at the group. "They all wanted to come along for the ceremony. Is that okay with you?"

Her nostrils flare. "And if I say no?" she demands.

She's testing me. She wants to see how restrictive her golden handcuffs really are. She tested me this morning when she stopped me from kissing her. Now she wants to know how much agency she has over how things go down.

I want to pass her test even though I think the experience will probably be better for both of us if my friends attend.

Lili reaches for Lara, touching her arm. "Hi! We haven't met yet. I'm Lili Baranova, Ben's sister." She tilts her head to the side. "Soon to be your sister."

"Oh." Lara looks back at her without moving. I can tell she wants to hate Lili, too, but my sister is too sweet and innocent to hate.

"So this is kind of my fault." Lili sweeps a hand at the gathering. "We both just found out about the sudden, um, acceleration of marital plans, and I told Ben I wanted to come. I mean, we're going to be family." She sends an apologetic look. "And once I said I wanted to go, everyone else jumped on the bandwagon. But if you don't want us there, it's okay. We can wait for you here with champagne."

Lara scans the faces of the group, arriving at Anders, who pulls a bottle of champagne from the case he bought today to show her.

"Why don't we start the champagne now?" Lara asks.

The tension breaks. "Aha! Now we're talking!" Anders exclaims but looks at me for confirmation.

"Bring it along," I concede. "We have to get to the courthouse before four-thirty."

We split up and pile into my Range Rover and Leo's

BMW X7. Lara chooses to ride in the back with Lili and Anders, leaving Anya to ride up front with me.

I hear the pop of a cork. "Spill that, and you'll be shampooing my upholstery," I growl from the front seat even though I can already hear the sound of liquid pouring onto the floor and Lili squealing.

"Oops," Anders laughs.

I glance in the rearview mirror to see him trying to pour the champagne in a glass. Lara reaches over and takes it from him, drinking straight from the mouth of the bottle.

"Okay! The bride is quelling her nerves. Nothing wrong with that," he narrates.

"Pass it over here." Lili takes the bottle from Lara.

"Uh...am I supposed to let your underage sister drink?" Anders asks.

Lili makes a popping sound when her lips come away from the bottle. "Fuck you, Anders."

"I trust Lili to be responsible."

It's not true. I don't trust Lili, and I don't trust anyone *with* Lili. In my mind, she's still that six-year-old with a gun to her head. The one I had to save from being murdered.

It's why I'm so overprotective now.

But I can't put restrictions on her, or it will only drive her further away from me. She chose not to live in Baranov House, which already makes me insane.

So I say I trust her to make sure she understands I have expectations of her. She's smart and driven. But being away from home for the first time can be intoxicating. I don't want her to make a dumb decision that puts her in danger. But I have to remind myself that Thornecroft is one of the safest places she could be. And that I'm not going to let anything bad ever happen to her again.

"See?" Lili raises her brows at Anders. "He trusts me to be responsible."

Lara takes the bottle back from Lili and chugs some more before passing it back.

"Don't drink it all." Anders intercepts and takes a long swig.

"So why did I have to hear from my friends that Baranov House is having a party next Friday?" Lili demands.

I don't answer.

"They want invites," she presses.

I knew this would come up. I don't want my sister at our parties—there are things that go down there that I'd rather she not be involved in. But forbidding her from going will only create more problems. Besides, I want my sister protected by my reputation as a dangerous killer. Acting like we aren't family doesn't offer her that protection.

"You are a Baranov, so obviously, it's your house, too. No invitation is needed to get through the door. You may choose to bring anyone you want, but they have to come with you. No one dropping your name at the door is going to be let in. Understand?"

"Can I bring *as many* people as I want?"

"Yes. But they have to come with you." I meet her gaze in the rearview mirror, and she nods. "And you take responsibility for each of your guests."

"What does that mean?"

"No drinking if they're underage. No drugs. No bad behavior."

"Doesn't sound like much of a party."

"Then don't come."

Lili rolls her eyes.

Whisper is a small town, so we're at the courthouse in seven minutes, and during that time the three in the back completely drain the first bottle of Champagne. I climb out and hold the door open for Lara, who surprises me by taking my offered hand to jump down.

I'm in a suit to show respect for the day. She gives me an appraising look, as if just now noticing. When she glances down at her outfit, she fingers her cream-colored blouse. "Well, I guess I'm wearing a bit of white."

I tug the hand she gave me to bring her closer to me, then loop an arm around her back. "This is just paperwork," I tell her softly, not wanting the others to overhear. They take the hint and head into the courthouse. "We'll have a do-over later. You get to have the ring you want. And the dress you pick out. Flowers. All your friends and family with us to celebrate."

Her eyes grow bright with tears, and it makes my gut twist.

"Today is just—" I look past her, struggling to find words. "Today is paperwork. We're signing the contract. We can make tomorrow into whatever we want."

————

Lara

My breath shudders in on a sob.

I've been holding in my emotions, using rage and right-eousness to tamp down my fear and grief.

But Baron verbalizing just how wrong this ceremony is, without the dress or flowers or friends, brings it all storming to the surface.

Because I need to keep it together until after we sign the "contract," I push him away and march toward the courthouse.

Leo holds the door open for me, meeting Baron's gaze over my head.

I keep gulping in air, pushing back the torrent of tears threatening.

Lili glances at my face. "Too bad we couldn't bring the champagne in here, right?" she mutters with a wry smile.

I give a watery laugh in agreement.

We head into the assigned courtroom and wait to be called forward by the judge. Lili and Leo volunteer to be our witnesses. Zoe thrusts a bouquet of white roses wrapped up in ribbon in my hand.

We stand in front of the judge as he looks through the paperwork and then looks us over. "You wish to take your husband's name?"

Ben nods, but the judge is looking at me. I manage to nod my head. I'm feeling dizzy from drinking the champagne on an empty stomach.

"Do you have rings?"

Benjamin nods.

"Are you doing a kiss?"

Benjamin darts a glance my way. "Of course."

My stomach churns.

The judge begins. "Benjamin Baranov, do you take Lara Tur...Tour-Geneva" –he butchers my last name, making it sound like the city in Switzerland– "to live together in the honorable estate of matrimony, do you promise to love, honor, and comfort her in sickness and health, do you promise to be faithful and keep yourself only unto her as long as you both shall live?"

"I do."

The judge turns his attention on me. "Lara–"

"Turgeneva," Baron interrupts to pronounce my last name correctly.

The judge repeats it, "Lara Turgeneva, do you take Benjamin Baranov to be your husband, to live together in the honorable estate of matrimony, do you promise to love, honor, and comfort him in sickness and health, do you promise to be faithful and keep yourself only unto him as long as you both shall live?"

I look balefully up at my groom. My heart pounds against my chest.

Baron's expression is inscrutable. His brown eyes are steady beneath his unruly blond hair.

What if I say no? I got on the plane because my dad put me on it, but he's not here now to make sure I go through with it.

But the memory of his pinched expression returns to me. He was overprotective growing up, but I never saw that level of concern before. If I said no, would I be putting his life in danger? Or my mom's?

Baron seems unperturbed, but the tension from Lili is palpable, like she's holding her breath for Baron.

I clear my throat. "I do." My voice sounds rusty.

"By the authority vested in me by the State of Illinois, I now pronounce you husband and wife. You may exchange rings."

Baron pulls a pair of rings from his pocket and slides a thin gold band on my fourth finger, then puts a thicker one on his.

"Okay." Baron says the word with finality, his arm lightly draped behind my back. Like, *box checked. Wife acquired.*

"You may kiss your wife."

His wife. I'm now somebody's wife. This is insane.

Baron looks down at me, and I tense. Do I have to let him, since we're in front of a judge, and he wouldn't want the judge to know this marriage is against my will?

As if sensing I will refuse to be kissed, Baron sweeps me up into his arms in a honeymoon carry. His friends laugh and cheer.

The conqueror has conquered. I'm clearly a spoil of war. His to carry off and...

I glance at his handsome face, which is far too close for comfort.

He starts to walk out of the courtroom.

"Hold up," the bailiff calls. "You have to sign the certificate."

Baron spins me around—an extra time, fast, which makes my arms fly around his neck and a reluctant laugh spill from my throat—and carries me back.

We both sign the certificate. Leo and Lili add their signatures, and it's done.

I'm married to Benjamin Baranov.

"*Pozdravleniya*," Lili says.

"*Pozdravleniya*." Zoe, Anya, and Leo chorus.

"I'm guessing that's congratulations," Phoenix says. "So, what they said."

"*Gratulerer*," Anders adds in Norwegian.

I catch Baron looking at me, and my breath leaves my chest. He brushes the hair back from my face with the backs of his fingers then cradles my cheek. "May I kiss you?" he murmurs in Russian.

I want to say no out of principle. But my body says yes. My battered, lonely heart says yes. I crave human connection, even if it's with the man who caused all this strife to begin with. I tip my face up to show my silent consent, and he lowers his mouth to mine.

His lips brush lightly across mine, barely touching.

Mine fall open.

He kisses me harder, his hand shifting from my face to cup behind my head.

I don't *want* to like it. I don't want to surrender to him or this moment, but it feels too good. He's an expert kisser, confident yet nuanced. My body heats under his touch, nipples tightening, every cell electrifying. The courtroom spins. I'm free-falling into Baron. Into something foreign. I can't stop this new chapter of my life from unfolding, but I have to admit, it's not that terrible.

At least, not yet.

Baron lifts me into his arms again and carries me outside, still kissing me.

"Baron." Leo interrupts in a low but urgent tone.

Baron breaks the kiss and looks at his bratva soldier, who slightly lifts his chin in the direction of a sleek gray electric car parked across the street.

Baron's gaze follows as the car pulls away from the curb and disappears. He and Leo make eye contact for a moment and some communication passes between them.

Someone was watching us.

Someone witnessed our marriage. A member of the Chicago Bratva checking up to make sure Baron completed the deed? Most likely.

A cold chill brings me back to reality.

I just married an extension of my father. A gilded cage in the form of a soldier. A *pakhan* in the making. No amount of charm or good looks or perfect kisses will change that.

CHAPTER SEVEN

Baron

She let me kiss her.

I keep reminding myself of that fact as Lara downs more and more champagne in the living room of Baranov House.

Her phone started ringing with calls from Brash about five minutes after that *svoloch* who asked her to have a drink last night drove away. He's Brash's spy, I'm sure of it.

She didn't take Brash's calls, but she turned cold again after that, refusing to sit up front with me on the drive home. Phoenix offered to drive, so I could ride in the back with her, which I reluctantly agreed to. I don't like to be the guy riding in the back, subject to someone else's driving, but the situation seemed to call for it. I opened more champagne, and Lara drank—thirstily.

When we got back to the house, Emma had set out a spread of hors d'oeuvres—I guess someone told her I was getting married—and the whole rest of the house was gathered with more champagne bottles and proper glasses for a mini-reception.

I gnash my teeth, wanting to carry her upstairs to our

room and figure out how to get back to the place where she let me kiss her. But that moment is gone, and the boisterousness of my friends seems to be a welcome distraction for her.

Leo leans over to speak in my ear. "Melinda Tracy is outside."

Fuck. I don't need this right now. Melinda had texted me this morning while I was taking Lara on the campus tour, and I hadn't bothered to answer.

She's not my girlfriend. I owe her nothing.

I shake my head. "No entry."

"I told her. She insists on talking to you. Says she won't leave until you come out."

Blyad'. I know what she wants.

"I'll take care of her," I murmur, glancing at Lara.

She notices. She's tipsy but not drunk.

On the front stoop, I find the daughter of Illinois Senator and Vice Presidential hopeful Gabe Tracy.

I lean in the doorway, barring her access to the house.

I instructed the members of my house not to give her entry this year because the last thing we need is the press or Secret Service following her here or doing background checks on any of us. Not that we personally have records. Still, I'm fairly certain our deep bratva roots will come up in their system.

She throws her hands out in an exaggerated question stance. "What's the deal, Baron?"

Melinda's irritated with being refused entry, but she wants what I have to offer more than she cares about being mistreated. Of course, mistreatment is always on the table with her. "Baron—Ben—please." She uses my real name rather than the moniker most everyone at Thornecroft calls me to infer intimacy. "Don't be a dick. I *need* this."

I don't allow drug addicts to hang out at Baranov House, but Melinda's drug of choice is pain. And she knows—intimately—how our house got its nickname, "The Gulag." She's taken more trips to our dungeon than any other non-house member on campus.

Melinda's not my girlfriend.

We don't have that kind of relationship. I've never even kissed her.

But I do have a certain penchant for delivering pain. And her straight A, over-achiever double major/triple minor personality requires a certain form of stress relief. One that usually comes in the form of a long session at the receiving end of a belt or riding crop.

"You can't come in. You know why."

"He hasn't been elected yet. No one cares what I do."

"You know that's not true."

Her brown ponytail is pulled up too tight on the top of her head. She's jittery, like she had too much caffeine, her brown eyes too bright, her body movements quick and jerky. She's in sneakers and yoga pants with a matching Lululemon sports bra like she just came from a run. Her ribs show above the neckline. If I had her in the dungeon, I'd demand to know what she ate today. But I can't take that role with her ever again. I'm married.

"I need this."

"Find someone else."

"Who? You're the only one I trust. *Especially* with my dad's nomination."

I shrug. I want to suggest she talk to Anders because I know he has a thing for Melinda, but that would put her back in our sphere, which I can't have.

"Not me. Even if your dad hadn't been chosen as a presidential running mate, I'm out this year."

Her eyes narrow. She's bright enough to need to understand everything at play. "Why?"

"I'm married."

Her jaw drops at that. "*What?*" She looks offended, which makes me frown. I never gave her any reason to think she had a claim on me. But I don't think she's attached to me that way. It's only ever been transactional between us. I hurt her because I enjoy honing my practice on a willing partner. She craves it for the endorphin release. Nothing more, nothing less.

"My bride flew in from Paris this week. She transferred to Thornecroft."

Melinda cocks her head. "Bullshit."

"Truth. I had an arranged marriage to a Russian bratva princess."

I know part of the mystique of Baranov House is that everyone knows or believes we're bratva heirs. I play it up when I can, not because I'm a tough-guy but because that reputation does more to spark business and alliances and command respect than me trying to prove we're legit.

Besides, we're not legit. We may not be in our parents' business, but we created our own enterprises.

Now Melinda's sure I'm lying to get rid of her. Her nostrils flare. "Fuck you, Baron. You're an asshole."

"It's true," I say mildly.

A flash of uncertainty shows under her mask.

I don't want her to think I'm playing games with her—that's not my style. "It's the truth, Melinda." My tone is gentle. I show her my hand with the shiny new gold ring.

This time, my words seem to settle over her and land, lowering her shoulders and relaxing her face. "Seriously?"

I nod. "Yeah. It's been arranged since we were babies, but the timeline got moved up."

"Why?"

"She had interest from another party."

I probably shouldn't have shared that part, but Melinda can be counted on for discretion. I know many savory secrets about her that she wouldn't want discussed on campus.

"That's just between you and me," I say to be sure.

She relaxes a bit more now. "Yeah, I'll be sure to keep my mouth shut around all my other Russian bratva contacts."

"I mean it."

She mimes zipping her lips and throwing away a key. "All right. Well, I would never mess with a married man, so no worries."

I nod. "Glad you understand."

Hearing the voices of my friends, she tries to look past me into the house. "You can't come in here," I reiterate.

"What about for parties?"

Ugh. I don't want to ruin her social life, but I also don't want any attention on Baranov House. I relent. "Twice a semester. For the biggest parties only."

She rolls her eyes. "You're a dick."

As she turns to walk away, the part of me that needs to protect everyone around me surfaces. "If you're ever in trouble—"

She looks back over her shoulder and sends me a forgiving smile. "You'd be the first guy I came to."

I enter the house and find Lara stationed in front of the large picture-glass window. She'd seen everything.

Had she overheard? No. No way. We sound-proofed the house for parties. Sound wouldn't carry in or out.

"Who was that?" she demands.

I hide the satisfaction her question brings. She cares. I doubt she's jealous—she doesn't care about me enough for that yet—but she staking her claim.

I walk over and lightly rest my hands on her waist. She skitters to the side but then settles, letting me touch her. "That's Melinda Tracy." I know the more truth I can offer Lara, the sooner she will learn to trust me.

"Her dad is running for Vice President, so I banned her from the house this year. She was pissed off about it."

Lara stares up at me. Her eyes are the most stunning shade of blue, enhanced by the dark brown shade of her hair. I want to kiss her again.

Desperately.

I want to break down her walls as much as I want to strip off those clothes.

"Because illegal things happen here," she surmises.

I shrug. "I don't want undue attention on us. I would also hate for anyone to draw connections between her father and mine."

"You've slept with her."

"No," I answer instantly to put her mind at ease.

Lara's eyes narrow. "You showed her your ring."

Right. She saw that. I consider my next words. While truth is the best policy, I'm not sure she's ready to learn about the dungeon and the things I do—or used to do—down there.

"I did. She wanted something from me. Something I've given her in the past. But as you saw, I showed her my ring and ended things. You're my wife. I'm not going to fuck around on you."

Confusion scrambles her forehead. "*What* did she want from you?"

Gah. I hesitate.

She pushes my chest, and I drop my hands from her waist. "Hang on," I say, but she's already moving away from me.

She marches up the stairs, her perfect ass swaying with each step.

I follow. This is what marriage is about, right? Resolving differences?

I mean, fuck if I know. I've never even had a serious girlfriend.

When we reach the bedroom, her phone rings again.

Fucking Brash. She looks at the screen and sends it to voicemail.

"Is that your boyfriend?" My voice sounds dangerous. I don't mean to show this side of myself to her.

I get my violence under control. It's time I broached this subject with her. "Did I see the name Brash?" I pretend I don't know who she was dating. "Not Brash Rostov, the oligarch's son?"

Lara turns, surprised I know him.

"I went to boarding school with him." I shake my head, remembering the torture I'd found him inflicting. It had triggered my PTSD, and I'd gone nuclear. If a monitor hadn't caught us, I would've killed him with my bare hands. Instead, I got expelled.

How do I tell her that she's in more danger from him than me?

"The Rostovs aren't who you think they are. They're... worse than bratva."

She snorts, her eyes narrowed. "That's ripe coming from you. Brash has been nothing but kind and generous with me." There's a defensive note in her voice. "I'm in more danger with you than the Rostovs."

Blyad'. She has it backward, but I don't know how to make her see that. I have to wait until she trusts me more than she trusts him.

"Did you end things with him now that you're married?"

She stiffens and whirls to face me. "Fuck off."

I dial down my control issues and switch gears. She's never going to trust me if I can't make her fall in love.

"Uh-uh." I close the distance between us. She flinches when I reach for her, but all I do is pull her into my arms. "We don't talk to each other that way."

"*We* just did."

I back her up until her ass hits the dresser and then cradle her nape to lift her face to mine. "We don't." I murmur the words against her cheek as my thumb caresses her cheek. "Is that how you want me to speak to you?"

She doesn't answer. Her body trembles against mine—whether it's from fear or desire, I can't be sure.

I know from the dungeon that both can work in my favor.

I slide the hand behind her back down to explore the curves of her ass and squeeze. "Hm?"

"Get off me," she whispers.

I hesitate. My experience as a dom tells me this is a moment to push, not to give her sovereignty. But she's not a consenting sub.

She's also not a consenting wife, but we're married just the same. Breaking down her barriers and forging something tender between us is the best—possibly the only—way I can keep her safe from Brash.

"Should I show you what Melinda wanted from me?"

I catch that confusion swirling in her eyes again. "What is it?"

"Turn around," I murmur, at the same time I gently rotate her.

Miraculously, she lets me.

"Hands on the dresser." I pick up one hand and flatten it on the surface of the dresser then the other.

I unzip the back of her skirt and let it tumble to the floor.

———

Lara

I look over my shoulder, starting to straighten, but Baron pushes my torso back down. "You said you didn't have sex with her," I accuse.

I don't know why seeing Baron with that woman set me

off, but it did. I know she's an ex-girlfriend or at least someone he's slept with, I can tell. Call it women's intuition.

"I didn't," he maintains.

I'm shivering, my knees quaking, my breath quick. I wish Baron wasn't so damn seductive. I don't know how I ended up standing in my panties, bent over a dresser when I was resolved to not even let him kiss me.

He slaps my ass, hard.

I shriek and try to turn, but he holds my hip in place.

"This is what Melinda wanted from me."

I stop struggling, listening.

He slaps the other cheek equally hard.

I squeal again. Heat rushes between my legs. My pussy tingles, moisture gathering.

Baron stops and rubs my stinging flesh. "She's a masochist who uses pain to cope with the stress of overachievement."

I remember the girl at the cafe asking about a dungeon. Is this what she meant? There's a BDSM dungeon at Baranov House?

That's...wild.

He delivers a flurry of light, quick slaps. They don't hurt, but they warm my ass.

It feels wonderful. Not the first two spanks—they were stingy. But this...I can see the appeal. Every slap sends a jolt of sensation straight to my core. The mixture of danger and pleasure, of pain and seduction, intoxicates me more than the champagne I drank.

Baron knows what he's doing. He's done this before. With that woman.

"Did you fuck her?"

I guess I'm jealous. Even more so after hearing he's done this with her.

"Never, *malyshka*. I haven't even kissed her."

"Kiss *me*." Funny how I was determined to refuse his touch, and now I'm suddenly demanding it.

Baron rotates my hips, turning me to face him, then picks me up and sets my heated ass on the top of the dresser. He pushes my knees wide and invades my personal space, grabbing my ass with both hands and yanking my core right up against his body as he dips his head for the kiss.

My core contracts, knees clamping around his waist as his tongue delves into my mouth.

This time I'm eager for it. I kiss him back, my lips sliding over his. My hands come to his chest and coast over his pectoral muscles. I work the buttons on his shirt.

He catches my wrists, and I go still, catching his gaze to interpret why he stopped me.

"Good girl," he praises. My belly flutters in response. I shouldn't love it, but I do. "Now lean back on your elbows."

I try to figure out what he means. He puts a finger in the center of my chest and presses backward. I fall on my hands first, then, finally understanding, lower to my forearms.

"That's it, *malyshka*. So fucking beautiful." He slides his hands under my knees and reaches for my ass, forcing my legs wider, dangling over his biceps. One firm yank, and my ass is right at the edge of the dresser.

I gasp at the sudden movement then gasp again when he yanks the gusset of my panties to the side, ripping the pink lace. "Oh."

I've had sex before. I'm not a blushing virgin bride, but this is something different.

Baron has the skill and confidence of a man who's had a hundred lovers. And I hate all of them.

Except the moment his tongue makes contact with my lady bits, I'm grateful for his skill. He traces my inner lips, sucks the outer ones. He finds my clit and laves it with his tongue.

I cry out, tension building. My inner thighs shake and tighten against his shoulders.

He takes his time, dropping to his knees to improve the angle, penetrating me with his tongue. When he manages to suck my clit, it's too much. I rock my hips, pressing my wet heat into his face for more.

But then some part of me doesn't want to shatter. I don't want him to succeed. I need to maintain my strength.

"How many?" I demand.

He lifts his head, his mouth glossy with my juices and raises his brows in question.

"How many women have you...done that with?"

His lips twitch with faint amusement, but then his expression returns to the serious, inscrutable one he usually gives me. He slowly rises, and I regret my interruption. I want his mouth back on me, teasing me, winding me up to orgasm.

He steps in close, and I start to sit up. "Ah ah," he tuts.

I freeze, caught in his commanding brown gaze, then ease back down to my forearms.

"Good girl." He rewards me by sliding the pad of his middle finger through my juices. He continues the slow glide, up and down along my slit, then dipping into my entrance. "You want to know how many submissives I've mastered?"

Do I? Part of me feels a little sick about it. But the rest of me needs to know.

My indecision is made worse by his full penetration with two fingers. He curls them into me, stroking inside, setting me on fire. "Wait."

I'm going to come, but I don't want to. I can't take the vulnerability. Or giving Baron the win.

I start to sit up, but he distracts me by pumping quickly, the tips of his fingers hitting the place that drives me wild every time.

"Baron—"

"Take your finger-fuck and show me how you let go when you come." His voice has a stern, commanding tone he hasn't used with me before.

I squirm on the dresser. "I can't—"

"Take it, or I'll turn you back over and spank you until you scream."

The threat breaks something apart inside me. The orgasm rips through me without warning, and I spasm around his fingers, crying out in surprise.

He stops pumping his fingers and holds them inside me, his warm palm molding to cup my mons. The heel of his hand presses against my clit, wringing even more of a release from me.

"*Gospodi!*"

"Mmm. That was pretty." Baron starts slowly fucking me with his middle finger, while keeping the heel of his hand against my clit. "You took it so well, *malyshka*."

I'm panting, the spinning room starts to right itself again. As it does, awareness of the fact that *I* was the one who came undone while he stayed fully dressed and in control creeps in.

I don't like the gash of vulnerability that cuts across my chest.

Baron must sense my exposure because he slips his fingers out of me, loops an arm behind my back and pulls me up to straddle his waist. "Come on. Let's get in the shower."

A shower sounds good, so I don't protest. There's something easy about letting Baron take charge, especially because he has an uncanny sense of what I need in the moment. Like the way he commented on the ride home that we should get some food in me before the champagne went to my head. He's good at reading me and responding to what he sees, and there's relief in that.

I let him carry me to the bathroom where he sets me

down and pulls my top off over my head. I unbutton his shirt as I kick off my boots.

This is fine, I tell myself. I deserve some good sex. It doesn't mean I've accepted Baron or our marriage.

"You want to know how many," Baron says.

I meet his gaze, startled. Wow. I admire the hell out of him for addressing the uncomfortable question I already let drop.

I work open his belt buckle, avoiding his gaze.

"The answer is I don't know. There isn't a number. It's not something I counted to notch on my belt."

Gospodi. That means it's a lot. He's been with a lot of women.

I mean, I suspected it, but this is confirmation.

"But that was all before." He reaches for me, and when he yanks me against his body, he's rough.

I gasp and look up to search his face.

Lust blazes in his gaze. Lust for *me.*

He grips my head and steals a fierce kiss. A claiming kiss.

I yank his shirt off his broad shoulders. I'm in nothing but my bra and panties, and he still has more clothes on than I do.

He breaks the kiss, holding my head captive in a steel grasp. "It's just you now." He holds my gaze. "I made a vow today to be faithful, and I won't break it. I'm a man of my word."

I don't know how to answer. I made a vow because I had to. I would break it tomorrow if I thought my family wouldn't get hurt. I don't know if I believe him anyway. He's obviously a player.

As usual, he seems to read my mind. "You don't know whether you can trust me. You can, Lara."

He releases me to shove his pants and boxers off. His body is gorgeous—all lean, powerful muscle. His skin is golden, his sculpted chest covered in soft curls. My eyes trace down his washboard abs and the natural taper of his waist to the enormous erection pointing at me.

Damn.

It looks demanding. And he likes to get rough. Will he hurt me with that beast? Do I still have a choice, or are we way past that now?

He sees me looking. I must appear daunted because he immediately, dismissively pronounces, "You don't have to take my cock tonight."

I drag my gaze up from his dick to his face.

He steps closer to me, the lion cornering his catch. His hands grip my hips. "I'm going to do my husbandly duty and get you off on your wedding night." He unhooks my bra and slides it down my arms. "I don't care if it's by riding my cock or with my mouth and fingers. All I know is you're going to be fucking *satisfied* by the time I'm done with you."

The way he says *satisfied* seems to signify something I've never before experienced. My knees buckle a little. My pussy drips through the rip in my panties onto my inner thighs.

Am I swooning? I might be swooning a little.

"Now lose your panties before I tear them off you."

CHAPTER EIGHT

Baron

I watch with heavy-lidded eyes as Lara steps out of her panties. She's perfect—her pale breasts adorned with a set of taut, dusky-rose nipples that tilt upward. She's trembling, her breath coming in shallow pants, but her pupils are dilated, telling me she's turned on, not afraid.

Fear makes the pupils contract. Lust blows them wide.

I turn on the water then slide my forearm under Lara's ass and lift her into the large walk-in shower.

"Tell me about your preferred birth control, *printsessa*."

When she doesn't answer, I pin her against the tile wall, crowding against her, letting her feel my size, my strength. Warm water sluices over our heads, adding to the sensory experience.

The hard points of her nipples brush against my ribs.

I kiss her hard. My lips move over hers, not teasing—punishing. *Claiming*. My tongue lashes into her mouth. My dick presses insistently against her soft belly.

I meant what I said, though. Even though I'm asking

about birth control, I'm not going to fuck her if she doesn't want it.

Right now, she seems agreeable, but if she says no, I'll respect that boundary.

"I'm on the pill," she gasps when I finally break the kiss.

Jealousy spikes through me. For him? For Brash?

No. They didn't seem that intimate. She still hasn't taken his call or texted him back.

"I'm clean." I kiss her some more. Without breaking the liplock, I reach for the soap, rolling it in my palms to build a lather then stroking them across her shoulders. Around her tits. Down the sides of her rib cage. I slide them around her ass, circling.

"Let me see this gorgeous ass." I turn her around to face the far shower wall, so her face is out of the spray. "Hands against the wall, *printsessa*."

She doesn't obey.

I smack her ass. It's still pink from the spanking I gave her in the bedroom, and the water makes my slap stingier—I know because it stings my palm.

She gasps and whirls to glare at me over her shoulder.

I crowd in close again, gripping her nape to kiss her thoroughly. "Show me your pretty ass," I murmur, more coaxing this time, while my hold on her is firm. I turn her to face the wall again, catching her left wrist to press her palm against the tile. "Other hand," I prompt.

She lifts it then stops herself, pausing midair, as if she obeyed automatically then wanted to show me I'm not her master.

I wrap my larger palm over her hand slowly, and interlace my fingers over the tops of hers. I kiss her temple, her jaw, the side of her neck, and I ease her second hand into place against the wall. "Good girl," I murmur against the shell of her ear.

A shudder runs through her.

"Did you just come, *malyshka*?" My voice is a low rumble against her skin. I bring my fingers between her legs to feel what's going on. "Are you clenching down here for me?"

Her pelvic floor lifts and lowers, fluttering with a small climax.

"That's good, angel. You're so perfect." I kiss her shoulder. "So responsive."

I pick up the bar of soap and get more lather then soap her back, her waist, the crack of her ass.

She moans, pitching forward more, arching for me.

"This is what I wanted to see." I stand to the side and stroke a loving hand over her plump ass, exploring every centimeter. "Fucking gorgeous."

When I slide my hand over her pussy again, she moans.

"That's it, pretty girl. I like it when you let go." I crowd against her, grasping her breast with one hand as I tease her clit. My teeth graze her shoulder as I pinch her nipple hard enough to make her gasp and her pussy clench.

"Turn around." I'm suddenly rough. Commanding. I spin her and push her back against the tile, then squat and lift one of her legs over my shoulder.

"Oh!" She clutches my head for stability as I bring my mouth to her dripping core.

I penetrate her with my tongue. "You need me here?" I demand, my voice rougher and deeper than normal.

"Oh!"

I reach up and pinch the other nipple. "Answer me, Lara-Love."

Her core squeezes. I know she's beyond turned on. Deep in the physicality. Almost in sub-space. Or maybe she's there now. She offers no resistance other than not speaking, but loss of language can be a result of sub-space.

"What?" she asks in Russian, sounding dazed.

Good. She's there.

I take over, releasing her from the obligation of speech or decisions. "I'm going to fuck you with my tongue," I tell her. "And then I'm going to decide if you get my fingers or my cock. And you're going to be a good girl and take it. Understand?"

"*Da.*"

I'd prefer a *yes sir*, but I won't ask for it tonight. Tonight is about her pleasure. Teaching her to yield to my lead. Showing her how well I can take care of her needs.

I need her trust to keep her safe.

But I desire her full surrender.

I want her on her knees every night for me, begging for my touch. My praise. For her release.

I don't want to own her contractually. I want to fully possess my wife—body, mind, and fucking soul.

"That's good." I rub her clit with my thumb, and she jerks and whimpers with need. I lick into her, bathing her with the flat of my tongue, sucking her labia, penetrating. I penetrate her with my thumb and suck her clit, and she starts to cry out in short, staccato beats.

"Oh, oh, oh, oh."

"That's it, beautiful." Time to switch things up. I want to keep her in a prolonged state of arousal before I let her come. It will make the orgasm all the juicer.

I stand and whip her around to face the wall again, delivering several medium-hard spanks to her round ass—right, left, middle.

"Oh! Wait! Why?" she cries out.

I grip her hips and twist her back to face me, pinning her pelvis against the wall and lifting her thigh to give me access to her core.

"Why what?" I kiss her hard, bending my knees so the head of my cock prods her entrance. "Why did I spank you?"

I pull my face back enough to find her gaze and see confusion there.

I celebrate the fuck out of it. It means she was trying to please me. I tamed her, at least for this moment. This scene.

"Because your ass is too perfect not to spank, angel. Because it gives you fresh stimulation."

I grip my cock and rub it across her cunt. "Feel how wet you are?"

I kiss her with bruising force, my teeth scraping her lips. She moans into my mouth. I suck her lower lip as I pull away.

"And because I wanted to. It's for my pleasure and yours." I lean my forehead against hers. As our breath mingles, I work the head of my cock into her entrance. "You want to ride my cock tonight?"

One last chance for her to refuse. I know she's not going to, but I want her to understand it's her choice. I may be dominant, but it's always consensual.

She reaches for my waist and pulls my hips toward her.

"Say it," I demand even as I press forward, parting her to take me.

"*Da.*"

I might have to learn to dirty talk in Russian for my bride. I'm better listening and reading it than speaking, and I obviously never picked up sex talk from my dad. I make a mental note to watch some Russian porn.

I ease slowly into her. She's sopping wet, but her channel is tight, and my dick is big. I don't want to hurt her. As I push in, inch by inch, my palms rove over her body—along her sides, across her breasts, down her back to grip her ass.

I trace my middle finger down her crack and press against her anus when I fill her to the hilt.

Her nails score my shoulders as she cries out.

"That's right, *malyshka*. Take your husband's cock."

———

Lara

This is the hottest sex I've ever had in my life.

This is *so*...beyond.

Beyond anything I even imagined.

If you asked me before, I wouldn't have said I liked or wanted any of this. The dirty talk, the rough treatment, the spanking. The dominant mastery.

But my body responds to Baron's every word. Every look. Every touch. My body craves everything he has to give. I'm *dying* for it.

I lean my shoulders and head back against the tile and press my hips up and forward to take him deeper. He's big–both in girth and length, and he fills me beyond what I would've thought possible.

Thank God he's going slowly.

But I'm starting to trust him. Even when he's rough, he seems very aware of what he's doing. He didn't bang my head against the tile. He spun me fast, then went slow for the press. And the spankings don't really hurt. Just a momentary sting.

He holds my knee up now, pushing into me as one of his fingers presses against my back hole.

It's crazy. Insane. So much sensation at once. The nudity. The water. The passionate kisses. The titillation of all my erogenous zones at alternating times and intensities.

I've been with a few guys before. Three, to be exact. *Nothing* felt like this. Our encounters were lights-off, under the covers explorations. There was no dirty-talk. No devious commands. No praise. Certainly no punishments or rewards.

I'm intoxicated by it all–every nerve ending attuned to Baron. I moan, needy for more.

He continues to penetrate me with his thick cock, in and

out, plowing deep. I tip my pelvis up to meet his thrusts, rubbing my clit against his loins, taking him deeper.

"Good girl." He claims my mouth again in a jerky kiss. "Good fucking girl." His tongue plunges in between my lips at the same time he thrusts into me.

"Baron!" I cry out. "Benjamin."

His chuckle is a deep, satisfied rumble, like he enjoys hearing me call out his name.

I get dizzy—the warm water combined with hot sex makes spots appear before my eyes. "It's too much," I gasp.

He shoves in, spearing me with his erection and lengthening his knees, so I'm lifted on my tiptoes by his cock.

I hang there against the wall, spread open to him and desperate.

His hands brace beside my head as we pant together.

"Too hot, *printsessa?*"

I nod, my head wobbling on my neck.

He looks down between our bellies where we're joined. "You're going to come for me, *malysh*. And then I'm going to carry you to our bed where I'm going to fuck you until you scream. Understand?"

His words make me moan.

He reaches down between our bodies, sliding his finger into the apex of my folds and rubs.

I jerk, crying out with the jolt of sensation that zings straight from my clit to my pussy. I squeeze around him, muscles spasming in another orgasm.

He's incredible. I've never known such pleasure. Never had more than one orgasm in the same night.

I open my eyes when he gently lowers me to my feet and eases out of me. I'm still light-headed, and now my legs won't hold me up.

"Come here." He wraps his arm around me and pulls me under the spray of water, turning the heat down, so it's cooler.

Still holding me up, he pops open the top of my shampoo bottle and squirts a large dollop in his palm.

He draws a deep breath through his nostrils. "Mmm. This is why you smell like butterscotch." He rubs his hands together then brings his palms to my head. "You have the most beautiful hair, *printsessa*. I love it. It's so long. So thick."

His praise is starting to seep into the cracks in my armor, and the most vulnerable part of me sops it up like a sponge. I've worked so hard to be strong and independent, living in a different country from my parents, but having someone take care of me this way reminds me of just how alone I often felt. Especially over the last few days. Even though I know it stems from his control issues, Baron's nurture and praise feel far too necessary right now to refuse, so I let go and enjoy.

I close my eyes and drink in the pleasure of having my scalp massaged. Of being held up when my knees are weak. Of not having to make decisions for myself when I've been in a state of survival panic since my dad showed up and told me I had to marry this man.

Before he finishes washing my hair, though, Baron spanks me again.

My eyes fly open in surprise. I'm the type who likes to get things right. To be kind and considerate and avoid judgment from others. But then I remember what he said last time. This is for pleasure. It's not punishment.

"I'm not done with this ass yet," he growls, tipping my torso forward.

I catch the edge of the shower's entryway and hang on.

"Spread your legs. I'm gonna spank that sweet pussy."

I obey, despite my mind rebelling at his statement. My body must want it. Must trust that I'll like it.

He slaps lightly between my legs. A jolt of sensation goes through me, registering in three places at once—my clit, inside my pussy, and my anus.

"Oh!" I cry out.

He peppers my ass with spanks that are hard enough to make me jerk and jump then slaps between my legs again. "I'm gonna pound into this pussy when I get you in our bed," he says, tugging me back under the water to rinse off the shampoo.

I moan, all turned on again. Baron is brilliant—keeping me wildly turned on and on edge, even as he gives me a break. He quickly smooths conditioner in my hair while I rub myself. I'm shocked at how different things feel down there—my pussy is plump and swollen. Slick and open.

"Uh uh." Baron catches my wrist and moves my hand away. His body molds against mine from behind, his hard cock pressing at my lower back. "That's my job." He rubs between my legs.

I like giving him the job. His fingers are larger. More skilled. He squeezes one of my breasts, and I lay my head back against his chest and let him explore between my legs.

"You liked your spanking." He rumbles the words right against my ear—a dark seductive taunt.

I want to protest, but then he says, "I'm gonna learn everything you like, my beautiful wife."

Something about him reminding me that we're married drains away some of the passion. A sense of defeat washes over me.

I *am* married to this man.

We are *married*.

It already happened, despite my wishes.

In this moment, I no longer have the desire to fight. I surrender to my fate. To this reality.

Baron senses the change and rotates me in his arms to face him. "I know."

He pulls me against his chest and then rocks me side to side. We're slow dancing in the shower to the rhythm of our heartbeats. I want to push away, but I don't have the energy. I don't even *want* to fight him anymore.

I just need to grieve.

"I know you didn't want this. I didn't either." Baron's voice has a different tone to it. It's not the commanding one he was using a moment ago. Nor does it carry that quiet confidence he wields so well.

It sounds...real. Like I'm getting the real Baron for the first time.

"But Lara, the moment I met you, I felt—" He breaks off, and I go still because I sense that whatever he says—if he drops his control and lets himself say it—will be something I can believe.

I don't lift my head from his chest even though I'm dying to search his face. I'm afraid if I do, that impregnable mask of his will slide back into place.

"You felt familiar. Like my body recognized that you've belonged to me all along."

I push him away, shaking my head.

Belonged to him?

What the actual fuck?

He realizes his faux pas. "I don't mean it that way. I just meant that it felt like it was meant to be."

"Of course it was meant to be for you. Your father hands you a bride, and you're happy to jump to his bidding. The *pakhan* in training. I had a life and dreams, and none of them involved marrying a man like my father or yours. I don't want this life. I don't want to be married to the bratva. We are not *meant to be*. Don't write pretty stories in your head about us being *meant to be* just because I like being fucked by you." I gesture him out of the way and step under the water to rinse out the conditioner.

When he leaves the shower without another word, I register the loss of him in every cell of my body.

Regret leeches in, but it's too late.

The magic is gone.

Mood broken.

And I refuse to be sorry for offending the man who calls himself my husband.

CHAPTER NINE

Baron

"What did you find out about that little fuck moving in on my wife?" I demand, falling into step with Anya as she heads out the door for class the next day.

Lara already left, giving me the polite but mostly silent treatment for the rest of last night and this morning.

Anya sends me a startled look.

Blyad'. I let my emotions show through. I'm usually measured and controlled. It's the reason my friends trust me to lead.

This frustration is a result of going to bed with blue balls and having to share the bed with a beautiful woman who hates me.

Lara's hurting, I know that. She's using anger and righteousness to glue herself back together. I'd rather she let me mend the shattered pieces, but that's not going to happen anytime soon.

"His name is Denis Penkin. I'm still digging, but I haven't found a connection between him and the Rostovs. He's not part of the oligarchy, but his family does seem well-off."

I grunt, dissatisfied.

"I also didn't find his application to Thornecroft in the pool submitted last spring." Anya raises her brows.

It takes me a second to process. "Meaning someone pulled strings to get him in here."

"Right."

"Last-minute strings."

"Probably."

Just like the ones my dad pulled to get Lara transferred and into the necessary classes on short notice.

"So he's definitely a spy."

Anya shrugs. "I don't know if I'd say definitely, but I thought it seemed suspicious."

"Good work," I tell her. "That was smart thinking."

Anya flashes me a quick smile as she pretends to buff her nails on her shirt. "I know, I'm a genius."

We reach the end of the block, and Anya points to the left. "I'm going this way."

"I'll see you later. Keep digging for me." I walk north to my statistics class.

"Yes, *pakhan*," she calls over her shoulder.

I point in warning as we walk farther away from each other. "Don't call me that."

"Just accept it."

———

Lara

After my last class, I walk toward Whisper's End, the bar Denis named to meet him.

Like yesterday, I avoided Baranov House all day. I have time between classes or at lunch to walk back there, but instead, I ate at the food court and studied in the library.

I don't really want to. I'm having a pity party for myself, and it's definitely a party of one.

My phone rings as I'm walking with a Facetime call.

I check the screen and sigh. It's my mom. She's probably desperate to know whether I'm still alive. I stop under the shade of a tree and answer. "Mama."

"Lara, thank God," my mom exclaims in Ukrainian, her native language, and bursts into tears.

I immediately feel terrible for not taking her calls. I also still feel a little bad about ruining my wedding night.

And I'm homesick. Seeing my mom hits hard.

I sink onto a park bench under the tree, uncontrollably crying. "Ah, Mama," I tell her, "this is why I didn't call you yesterday. I knew you'd make me cry."

My mom wipes her tears. There's a clay smudge on her face. I can see she's calling from her pottery studio. "Sweetheart, I was so worried. Are you okay? I'm so sorry for everything you're going through."

I let the tears out since there's no stopping them now, and, surprisingly, they pass after just a few moments. When I can calm down and breathe, I show her the wedding ring. "Well," I draw in a terraced breath. "I'm married."

"I know, my love. Is he decent enough? What's he like?"

"I don't know," I moan. That bit of regret over last night surges again, and I firmly remind myself that I am the victim here.

My mom wipes her tears and cocks her head at me, peering into the screen like she wishes she could climb through and hug me. "He must not be that bad."

I frown, offended that she would defend him. "What makes you say that?"

"Well, you sound conflicted. That means you like something about him. What is the conflict? Are you missing the guy you were dating in Paris? Abrasha?"

"Brash? No. He keeps calling, though." I sigh. "The conflict is that I don't want to be here. I don't want to be married. I'm scared for you and Papa and for me."

"We're safe. We're *all* safe. Your father believed this was the best way to ensure our safety." I hear the disagreement in her tone. "But tell me about Benjamin. I haven't seen him since he was in preschool."

"He's..." I think of what I went to tell my mother. I return to my complaints. "Mama, Baron—that's what they call him here—thinks he owns me. *Owns* me."

"Mm." My mom makes a noncommittal sound. "Bratva men are protective."

"Not just protective. He said I *belonged* to him."

"So what's the good part?"

"There is no good part!" I exclaim, exasperated.

"I can tell there is. I heard it in your voice. You like him, despite your objections."

"Like him? No." I sulk.

My mom waits. "Is he good-looking?"

The image of him standing naked in the shower pops into my mind, and my body instantly heats. I think of the bulge of his muscles. The confidence in the way he touches me. "Yes," I keep my voice neutral. "He's handsome. And...he is good in bed. Well, we haven't done it in the bed, but he's, um...he knows what he's doing."

My mom gives a light laugh. Seeing her smile relaxes the tight knot between my ribs. My mom is an artist—a fun-loving, wild, and wacky woman usually full of laughter and overflowing with love. That's why her tears killed me. "Well, there's something to be said for that. So does your fa—"

"Stop!" I cut her off. "I don't want to hear that. Ugh."

She chuckles. "Well, I will tell you that attraction was all we had at first, too. It started with sex. Your dad kidnapped me, and I seduced him."

"*What?*"

"True story. And now here we are, madly in love twenty-five years later."

"What do you mean he *kidnapped* you?"

"It's a long story. I'd rather tell you another time in person."

"Oh my God, Mama. You just smashed my entire reality into little bitty pieces."

"The point is, as long as there's chemistry between you, the most difficult situations can be worked out. I believe it was all meant to be. If your dad hadn't wanted to kill mine, we never would have met, and I wouldn't be with the love of my life. Maybe you and Benjamin are meant to be."

I think about Baron. Not just the sex, but the way he washed my hair last night and brought me coffee this morning. How he holds doors for me. The way he anticipates and takes care of my needs. I could get used to a man taking care of me the way my dad does with my mom. A man who acted like the world revolved around me, and he would rip the heart out of every dragon or man who tried to come near me.

I could get used to it, but not with a man I can't trust. Not with a man who is literally holding me and my family prisoner.

I glance at the time on my phone. "Mama, I have to go. I have a date with a guy from Russia I met yesterday."

"A *date?*" My mom sounds appalled.

I roll my eyes. "Not a date-date. We're just meeting for a drink."

"That sounds like a date. *Lyubimaya*, Benjamin isn't going to stand for that."

The same sense of rebellion rises in me that made me agree to meet Denis in the first place. Benjamin Baranov thinks he owns me. I'm going to prove he doesn't.

"I don't care, Mama. I'm going to show him he can't control me."

I end the call with my mom before she can lecture me and walk to Whisper's End. Denis sits at an open laptop at a high-top table for two near the window opposite the door. A beer and basket of fries sit beside him, and his books sprawl across the table. He has a goofy, disheveled look, and his face lights up when he sees me. If my mom could see him, she would know that there's nothing about this guy that would worry Baron.

"Hi." I greet him in Russian and slide into the chair opposite him. "How was your second day?"

He slaps the laptop closed. "You came. I wasn't sure you would."

Wow. This guy is like a puppy.

His gaze goes to my wedding ring. I don't know why I didn't take it off. Maybe I was afraid it would provoke a battle I wasn't sure I could handle. "Is...that new?" he asks. "I mean, I didn't notice a wedding ring yesterday. That *is* a wedding ring, isn't it?"

I finger the thin gold band. No words come out of my mouth.

How do you explain to a stranger that you just got married to another stranger because your dad basically sold you off as a child? Is that something you share with a guy you just met? Probably not.

In fact, it's probably not something I should share with anyone.

For one thing, I don't like the way it makes me feel. My self-image doesn't have room for the idea of me as chattel.

I draw a deep breath and sigh it out. "Yeah. I got married yesterday, actually."

I must sense the storm that is Benjamin Baranov barrelling toward us because my gaze pulls to the glass door moments before he yanks it open. He stalks straight toward us with a scowl firmly in place on his handsome face.

My stomach draws up into a tight knot, regret for my choices worming past my justifications. Not because I'm afraid of Baron—although I am, a little—but also because whatever this turns into doesn't feel worth it. I didn't really want to meet this guy for a drink. It was a pity meeting because he seemed lonely, but I don't have the energy to spare right now for extra battles.

"Oh good." My voice is flat. I don't take my gaze off Baron's approach as I speak. "Here comes my husband now."

CHAPTER TEN

Baron

I'm going to kill the fucker. He will die wishing he never knew my name. He will bleed and cry and beg me to forget that he came after what was mine.

I keep all of that from my face. At least I try to, but violence probably leaks from every pore. Maybe I reveal that my body is a lethal weapon in the way I stride across the bar, grab a chair from another table, and smoothly sit between the ass-cake and my wife.

I sit and reach for the basket of French fries beside Denis, pulling it toward me and eating one as I look at them expectantly.

I'm staking my claim. Making sure they both understand—to their bones—that I belong in this conversation. I belong anywhere my wife goes. I will follow her on every appointment, hangout, or meeting. I will vet every person she comes in contact with. And I will never, ever, allow Brash or his spies to fucking touch her.

I notice Lara's eyes are red, which punches me in the gut. She was crying—and not on my shoulder.

On this flaming fucker's?

The edge of jealousy creeps up in me, twining with guilt over Lara's pain to make a foul dish of violence.

I should say something to her. Ask if she's okay. Except she's not okay, and I'm the cause of her pain—at least from her perspective.

"Denis, this is Benjamin Baranov, my husband." Lara introduces us in Russian.

His brows raise as he holds out a hand for me to shake. "Are you Russian?"

I ignore the hand. "Half." I let him see the menace in my eyes.

He flinches and withdraws his hand.

Eric, the owner of the bar, spots me and comes out from behind the bar. Once or twice a year, I organize events here at Whisper's End. It's good to change things up and support local businesses. I compensate Eric well, so he's eager for more.

"Baron." He holds out his hand.

His, I shake. "Good to see you."

"Thanks for coming in. What can I get you to drink?"

"I'll have the IPA on tap." I look over at Lara. "What are you drinking, love?"

My tone is anything but loving because the desire for murder courses thickly through my veins.

Lara tucks her hair behind her ear and glances at Denis' half-full beer. The *mudak* didn't even get her a drink when she arrived. That's reason enough to shove my thumb through his eye socket.

"Um, I'll have the same."

"This is my wife, Lara." I tip my head toward Lara. "Lara, this is Eric. He owns the place."

"Oh! Didn't know you were married. Nice to meet you."

Lara's face is pinched and unhappy, but she forces a smile. "Nice to meet you."

I don't bother introducing Denis, and Eric takes my cue and ignores him, too, walking away. As soon as he's gone, Lara slides off her barstool. "I'm going to the ladies' room."

I nod coolly. The moment she's out of sight, I shift my weight off my barstool to one leg as my hand shoots out and grasps Denis by the hair. I slam his face down against the table and release him, sitting back in my seat as if nothing happened.

Eric shoots a glance my way at the sound, but Denis' back is to him, and my face is a calm mask.

Blood pours from Denis' broken nose. He grabs a napkin and holds it, dropping the bumbling nerd act and glaring at me with blazing eyes.

"I'll give you a choice." I flex my hand to flash the tattoos on my fingers—the ones that prove I'm lethal. "Leave before she comes back or stay, and I'll beat you over the head with that laptop to see which breaks first."

He stacks his books with one hand, keeping the other clamped with the napkin on his nose.

"Don't talk to my wife again."

He shoots me another glare.

It occurs to me I shouldn't have shown my hand. I should've had Alex and Feliks pick him up later and torture the truth out of him. Found out what Brask knows. What his plans are. Why he sent a spy here to watch Lara.

But that would've required me to sit here for another moment observing this jellyfish of a man sitting next to my woman.

"If you or your sick friend ever touch her, I will *end you both*."

"You're fucking crazy," he mutters in Russian, scooping his

laptop and books against his chest and hustling out of the bar.

I pick up another French fry and pop it in my mouth.

When Lara returns, she sends me a suspicious look. "Where is Denis?"

I eat another fry. "He had to go."

The puddle of blood on the bar catches her eye, and she gasps. "What did you do to him?"

I stare back blithely. I know I need to switch gears. I'm not going to woo my wife by being an asshole or scaring her, but my blood is still hot. The need to protect her with violence still too strong.

Eric walks over with our beers, and I toss a spare napkin on top of the puddle of blood.

"Thanks, man." I pull a twenty out of my pocket, but he shakes his head.

"On the house. I'm looking forward to working with you again this year."

"Me too, man." I lift my beer as if to toast him. "Thanks. I appreciate it." I drain half my glass and set it down to study Lara.

Her face is pale, but her lower jaw juts out in defiance. She doesn't touch her beer.

"What did you do to him?" she repeats. The words start out angry, but her voice breaks on the word *do*, and then her eyes fill with tears.

Blyad'.

I didn't mean to make her cry. I stand and reach my hand out to her. "C'mon. Let's get out of here."

She jerks her hands protectively to her chest. "I'm not going anywhere with you."

I slide back onto my barstool. "I'm not going anywhere without you."

We stare at each other. There is no contest of wills I won't win. I am the fucking *prince* of control.

Control is the only way to anticipate everything that might go wrong. To protect everyone who needs my protection. It's how I learned to deal with the guilt of having someone I loved gunned down while trying to protect me when I was a child.

Lara must see that in my face because she gives an exaggerated huff and stands. "Fine. Take me home. Seeing how you *own* me and everything."

She strides toward the door—a gorgeous bundle of rage and fear.

I should be sorry she's upset. I *am* sorry. But the man in me who needs to maintain control of everything to keep the people I love alive is satisfied.

My wife is where I need her to be.

Safe, under my watch.

CHAPTER ELEVEN

Lara

I should be glad Baron gave me space when we got home, and I stomped upstairs to our bedroom.

I was at first. But then I felt strangely abandoned.

Now, a few hours later, I feel terrible about putting Denis in a bad situation. I knew he was attracted to me. I also knew I was married to a dangerous man. I was acting out without thinking about the collateral damage of my toxic girl behavior.

I'm also just hungry. I guess I'll have to go downstairs at some point. I head down the stairs. Phoenix is working on a laptop on the couch in the same place he was when I came home.

In the kitchen, the two enormous guys, Alexei and Feliks, shovel ravioli into their mouths.

"Hey," I greet them. "Is there any left?"

"I'll get it for you." Feliks surges to his feet.

The deference everyone shows Baron, and me by proxy, continues to surprise me. I can't figure out if it's out of fear or respect. But actually, no one seems jumpy or nervous. The inhabitants of this house are comfortable here.

Feliks dishes me a plate of food and puts it in the microwave to heat while I try to decide whether I'm relieved or disappointed not to find my controlling, apparently violent husband down here.

Is he mad at me? We didn't speak on the ride home. I half-expected a war. Some kind of retribution for making and keeping a date with another man. I was ready for it

I wrapped my anger around me like a blanket, planning to use it as a shield for whatever he threw at me, but he left me alone.

The microwave dings, and Feliks pulls out the warm plate and hands it to me.

"Get her a fork, dumbass. She doesn't know where anything is here," Alexei chides his younger brother.

Feliks opens a drawer and pulls out a fork. "Sorry." He hands it to me.

"Thank you." Not wanting to sit with them, I head out to the couch and drop into a seat near Phoenix to eat.

He glances over. "Hey."

"Hey."

"You okay?"

I look over, surprised by the question. Is he for real?

"No. I'm not."

Phoenix's shoulders round more over his laptop, as if my anger landed as a physical assault.

I instantly regret being combative. Maybe he is genuinely concerned.

"Sorry. It's not your fault."

"No, I get it. You're in a new place with a bunch of strangers, and you have no idea if you're safe or not. I know how that feels."

Some of my walls start to crumble. "Yeah. You probably do."

"I registered to live in a men's dorm at Thornecroft when I'd just started my hormonal transition. To me, it felt like a new chapter. Starting college as the gender I always knew I was. But then I got here, and it was scary as fuck.

"I had this tatted-up alpha male roommate from Chicago who didn't say much. Rumor had it the guy was in the Russian mafia. I was fucking terrified.

"Baron was your roommate?"

Phoenix nods.

A part of me that was bracing against some awful story relaxes. Baron didn't hurt Phoenix. He wouldn't be living here if he had.

"Turns out, it wasn't my roommate I needed to worry about."

I tense again.

"During orientation week, three guys accosted me in the shower."

"What?" I shove my plate on the coffee table, no longer hungry.

"They grabbed me and forced me down on the floor. I think they were going to gang rape me."

"Oh my God."

Phoenix shakes his head. "They didn't succeed. Because Baron appears out of nowhere with the plastic bag from the garbage can, which he whips over the head of one of the guys."

My lips part in shock.

"He pulled it tight over the guy's face, so he couldn't breathe. There was something about the calm way he wrestled with the guy that said he'd killed before, and he'd be happy to do it again."

I've killed. And I'd kill again—for you.

My heart thuds against my chest. "Did he?"

I'm not sure I want to hear the answer. It's like watching a horror movie where you want to hide and peek through your hands at the same time.

"The guy was suffocating, and before the other two jumped Baron to get him off because they could have—I mean, it was three against one—he orders them to drop to their knees, or he'll kill their buddy. And they're scared shitless because he looks like he does professional wet work and enjoys it, so they do it—they kneel.

"Wet work?" I don't understand this English turn of phrase.

"Wet for blood. Hitmen do wet work."

"Oh. Then what happened?"

"Baron keeps suffocating their friend with the plastic bag, right up to the point he almost passes out, and then he lets go. The guy slumps on the floor, gasping. Baron's still totally cool. Not mad. Not like he almost killed someone. He doesn't raise his voice when he calmly tells the three of them if anyone so much as looks at me again, he'll tie them to their beds and burn them alive."

I let out a shaky breath I didn't know I was holding.

"And then he tosses me a towel and helps me up. He asks if I'm hurt or want to file charges. I'm not interested in guys, but if I were, I would've fallen in love with Baron right then.

"I mean, I guess I did anyway—bromance-wise.

"After that, word got around that I was under Baron's protection, and no one has ever fucked with me again."

My lips tremble, eyes burning for Phoenix. "I'm sorry that happened to you."

I catch the pain in his eyes before he drops his gaze. "Yeah, it sucked. But it created this" —Phoenix waves his hand to indicate the house— "so I guess I can't complain."

I cock my head. "What do you mean?"

"Baron decided he needed his own Thornecroft society house, so he could keep the people under his protection safe. That was why he cooked up the plan to purchase and donate this property to the University under his father's name.

I stare at Phoenix. "Baron bought this house?" I had definitely assumed his dad bought it for him.

Phoenix nodded. "Well, he worked out something with his dad to front him the money, but he makes payments every month. He's also figured out ways to generate income to cover most of the occupants' room and board. Plus a full-time cook and housekeeping. He's a genius.

I stare at my half-eaten dinner, letting it all sink in. "A dangerous genius."

Phoenix nods. "For sure." He peers at me. "Are you scared of him?"

"He did something today," I say, not elaborating.

"Yeah, I saw you looked pissed when you came home."

Phoenix is too respectful to pry, which I appreciate. But he just shared a vulnerable story with me. It feels like I could trust him.

"I was meeting with this Russian guy who said he was homesick. It wasn't a date—he's just a dorky kid. I wasn't going to cheat on Baron or anything."

Phoenix winces.

"What?"

"I'm already sensing where this is going."

I throw my hands in the air, some of my ire returning. "Yeah, so Baron shows up—I don't even know how he knew where to find me—and he just sits down with us and starts eating Denis' food."

Phoenix's lips twitch.

"Then I get up to go to the bathroom, and when I come

back, Denis is gone, and there's a puddle of blood on the table in front of where he was sitting."

Phoenix winces again.

"Blood!" My voice raises, and I throw my hands up. "I don't even know what Baron did to him."

"Well, in my experience, anyone Baron hurts has it coming."

"*Nyet.* This guy did *not* have it coming! He's just some new student like me, who happened to invite the wife of a bratva prince to have a drink with him on the first day of school."

Phoenix scrubs a hand over his facial hair. "The thing to know about Baron is that he's ultra-protective of the people he cares about or feels responsible for. And he believes that in order to keep everyone safe, he needs to control everything around him.

"I'm sure having a wife to protect is next level for him. Here I was afraid he was going to drive his little sister crazy this year."

"I didn't need his protection! I *don't* need his protection."

"Yeah. Well, maybe in the future, communicate with him when you're meeting with someone, so he doesn't go off the deep end."

I frown, and Phoenix holds his hands up in defense. "I don't mean to butt in or give advice. I'm here anytime you want to talk. I can give you my perspective, or you can tell me to shut up, and I won't say a word, I'll just listen."

The defensiveness rising up in me softens. Phoenix really does seem like a good guy. "Thank you."

A door opens, and Benjamin emerges. It's a door to what I thought was a closet, but now I see the flash of an inner door guarding the entrance to stairs descending downward. A secret staircase!

Was he in the dungeon?

With that girl?

But no one else emerges.

His gaze flicks over to the couch, but he doesn't acknowledge either of us, he just walks up the stairs.

There's a heaviness in his walk. Strain in his expression. For a moment, I don't see an aggressor—I see a young man with far too much weight on his shoulders.

CHAPTER TWELVE

Baron

I walk up to the bedroom after studying in the dungeon. It's soundproof down there, and I needed a place to concentrate.

I needed to be away from my looping thoughts about what went down at Whisper's End. Wrestling between my anger and guilt.

I had the heads' up from Leo that Denis the fucking menace had asked her to meet him, and I have a tracker in her phone, her purse, and every pair of shoes she has, so it was easy to find her.

Still, I wanted to kill that little *mudak* for even breathing the same air space as my wife. I hope he's only here to find out if our marriage is real. But the part of me that has to go through and plan the very worst possible scenario foresees Brash kidnapping Lara and ransoming her life in exchange for Adrian's full future cooperation with the Rostovs.

I can't let that happen.

On top of it all, I need to make sure I've covered every base for Friday's party. The Titan House wants to shut us down this year, which means they'll call the cops or the fire marshall or the Chancellor with noise complaints or over-occupancy alerts or whatever they can think of to shut our party down prematurely.

In the bedroom, I stop and stare at Lara's open suitcase, which she still hasn't unpacked. I ordered the dresser for her, and it should be delivered tomorrow. Somehow I doubt it will make this room feel any more like it belongs to her.

She's uncomfortable.

It was probably wrong of me to insist she share my bed.

I can't bring myself to make any other arrangements, though.

Last night, I tasted her. She came riding my fingers. I would've come too if I hadn't fucked things up.

The door opens, and Lara steps in. She doesn't ignore me, as she did this morning. She just stands there, looking at me. There's an uncertainty to her stance that activates the dom in me.

"Come here." I open my arms.

I give it a less than twenty percent chance she'll accept the invitation, but to my shock, she walks forward.

I meet her halfway, wrapping her up in my arms and dropping my face into her hair. It smells like her butterscotch shampoo, which makes my dick chubby remembering I was the one who washed it.

"Let me kiss you," I murmur. I know we should talk, but I can't think of what to say. I can't explain why she needs to stay away from Denis, and I'm not going to apologize for doing what I had to do.

All I know how to do is touch her. That's what I'm good at. After last night, it's what I live and breathe for.

I celebrate my blessings when she lifts her face. I cup her cheek in one hand and lower my lips to hers, my other arm wrapped firmly around her back. The first kiss is soft. Exploratory. My lips moving across hers lightly.

I sense surrender in her. I'm guessing she's tired of fighting me. Probably a little scared. She needs reassurance, and she's turning to *me* for it, even though I'm the enemy. It's classic Stockholm Syndrome, but I'll work with whatever I can get.

I deepen the kiss, slanting my mouth over hers and prying her lips open with my tongue. She's in another skirt today— this one is a soft cotton that molds to her hips. I slide my hand around the curve of her ass and squeeze.

She melts into me, molecule by molecule. Her hands brush my chest and slide up to my shoulders.

I tug the hem of her skirt up her thigh until I touch skin, then slide my hand beneath it to cup her ass. She's wearing panties that floss her ass, leaving the entire cheek exposed for me to stroke. I knead it as my tongue explores her mouth. When my middle finger traces the thin ribbon of fabric that plunges between her cheeks, she moans.

I forget to go slow.

I hoist her up, legs around my waist, and carry her the few steps to the bed where I drop her. "You were a bad fucking wife today, *malyshka*." I reach behind my back with one hand and yank my shirt off over my head.

I probably should dial back the dominance considering it was that kind of talk that completely shut her down last night, but the switch has been flipped. Gentle mode is off. Dark mode activated.

And I know how well her body responds to it.

She looks up at me with those big blue eyes, and I want to fucking ravish her. I reach beneath her skirt and yank her panties off in one rough motion.

"Spread those legs for me, Lara. I'm going to eat that

pussy." I don't wait for her to obey. I push her knees wide, forcing her to fall back on her forearms.

Her pussy is groomed with a neat little triangle of silky dark hair. I rub it with my thumb as I lick into her. She gasps, jerking at the wet contact.

I give it to her good, tonguing all along her slit, inside and out—sucking, nibbling, and tasting her. When I bring the pad of my thumb between her ass cheeks and twist it over her anus, she squeezes her cheeks, lifting her pelvis off the bed.

I lift my head, but keep my thumb firmly in place. It's a mild threat.

"Are you allowed to date other men, Lara?"

Her pussy squeezes, like my stern-dom voice is going to make her come. She looks at me, a mixture of lust and fear swirling in the depths of her dark-lashed eyes.

I slide my other thumb into her pussy and pump, giving her a little pleasure.

Her head lolls to the side, and she moans.

"Hmm?"

When she doesn't answer, I remove my thumbs and roll her to her belly. "The correct answer is *no, lyubimaya.*" I pin her down with my hand in the middle of her back and deliver three hard spanks.

She squeals and kicks her legs. She looks fucking gorgeous with her skirt pushed up and her ass bare. It's giving Catholic school girl vibes, and my dick gets marble-hard.

I grasp a handful of her ass and squeeze, making a growling sound in my throat. "You have the best ass, *printsessa.*"

I slide my fingers between her legs and find her sopping. Nothing gets a girl wetter than a good spanking, in my experience. I deliver two more spanks, this time to the backs of her thighs, below her ass where there's less padding.

"*Ou!*" she protests.

"Let's try this again." I rub two fingers slowly between her legs, rewarding her, even as I wind up for more punishment. My thumb fits between her ass cheeks, resting over her anus. She squirms beneath me, letting out a low moan.

I slap her ass several times in quick succession—striking her right cheek, left cheek, then spanning them both in the low center, right over her glorious pussy. I repeat the pattern twice and then stop with my hand resting on her ass, gripping it possessively.

"Are you *allowed* to date other men?"

She reaches back and covers her ass. "It wasn't a date!"

My grip on her ass gentles, and I lean forward to push her shirt up and kiss along her spine. "That's good," I tell her between kisses. "Because I don't want to have to take you to the dungeon."

She stiffens, probably believing terrible things happen there.

"Roll over and give me that pussy again," I command.

She's quick to comply, and my heart lurches a little at the sight of her flushed face, obscured by her disheveled hair.

I did that. I gave her that freshly-fucked look, and I'm just getting started.

I return my attention to her pussy, sucking more forcefully. Finding her clit and swirling my tongue around it.

Lara arches her tits up toward the ceiling, her head falling back, mouth open.

"I'm going to fuck you tonight, *malysh*." I rise to my knees and unbutton my pants. "And you're going to be a good girl and take it." I free my throbbing erection. "Because I need to show you who you belong to."

I barely register that I've said the words that pissed her off last night. I'm speaking my truth, and she needs to hear it.

She *does* belong to me. She's my wife. I gave her my name and my protection, and now she's mine.

I take a moment to shuck my pants and boxers and strip Lara out of her remaining clothes.

"That's right," I praise her when her bra comes off, and she's fully naked. "This is how I'm going to need you every goddamn night." I kneel between her legs, nudging them open to give me access. "Naked and beneath me, *printsessa*." I rub the head of my cock along her slit. "Screaming my name every time you come."

I shove into her with a single stroke, and she gasps, her fingernails clawing at my forearms. "Are you close to coming, Lara?" I ease back and push in again.

"Oh...*au*."

I'm being too rough. "Sorry, *malyshka*." I stop moving to give her a moment to get used to my size.

She pants beneath me. Her gaze slides off to the side.

I catch her jaw and turn her face to mine. "Are you okay?"

I see a trickle of relief in her expression at the connection. At the fact that I stopped playing my dominance games and met her where she was. She nods.

I ease back an inch and push in slowly, watching her expression for signs of pain. I see none. "Ready for more?"

She nods again.

I lower my head to flick my tongue over her nipple then take it fully into my mouth and suck, hard.

She squeezes around my dick, and I nearly lose control.

I rest my weight on one hand propped beside her head and fuck her slowly, watching her face the entire time.

When she closes her eyes, I say, "Eyes on me, princess. I need to see what you're feeling."

———

Lara

"I'm okay." I lift my hips to take Baron deeper. My voice

sounds breathless. I force myself to meet his gaze even though it does crazy things to my chest. To my heart. "It's good."

It's insane that I'm reassuring him after he just rolled me over and spanked me for cheating on him, but he's paying close attention to me.

He saw me wince when he first thrust in and apologized. So I know that as much as he's acting the role of punisher right now, he's not going to really hurt me.

That's when I decide I want it. Whatever he has to give me tonight—I want it all.

I was on board before, but part of me was holding back. I was scared and defensive and still mad at him over whatever he did to Denis.

But I feel safe now, as crazy as that seems.

Maybe it was hearing Phoenix's trust in him. Maybe it was his apology. All I know is that my body is in receiving mode, and I want everything he has to give.

"Please."

Triumph curves Baron's lips. He likes me begging.

Of course, he does.

"You want more, *malyshka?*"

"Yes. Give me more."

He pumps faster, his muscles flexing in a glorious display of manhood, like a beautiful stallion running. "I should fuck your ass tonight, after what you did. But you're not ready for that, are you?"

I shake my head, but I can feel an orgasm starting, triggered by his threat. My inner thighs tremble, the coil of need winds tighter.

"I'm going to fuck you hard, though." To prove it, he picks up his pace even more. The stallion galloping.

It feels perfect—his rhythm matching my need, the slide of

his cock hitting every nerve ending inside my channel and out.

"My balls were blue all day remembering how fucking *gorgeous* you looked last night in the shower."

My moan takes on a higher pitch. I feel beautiful. Desirable. Worshipped, even.

His attention intoxicates me. His cock is *wrecking* me. I feel him so deeply, I swear he will split me in two.

"Take it, *malysh*. Take it like a good girl," he commands.

He knows it's getting challenging for me. The pace, the intensity of his thrusts.

"Please," I beg.

"You don't come until I come." His voice is stern. Forbidding.

It makes wings flap with excitement in my tummy.

"Please," I repeat.

My begging seems to undo Baron. A muscle jumps in his cheek. He slams into me harder and harder, driving me upward with the force of his thrusts.

"Fuck," he mutters. And then he unleashes a torrent of praise and dirty talk. Like now that he's close to coming, he can't hold it back. "Fuck you're beautiful. You feel so good. So tight and wet and perfect. Are you gonna be my good girl, Lara?"

"Please," is the only syllable that will come out of my mouth.

Baron roars and slams in deep. "Come, baby. Come for me now." He licks the pad of his thumb and brings it between our bodies, rubbing my clit.

I go off like a geyser. My muscles spasm around the thick girth of his dick, milking it for every last drop of his cum. I cry out, still squeezing. My pelvis lifts. My feet stomp into the covers. My inner thighs tremor and quake.

"That's it, baby." Baron eases out when the last of my tremors goes quiet. "You're so perfect."

He flings the blankets back for us and settles behind me, wrapping one strong arm around my waist to pull me snugly against him. His big spoon into my little one. He kisses my head.

"You're perfect," he murmurs again against my hair.

My eyes drift closed. I've never felt so satiated in my entire life. And it's with the man I've sworn to hate.

Maybe my mom was right. Maybe good chemistry can really overcome a mountain of conflict.

The intimate connection forged through mind blowing sex becomes a bond. We haven't worked out a single difference, and yet I feel safe. Held. Loved, even.

But that's probably just the endorphins talking.

CHAPTER THIRTEEN

Lara

When I wake, Baron is gone. I remember him jerking awake in the night the way he does. I'd reached out and touched his chest, and he mumbled an apology. "The nightmares get to me sometimes."

It dented the privileged bratva prince image I'd assigned him. Something has caused him trauma. The same thing that makes his eyes look haunted at times, I imagine.

I sit up to the sound of my alarm going off beside the bed. Baron must've gotten up and plugged my phone in sometime during the night.

He also left a cup of coffee beside the bed in one of those thermal cups that stay warm or cold for hours. I take a sip, and the creamy goodness hits me like a drug. It's still hot. The milk tastes freshly steamed.

I groan in pleasure.

I remember moments in the night with Baron. His strong arms around me. Our legs tangling. My head on his shoulder.

It's like my body needed the close physical contact—craved

it—to make up for all the fucked-upness of this situation. I drank in comfort through my skin, and it must have lowered my cortisol levels because I slept like the dead.

I swing my legs out of bed and head for the bathroom. I guess you could say our marriage was consummated. I'm definitely sore between my legs and even inside—like my cervix took a beating.

But it *was* incredible.

I turn around and look in the mirror to see if he left handprints on my ass. No, it all faded. I find myself strangely disappointed, like I wanted to see proof of what he did to me. My belly flutters when I remember the things he said.

I don't want to have to take you to the dungeon.

This is how I'm going to need you every goddamn night—naked and beneath me.

I want to see the dungeon. Want to know what goes on down there. I want to experience everything that every other woman has felt at Baron's hands.

A sense of possessiveness grips me like fingers closing around my heart. Benjamin Baranov is *my* husband. He won't be giving his attention to any other woman.

I suppose this is exactly how he feels about me. Meeting Denis yesterday without telling him was asking for trouble. I told myself I was proving I wouldn't be caged like a bird. That I may have married him, but I'm not his possession. But I definitely knew I was poking a bear. And when I got the results I expected, I felt guilty over involving Denis in my ill-thought-out games and lashed out again at Baron.

Now I know for certain that he follows a code. He won't hurt me, not even when I act out. The spanking last night stung, but the flavor of the scene was sexual dominance, not torture. Not fear.

Phoenix's story about Baron proves he operates by a code as well.

It comes as a huge relief and a bit of a turn-on to know that my husband is dangerous—lethal, even—but not to me.

My phone rings, and I check the screen and sigh. It's Brash again. I guess I should take it or he'll keep calling.

I accept the call. "Brash, you keep calling," I say in Russian.

"Of course, I keep calling!" his voice explodes through the phone, filled with concern. "It sounds like you're in trouble, Lara. Tell me what's going on. I can help."

My pulse picks up speed. It's possible he could help. He is extravagantly rich. I know his father is part of the Russian oligarchy. That means he commands wealth and power. They might be able to keep me and my family safe from Ravil Baranov.

But do I want his help?

And why would he offer to help? What would he ask of me in return?

Somehow, after hearing Phoenix's story about Baron, I don't see Brash as the valiant rescuer of the weak. Brash strikes me as the kind of guy who's only out for himself. His interest in me always felt disingenuous, which is why I didn't take our dates that seriously. It's why I didn't even remember to cancel the date when I left.

He said and did all the right things and was a total gentleman, but it felt performatory. Almost like he's gay and was courting me to be his beard. The true spark wasn't there.

"I'm not in trouble," I hear myself say. I guess I've made my decision. I won't be asking Brash Rostov for a rescue. I'm going to figure this shit out on my own.

"It sounds like you are. You said you suddenly had to get married? What happened?"

I close my eyes and draw in a measured breath through my nostrils.

What do I say? Do I tell him the truth, or do I put him off?

I settle for a muted version of the truth. "I've been engaged to marry a stranger since I was young. It was a family arrangement. Our parents decided it was time to pull the trigger on the contract."

Surprisingly, Brash doesn't even take a beat to absorb that. "Like an arranged marriage? That's crazy. This is the 21st-century. You don't have to go through with it, Lara."

Again, I'm surprised he cares so much.

"It's too late. I went through with it. I'm a married woman now."

"You don't have to stay married. No court enforces *till death do you part*."

The idea of divorcing Baron and getting on a plane back to Paris has massive appeal. I was living my best life there. I had one year left to get my degree. I had just gotten an internship that would've provided me with the experience I needed to get a job as an interpreter after graduation.

Except...I'd be giving up Baron. The guy I thought was a bully, but I'm coming to suspect might actually be the guy who protects others from bullies. But how does that fit with the ruthless bratva family that demanded our immediate marriage? Maybe his dad is a bully, and he's resolved to protect me from him.

If I divorced Baron and let Brash help me, I'd be safer. Whether my family would be safe or not is unclear. And I'd be giving up the kind of sex I had last night.

The thought of having sex with Brash instead registers as a balloon deflating deep in my soul.

Pass. After Baron...

It's hard to imagine anyone else could hold a candle.

Still, am I going to pass up what might be my only chance to get out of this lifelong prison for good sex?

"Thank you for offering to help. I appreciate your concern. But I don't need to be rescued."

"You hesitated before you answered. Are you afraid, Lara?"

I suddenly feel dizzy. The bathroom swoops around me. Am I afraid? I certainly was. My dad seemed afraid—which terrifies me.

Yes, I'm afraid. But there's also a kernel of hope starting to germinate in the center of my heart. Some foolish piece of me wants to believe I might find love here in a monster's arms. My interest has been snagged enough that I don't want to run. Not anymore.

Maybe I'll change my mind, though. Maybe I'll find out all the horrible things Ravil Baranov and his son have done and wish to run as far and fast as I can.

Or maybe this arranged marriage will save everything, as my dad seems to believe.

"No, I am safe. But I'll let you know if that changes."

"Lara, you don't sound safe—"

"I'll let you know if that changes," I say firmly.

He stops trying to argue. "Where exactly are you? I'm coming out there. I need to see with my own eyes that you're not a prisoner."

I think of the blood on the table at the bar today. What would Baron do if my ex-boyfriend showed up with the intent to steal me away?

Something horrible, I fear.

He may be safe for me, but he's not safe for the men who want me.

I try to keep the urgency out of my voice by forcing a laugh. "Don't be ridiculous. I'm not a prisoner. I also don't want you to come. Like I said in my text—I'm married now. I can't see you anymore."

Brash is silent for a moment. "Promise you'll call if you

need anything?"

"I promise."

"Okay. Good luck, then. I hope to hear from you."

I hope he doesn't. That would mean that things had gone horribly wrong here.

"Goodbye, Brash."

I end the call with a queasy feeling in my belly.

I hope to God I made the right choice.

————

Baron

I go on proactive mode for the party, calling Edgar, the Whisper Fire Marshal, between my morning classes to let him know we're having a party and ask if he wants to inspect our alarms to make sure we're up to code. Baranov house made a generous donation and volunteered student labor for their chili cook-off fundraiser last winter, so I have some collateral to draw on.

Still, there's an impatient edge to his voice. "I inspected last year. Has anything changed?"

"Nope, just want to be sure. We'll use a counter at the door Friday to make sure we don't go over-capacity."

"Okay. Anything else?" He still doesn't know why the fuck I'm bugging him, so I just come clean.

"I'm going to be totally honest with you, Edgar. We heard one of the other society houses on campus was going to try to shut down our party, so I'm just trying to anticipate any direction that might come from."

"Ah. I see. Well, I'll bear that in mind if I get any calls, but we'll still have to respond if we do."

"I understand. I just want to assure you in advance that we will be following the rules you gave us."

"Okay, son. Appreciate that."

I end the call.

Well, that's all I can do. I don't know where else I can head off problems. If the police decide to come and search us, I can make sure they don't find anything, but having cops move through the house checking IDs will ruin the party vibe.

I did everything else by the book. Got a permit, registered the party with campus administration, ordered wrist bands to make sure no one underage gets a drink. We don't always follow those rules, but this time, we'll have to be totally above-board. No designer drug sales, no dungeon play.

My phone buzzes with a text from Anya.

> Brash called Lara this morning. Check the files.

Blyad'.

I stop and open the file folder on my phone where Anya sends all the records from Lara's phone. I quickly scan the transcript. There's a voice recording, too, but I don't have time to listen now.

She told him she's married now and refused his help. I hang onto that piece of information.

At what point is it safe for me to tell her the truth?

Not yet. Not until she's secure with me. She still doesn't trust me yet.

But the longer we go on with her believing this lie, the more manipulated she's going to feel. She's already furious about feeling like a pawn in her father's schemes. How will she feel when she hears he didn't trust her with the truth about it all?

Fuck. I hate all of this.

No, not all of it.

Because if Adrian hadn't made up the lie about Lara being betrothed to me, I may have never met her. I wouldn't have a beautiful, intelligent wife right now who feels like the person I've been waiting my entire life to meet.

I tuck my phone in my pocket and head to my next class.

As I walk up toward my statistics class—the one with Professor Vasiliev, who hates me—I slow my gait.

He's standing outside his door, and talking with him is a short dumpy kid with unkempt curly hair and medical tape in an X over his nose.

Denis Penkin. Talking to Professor Vasiliev.

Sure, they're both Russian. It could be that simple. Except they look over at me with a look of pure contempt.

Fuck.

They're in this together.

Vasiliev has ties to the oligarchs, too.

That's a problem.

Denis walks away before I get there, but I can't help it—the *mudak* brings out the violent side of me. I let Vasiliev see it. Gone is the respectful student. I show him what I truly am. What he already knew about me. I'm a killer. A criminal. A man who will use violence to protect what's his. I lift my upper lip in a snarl and stop in front of him.

"Friend of yours?" I growl in Russian, tipping my head in the direction Denis left.

He maintains his composure, uncowed by me. "Sit down, Baranov."

I hold my ground, staring him down. Showing him I don't give a fuck about his grades or his class or his opinion of me. If he's working with Denis Penkin to spy on or harm my wife, I will end him.

He looks balefully back at me.

Another student tries to get past, but I'm blocking the door.

"Excuse me," he murmurs, head down.

I release the lock on my muscles, smoothly moving into

the classroom and taking my seat in the front of the room where I have the perfect vantage point to stare the mother-fucker down.

No one screws with my wife.

Not if they want to live.

CHAPTER FOURTEEN

Lara

By Friday, all of campus is talking about the Back to School party at The Gulag–a.k.a., Baranov House. Baron's been in full *pakhan* mode all evening–giving quiet orders and directions to everyone who lives in the house as they make preparations for the party.

Except for me. He seems to have no expectations of me, other than that I bear his last name and am naked beneath him every night. I can't complain about the latter. It's been mind-blowing.

Baron apparently already updated the school's records with my new last name because I discovered yesterday that my record changed in my student dashboard.

Earlier today, when my French Lit professor called out "Baranov" to quiz me on the reading, the entire class turned to stare at me. Afterward, three young women stopped me to ask if I was related to Baron. I took a bit of smug satisfaction in their shocked disappointment when I said I was his wife.

"You're kidding, right?" One of the women had looked at

the others. "She's just joking." She looked back at me. "You're his sister. I heard he has a sister on campus this year."

"That's Lili," I explained patiently. "I'm Lara. His wife." I held up my ring.

Their expressions of jealous horror were epic.

Part of me can't believe I'm actually proud of it–that I'm showing the ring off for social collateral. But Baron is an apex predator on campus, and so long as I'm forced to live here as his wife, I might as well reap the benefits.

The doors to the party open at nine, and it's nine now. I stand in front of the mirror and survey my outfit. I don't know what Americans wear to college parties, but I went for French nightclub wear–sexy, but not too slutty, or the club doormen won't let you in.

I'm in a strapless black mini-dress that hugs my curves with a loose silver shell belt around my hips and a pair of black patent leather platform heels. I pulled my hair up to bring attention to my bare shoulders and decolletage. I went a bit heavier on the make-up, drawing cat-eyes with black liner and using a smokey grey powder to make the blue of my eyes pop. I dot a little berry lipgloss on my lips and rub them together.

I don't know what to expect, but I sense this party is going to be interesting, to say the least.

I open the bedroom door and walk down the stairs in my heels. The lights are off, except for mood lighting–a strip of tiny white lights line the stairs, so I can see where I'm going. They've probably always been there; I just didn't see them before. Music fills the house. It has a ska-reggae swing– upbeat but not dancey. It's probably just the warm-up music.

Downstairs, the house has been transformed. The lights are off except for the colored dance lights beaming on a disco ball hung from the ceiling. I don't know where the furniture went, but the living room is now completely empty and open to serve as a dance floor. Anya sits on a bar stool behind a DJ booth in the corner with a set of headphones around her neck. She gives me a wave when she sees me, and I wave back.

Baron swiftly walks through the living room giving orders although I don't see anyone around him and can't figure out who he's talking to until I realize he has an ear piece in.

Anya lifts her chin in my direction, and Baron swivels. I watch as he stops short, transforming from the cool, calculating leader to a hot-blooded male. "Fuuuuuuck."

Female satisfaction floods through me, reminding me that even in the darkest hours of the patriarchy, female erotic power is a stronger force than anything men could create. It's why they were so afraid of us. Why they sought to capture, contain, and own us.

"Your comms is on, Baron," Anya reminds him.

Baron reaches up and touches his ear, probably flicking off the device, and walks over to meet me at the bottom of the stairs.

Without saying a word, he crowds into me, pressing me up against the wall. His body heat registers beneath the fabric of my dress. His thumb brushes across my cheek, fingers sliding into my hair.

"My wife is so fucking hot."

He seems to love calling me his wife. The words still shock me every time I hear them, but it's hard to object when his obvious appreciation drips from his voice.

He's in a pale pink button-down shirt, unbuttoned at the throat and rolled up to his forearms. He looks more like a billionaire CEO about to get on his yacht than a college student, and he wears confidence as easily as the expensive clothes.

He covers my mouth in a possessive, claiming kiss. "What am I going to do tonight with you looking like that?" He leans his forehead against mine. "You look good enough to eat, and I have to run this fucking party."

"What do you have to do?"

His expression clouds, some of the lust draining from his gaze.

I instantly regret my question. I don't love his cool, distant persona—the one he usually wears—nearly as much as I like him turned on and growly.

"We have to keep things completely above-board tonight because we're expecting trouble from one of our rival houses."

"Oh." I blink. There's so much I don't understand about what goes on here.

"And we also have to keep the party interesting enough that people are dying to come back."

"How do you do that?" I ask.

He shrugs. "Mostly relying on rumors of illicit activities that aren't actually happening tonight. It will keep people coming back and hoping they're cool enough to be let in on them next time."

"Like what?"

He kisses me again. "I'm not sure you want to know, *printsessa*. And I don't want to make my wife an accessory."

A spike of resentment rises in me. I respect that he wants to keep me clean. My father is absolutely the same. My mother and I never knew about his bratva cell's activities.

But it seems like everyone else in this house—all of Baron's friends—are in on it. Everyone but me. I don't like feeling left out, even when it is for my own good.

I frown at him. "I *do* want to know."

He considers me. "You sure?"

"Yes."

"The usual sins—high stakes card games. Designer drugs. The dungeon downstairs."

I absorb that. "But nothing tonight?"

He shakes his head. "Not even one underage drink. Titan House wants to take us down, and we don't know how they're going to come at us, so we have to play it very cool tonight."

Wow. No wonder Baron looks like he has the world on his shoulders. He's not just in charge of his house, he's running a full-scale enterprise here. Plus, it sounds like he believes he's responsible for the safety and protection of everyone in this house.

This might be the first time Baron shared anything personal or important with me, and I like it. I appreciate that he trusts me enough to bring me in on it.

"What can I do to help?"

Something in Baron relaxes, and he flashes me a smile—perhaps the first I've seen on him. It makes him look boyish. Carefree. Heartbreakingly handsome.

He presses his weight against me and slowly moves in for a kiss, making me hold my breath in anticipation. His lips are supple; the kiss is perfect. "You can help me by circulating around here in this sexy little dress and making everyone wonder who this fucking gorgeous woman is who is the new queen of Baranov House." He kisses me again.

"Queen?"

"My *queen*. So don't be too friendly to the commoners—you're royalty in this house. Leave them guessing."

"Leave them guessing," I repeat.

"Yes. Extra points—you want to drop a few hints about our arranged marriage or that you're a bratva princess. It will only add to the mystique. You'll become a mystery they'll forever want to unpack." Baron's hands settle on my waist. He kisses my jaw. My neck. "You know what the most helpful thing you could do is?" His voice has a seductive rumble to it.

"What?"

"Let me take you upstairs, strip off this dress, and tie you naked to our bed, so I know what's waiting for me at the end of the night, and I don't have to worry about any *mudak* trying to touch you tonight."

"Hmm. Let me think about that." I pretend to consider. "*No.*" I give his chest a shove. "I'm the queen. Queens don't get tied up naked."

He gives me a mock innocent look. "Some do."

"So are you allowed to have fun at this party, or are you just working the whole time?"

His expression clouds again. "These things aren't playtime for me. They're business."

I look at my new husband—a twenty-two-year-old who seems to have entirely missed his youth. A man in a perpetual state of self-sacrifice for his father, for the cause, for others. He's clearly a natural born leader but one with the weight of responsibility for everyone who falls beneath him.

I want to lighten that load for him.

I kiss him. It's the first time I've initiated a kiss, and Baron doesn't miss the occasion. He holds perfectly still through my kiss then throws me back against the wall, his fingers wrapped around my throat in a gentle hand necklace as he delivers his own searing version of a lip lock.

It goes on and on until we're both breathless, and he breaks away and rubs his lips together, his gaze locked on mine."Thank you," he says reverently.

I practically hear my walls come crashing down to rubble around me.

My husband deeply values the gift of my affection. It couldn't be more clear. And it couldn't be more of a turn-on.

The music suddenly turns off.

"*Pakhan!*" Anya calls out, taking off her headphones. "They're trying to get you on comms. There's a line at the door of people waiting to get in, and they wanna know if they should open up."

Baron's hand slides from my neck up to grip my jaw, and he gives me one more rough kiss followed by a feral smile

My knees go weak.

He reaches up to his ear and flicks a button in his comms device.

"Let the party begin."

CHAPTER FIFTEEN

Baron

We're close to capacity by 10 p.m., which is about two hours earlier than when most campus parties fill up.

Anya has the music popping, and the dance floor is packed with sweaty, moving bodies.

Everyone's trying to work me from every angle, but I am the no-man tonight.

I press through the bodies, looking for my gorgeous wife.

"Boss," Phoenix speaks through the comms. He's working the door collecting the twenty dollar cover charge because he is my money man. He handles the accounting for our enterprises. Alex works with him as security. Feliks acts as bouncer inside, at the base of the stairs to keep non-house members from trying to go up them.

"Baron, Melinda Tracy is at the door. She says you told her she could come in."

I groan. I told her two parties a year, and she had to pick tonight? I shouldn't have made that concession for her.

"Tell her it's a waste of her time because the dungeon is closed tonight."

A moment later, Phoenix's voice returns. "She says she still wants in."

Christ, why? Well, whatever.

"Then let her in. I told her she could come to two parties a year so keep track. This is her first entry. She only gets one more. Remind her of that."

Phoenix returns one more time. "She's in."

I note Anders, who is presently playing host and will alternate jobs with Leo during the night, moving toward the front of the house. I imagine he's going to personally welcome Melinda.

I hope she finally notices his interest now that I'm not a distraction.

"Who has eyes on Lara?"

My wife has been hard to keep track of. After that kiss she gave me, I wanted nothing more than to cancel the whole party and take her upstairs to ravish her.

"I do," Zoe says. "She's helping me at the mocktail bar."

The mocktail bar is one of the ways we ease the wrath of the underage students denied alcohol. We serve them in the same-sized clear plastic cups that we serve alcoholic drinks. The only difference is the color of the straw. Then we pretend we don't know that they fill them with their own supply of alcohol.

It makes sense that Lara would end up with Zoe—it's not like she has any friends to hang out or dance with here. I should've foreseen her feeling out of place and assigned her a job. Except I don't want to be in the position of telling my wife what to do. She's already pissed off enough about marrying me.

Although that seems to be softening a bit, praise all the powers that be.

A tiny smile curves my lips as I head toward the back door of the kitchen where they are stationed. Leo's stationed at the main kitchen door serving alcohol drinks to party-goers wearing a wrist band. The kitchen itself is closed off to everyone else.

"Soda and lime?" Zoe asks, spotting me behind the line of people waiting to be served.

I nod. "And *my wife*."

Everyone in the line turns to look at me then looks back toward Anya. I hear their murmurs:

Did he say wife?

He's married?

"That's me—I'm his wife," Lara announces loudly in Russian, throwing her arms in the air.

My brilliant bride understood the assignment. The entire line of party-goers stare at her then at me as I push through and extend my hand to her.

"Come, *malyshka*."

Everyone gawks when she comes out from behind the makeshift bar (a rolling butcher block cart) and takes my hand as Zoe hands me the drink.

Did you hear that? Baron Baraonov has a wife, someone says as we move away.

"Would you like to dance?"

Lara shakes her head. "My feet hurt already. I might go up and change my shoes."

"I'll go with you." I press through the throng of bodies toward the stairs, but the impact of a body hurtling to the floor to my right makes me thrust Lara behind me and charge forward in that direction.

"Stop!" A young woman screams.

It's Lili.

Oh fuck.

Blood washes over my vision. My brain flips into warrior mode. I have to protect Lili, my little sister. Can't let her die in a pool of blood like Valentina, our nanny.

I'm a machine, ready to battle and kill. I've trained every day since I was ten years old for this fight. I've combated the nightmares with strategy. I've become an excellent marksman, learned MMA fighting, and kept myself in perfect physical condition for any fight.

I will not stand by helplessly while someone else I love dies in a pool of their own blood.

Leo hauls the guy on the floor to his feet with lethal intent. I barrel forward to help.

"Stop, Leo!"

It's Lili again. Why is she telling Leo to stop? I sweep in beside Leo, and the two of us drag the guy into the nearest bedroom—Phoenix's—using my thumbprint to open the lock.

"He tried to roofie Lili," Leo growls. We throw the guy onto the floor, and he scrambles to his feet. "I watched him put something in her cup when she walked away."

"I didn't! It was alcohol!" The guy yelps.

Leo shuts the door behind Lara and Lili. The five of us crowd in the small bedroom. I make a vague mental note to send the women out before we torture and kill him.

"I *asked* him to!" Lili exclaims. The fear in her voice makes me need to kill this guy soon.

She turns to Lara. "Help me stop Ben—please."

Stop *Ben*? That doesn't compute for me. Is the guy's name Ben?

Lili tugs my biceps. "He offered to spike my drink when I complained that Leo wouldn't give me alcohol. He did *not* roofie me."

I hear her, but the words have no meaning. I'm honed in on the guy, considering how I will hurt him. Problem-solving how I will get rid of the body.

Lili blocks my view of him, stepping right in front of me. Lara stands beside her, touching my arm.

"I'm *fine*." Lili waves her hand in front of my face. "Look at me, Ben. We're not back there. That's over."

Lara presses her body against mine. I'm still focused on the guy, trying to see around her, so I don't register her presence at first, but something about the softness of her body feels at odds with the hard contraction of my muscles preparing to fight.

"Are you listening, Baron?" Her voice sounds far away. She repeats the words. Instead of raising her voice, she speaks softly. Seductively, like the words are only for me.

"I need you," she says in Russian. "I need you to look at me."

My gaze leaves the target of my violence without my brain's permission, finding Lara's big, lovely eyes fixed on my face.

There's a moment of disorientation, like when disparate elements from your life mix in a dream. Why is she here?

Why is she looking at me?

My arm bands around Lara's back. I fucking love the way she fits against me. Like she's necessary to my survival.

"What did you say?"

———

Lara

There's something wrong with my husband. Something that turns him into a killer. And the switch has definitely flipped.

The proper response from me should be fear.

Instead, all I feel is an ocean of compassion. Something happened to him. To both of the Baranov siblings.

We're not back there. That's over.

Whatever it was must explain why he's so aggressively protective of the people he cares about. It explains the nightmares. Did he lose someone who meant something to him?

He looks at me now, withdrawing his gaze for the first time from the guy Lili is trying to save. The dead look in his eyes disappears. He blinks a few times, searching my face like he's confused about who I am and why I'm here.

For a moment, I'm not sure he knows who I am. I'm just grateful he heard me ask him to look at me.

His arm loops around me almost as if on instinct. Something hard in his expression softens. "What did you say?"

"Did you hear Lili? She wasn't roofied. You need to let this guy go."

I have mad respect for Baron, who shows nothing on his face as he looks from me to Lili's would-be suitor, then to Lili and Leo. I can practically see the wheels turning in his brain. Like he's trying to catch up without showing that he lost his grip on reality for a moment.

He releases me. "You put liquor in her drink." Baron says it like a statement, but he's watching the guy.

Sweat gathers at the poor man's hairline. A bruise blooms on his jaw where Leo must've punched him. "Yes. I asked if she wanted a shot of vodka, and she handed her cup to me and said she'd be right back."

He produces a metal flask from his back pocket. "I brought my own supply since I'm not twenty-one."

Leo snatches it from his hand, uncaps it and sniffs, then takes a swig and swishes it in his mouth. He passes it wordlessly to Baron, who does the same thing.

Baron puts a hand on Lili's shoulder. "This is Lili Baranov, my little sister. There's no member of this house who's going to let you pour something in her drink without trying to kill you for it."

The guy holds up his hands. "I-I get it. I was just—" he shakes his head. "I'm sorry."

"It's okay," Baron says. "It was a misunderstanding."

Lili's body relaxes like she'd been holding her breath.

Baron holds up the flask. "I'm gonna keep this because I don't allow outside liquor at our events, but you can go back to the party if you want."

The guy bolts for the door, ignoring Lili like he never wants to see her again in his life.

As soon as he's gone, Lili gives Baron a shove. "Jesus, Baron." She sends Leo an equally irate glare. "You guys are the worst."

"He could have roofied you, Lili!" Leo explodes. "You actually *handed your drink* to a guy you just met and gave him permission to pour something in it? Are you out of your mind?"

Lili blushes a deep red, turns, and stomps out of the room without another word.

Leo stares after her with a deep frown, like she's his problem, not Baron's. "Fuck. I left the bar unattended." He spins on his heel and follows Lili out the door.

Baron scrubs his face. He's looking in my direction, but his gaze is far away. I slide both my arms around his waist and lay my cheek on his chest. "Are you okay?"

His hand lifts to the back of my head, and he strokes me like a kitten. He doesn't answer.

"What happened to you?"

"What?" Baron sounds startled, like his mind was elsewhere, and now he can't figure out what we're talking about.

"What made you like this? Something happened."

A small puff of air leaves Baron's chest, and he steps back like I knocked him off balance.

I reach for his face, catching it between my hands. "Tell me," I murmur.

Baron's eyes cloud. For one heart-expanding moment, I

think he's going to open up and tell me something, but then a voice crackles in the comms in his ear.

"I'll be right there," he barks in reply.

Disappointment ricochets around my chest. I'm grateful that he doesn't move yet. He brushes a lock of hair that's fallen down from my face. "I'm sorry if I scared you."

"I've been scared of you since I arrived," I tell him.

That impenetrable mask slides over his expression.

I shrug. "It's no worse now."

"I have to go talk to campus security at the front door. You're going upstairs to change your shoes?"

I nod.

"Meet me on the dance floor?"

I nod. Disappointment over him shutting me out wars with pleasure that he wants to dance with me. Of course, it might just be to raise the mystique of his reputation over having a new Russian *mafiya* wife.

But no. He genuinely wants to be with me—I can tell. We are starting to connect on an emotional level. Or at least I thought we were going to. If he shared something with me—anything—I might feel like it was safe to be with him.

Except that I'm still essentially his prisoner. I'm still not sure why I'm here. He still hasn't told me why we had to suddenly get married.

I catch his hand as he turns away and tug him back. "Baron?"

"*Malyshka.*"

I ask the real question—the one I need answered even more than what made him into the tortured man he is.

"Why am I here?" I lift my face to him, pleading with my gaze. Unexpectedly, my vision swims with tears. Vulnerability buries me. I need to know why I'm a pawn in this game and what is the game? What use I serve? What do they plan to do with me?

A line appears between his brows. Regret washes over his expression.

"Lara." He cradles my cheek with one large palm. "You're here for me to keep safe. And I'll never let anyone hurt you—I promise."

I pull away from him, frustrated.

Damn him for not giving it to me straight. Damn his father—and mine.

Damn them all for using me as a pawn.

I toss my hair as I precede him out of the bedroom.

They can all go to Hell as far as I'm concerned.

CHAPTER SIXTEEN

Baron

Not surprisingly, my wife did not meet me on the dance floor after changing her shoes. She disappeared upstairs for so long that I assumed she'd gone to sleep for the night.

Except now, at one in the morning with the party vibe turning needy and people trying to find their hook-ups before the party ends, I spot her out on the dance floor.

With a guy.

Anya turned the volume down on the sound system to signal the wind-down of the party, and she's playing songs with more of a groove than a bop.

Technically, there are four guys dancing around her, moving in closer like they're planning some wild *menage à cinq*.

I'm already slicing my way through the crowd when one of the guys puts his hands on her hips from behind. I keep my head. Violence will be my last resort. I simply lay a hand on the guy's shoulder when I get there.

"You're dancing with my wife."

Lara spins around.

Luckily for the guy, he recognizes me and instantly jumps back. "Sorry, Baron. I didn't know."

I ignore him and step in front of Lara, taking his place with my hands lightly touching her waist as we move to the music.

She looks up at me. It's hard to read her expression because it's a mix of mulish resistance and vulnerability. Like I dented her confidence in us tonight, but she's holding out some hope.

"Are you punishing me?" I ask.

She nods, holding my gaze as her hips sway. She's still in the sexy dress, but she has on a pair of flats now, and her hair is down. For one agonizing moment, my imagination pictures her hooking up with someone during this party to get back at me, but I quickly discard that notion. My house members would've seen and told me if she was with anyone else.

I step closer, one of my hands sliding from her waist up her side to lightly hold her breast. I brush my thumb over the skin just above her strapless dress.

She doesn't resist me. Her body knows mine. She responds to my touch by softening. It seems she wanted this. Wanted to get my attention and throw a mini-rebellion to prove she won't fall under my command.

The problem for her is that her body already knows its master.

Me.

Bending my face down close to hers, I say, "I'm not sure you understand the way this works." I let my hands roam, one traveling behind her to grab her ass and the other massaging behind her neck.

"How does it work?" She has those electric blue eyes trained on me, which makes my dick get hard.

I keep my voice seductive. My lips brush her temple as I

speak close to her skin. "I do the punishing around here. And you've just earned a trip to the dungeon."

Her rhythm falters.

I slide my arm behind her back to pull her body up flush against mine. My fingers tangle in her hair. "You've been a naughty girl."

She looks over her shoulder toward the door to the closet that leads to the secret staircase downstairs.

At that exact moment, the door swings open and Melinda comes out, followed by Anders.

So much for my no dungeon decree tonight. But at least they both got what they wanted. Things didn't fall apart with Anders stepping away. No harm done. I didn't want any randos downstairs, but I trust Melinda. She's taken many trips to the dungeon and has as much to lose as we do if she's indiscreet.

The memory of Lara asking if I get to have any fun returns to me. I never indulge my own desires at these parties. But the world probably won't fall apart if I slip away for a bit. If I choose something for myself for a change.

I take Lara's hand and lead her toward the closet. "Anders, you're in charge of shutting the party down," I say into the comms. We typically shut off the music and kick people out by 2 a.m. Sometimes VIPs get to stay longer for a swanky after-party, which of course amps up the allure of befriending our house members to secure the special invites. My goal—which I achieved reasonably fast—was to change the entire social structure at Thornecroft from worship of the old monied legacy *mudaks* to making my house members the new royalty.

It's the reason Titan House is after us.

Which is why I probably shouldn't indulge in my dark desires with Lara right now.

But our marriage is important. Possibly more important

to me than my previous goal of building an empire. And my wife is in a sensitive, malleable state. If I don't use this moment to bond us together, I'll be driving us apart.

I pull her into the dark closet and shut the door after us. It locks from the outside, so no one will be able to follow without the proper thumbprint.

Once inside, I activate the secret sliding door that opens to the staircase. Yes, we do have a panic room down there, too. Safety was the utmost consideration when renovating this house.

I flick on the mood lighting—subtle strips of amber and red lights that run along the stairs— and lead Lara down the stairs. At the bottom, I flick on more mood lights. We set the dungeon up like a swanky lounge, with couches and chairs for voyeurs, and equipment for BDSM play. The back wall features floor-to-ceiling smoky mirrors so subs and doms can watch themselves or their partners. There are also private rooms with spanking benches and other equipment.

"This is where I bring you when you've been a bad girl," I tell Lara, guiding her to a spanking bench. "Take your panties off and kneel up here." I pat the padded area for her knees.

Lara blinks and works to swallow but doesn't move.

That makes sense. She's not particularly eager to please me tonight. She'd rather have me "make" her obey. I invade her space, sliding my hands down her thighs and hiking up the hem of her fitted dress. "I'll help you, *malyshka*." Circling her ass a couple of times with my palms, I murmur, "You can trust me."

It's crazy how much I want her to trust me. I'm fucking desperate for that deeper connection with her. I need this to be more than a hot scene in the dungeon. I want us to bond.

I hook my thumbs in the waistband of her panties and slowly slide them down, squatting at her feet, then trailing my fingertips up along her legs as I stand.

"Let's see how excited you are about your spanking." I slide my middle finger between her legs and pull my breath in as a hiss over my teeth when I find her sopping wet. "*So* excited." I put a heap of praise in my voice. "That's good, *printsessa*. Now—" I jerk the hem of her dress up to her waist and spin her around to face the spanking bench. "*Kneel up.*" There's a sudden firmness to my voice that makes her gaze dart over her shoulder to mine, like she's checking to see if I'm mad.

I wink to show her I'm not.

She climbs onto the platform, and I push her torso over the padded bench and swiftly fasten her ankles to the straps to secure her. I do the same thing with her wrists, sliding my finger inside to make sure the restraints aren't too tight. Then I leave her there to simmer while I put some sexy music on the dungeon's sound system and go to pick out my toys.

I choose a small starter butt plug, some lube, and a leather paddle. It's a favorite implement of mine because it makes a nice slappy sound and can easily be experienced as pleasure or pain depending on how hard I wield it.

I take my time, knowing that anticipation heightens the experience for both of us. When I return to Lara's side, I stroke her bare ass lightly, running my palm in circles around each cheek, then sliding a finger between her legs again spreading her slick down and around her clit.

Then I deliver a flurry of sharp quick spanks, alternating right and left cheeks, concentrating the spanks on the lower half of her ass where she sits.

"*Ou*," she exclaims.

"I know," I soothe, returning to caressing her ass. I love seeing the bloom of my red handprints on her pale skin.

"This is what happens when you've been naughty, Lara," I tell her, making my voice stern again. I pry her cheeks apart and dribble a dollop of lubricant over her asshole. She lets out a warbling mew that sounds like one part fear, one part arousal.

"I'm going to fuck your ass with this plug, *printsessa*." I bring the bulbous end of a stainless steel plug to her back hole.

She makes a little whine of protest, which I ignore. I nudge her anus with the head of the plug, applying a little pressure and then withdrawing. I set it down and spank her again with my hand a little harder this time.

"Are you going to take your ass-fucking like a good girl?"

"*Nyet.*"

I chuckle and rub between her legs, giving her the experience of pleasure before I return to her punishment. "Let me make it easier for you." I return to my cabinet of toys and pull out a vibrator. I rub it with lube and then tease her folds with it, gliding it up to her clit. At the same time, I lean forward and kiss, then bite one of her ass cheeks.

"Ahh-ah," she warbles.

I keep the vibrator at her clit, and with my other hand, bring the head of the plug back to her anus and apply gentle pressure. She squeezes against the intrusion. "Take a deep breath, *malyshka*." I wait until she complies. "Now, as you blow it out, push back on this plug, so I can get it in."

She freezes, breath held for a moment, then slowly exhales. I apply more pressure to the plug. She moans as her back hole yawns open to take the plug.

"Good girl," I praise. "You're doing so well. Keep pushing for me."

I get the fattest part of the plug past her entrance, and it seats inside her. "That's it, *printsessa*." I gently pump and twist the plug, providing sensation to all the nerve endings that ring the anus.

"This is how I punish my naughty wife. This is the position you will find yourself in every time you disobey me." I riff with the dirty dom talk. "We'll take a trip to the dungeon together. And when we leave, you'll be sore, and I'll be satisfied."

I'm probably going overboard. I know her body responds to dominance, but her mind rebels against my control. I could be royally fucking this up right now.

But she whimpers and moans and her arousal drips between her legs. *Goddamn*, her ass and pussy look so pretty presented to me over that spanking bench.

"That's my good girl," I praise. My dick is harder than granite. "Now it's time for your spanking."

"No," she whimpers.

"You're getting a spanking. I just found you with another man's hands on you, *malyshka*."

I pick up the leather paddle and give her two firm slaps across the middle of her ass. When she takes them without fuss, I continue, keeping it light and rewarding her with caresses in between. After a dozen, I stop and admire the pink hue of her cheeks and pump the butt plug again. As I unhook the ankle straps, I tell her, "Here's what's going to happen, *printsessa*. You're going to keep that plug in your gorgeous ass while you walk upstairs and wait for me in our bedroom." I free her wrists and help her up, sliding the hem of her dress down her thighs. "Understand?"

She doesn't answer. She tries to pick up her panties, but I snag them first.

"I'll keep these." I tuck them in my pocket. "I want that pretty ass naked except for your butt plug when you walk up to our room." I slide my hands around her shoulders and back, making sure she still feels held by me. Caressed. Cherished.

Making her go upstairs without me is a power move that she might not be ready for.

I nip her ear and make my voice dark and seductive.

"Hold that plug tight between your cheeks and think about what I'm going to do to you when I get up there."

She shifts from foot to foot, clearly getting used to the sensation of having the plug inside her ass.

"When you get upstairs, you can touch yourself if you need to." I stroke between her legs as a demonstration. Her hands fly to my chest, and I see her pupils blown wide with lust. "When I come up, I'm going to give you a good fucking, so you'll remember who you belong to."

———

Lara

Baron squeezes my ass possessively. There's a part of me that wants to resist all of this—a part that still wants to punish Baron for not being straight with me about why we had to get married. About what role I'm serving as the pawn in their game. I keep thinking if I could figure that out, I can figure my way out of this. But he's not talking.

But that part has been drugged by his dominance. No part of me doesn't want to be touched by him right now, in whatever way he wants to touch me. Even if that means plugging my ass and spanking me with a leather slapper. I'm beyond turned on—dripping wet and braindead.

The only part I don't like right now is the idea of leaving Baron. Everything feels right in these moments when his attention is on me. When he's directing me, dominating me, making me feel like I'm the center of the Universe.

But when he's not, I'm reminded of how alone I am here. How I can't trust anyone, and I don't have friends. How Baron will chase away any friends I make. At least any male ones.

"I won't be long, *printsessa*," Baron murmurs when we get

to the top of the stairs and exit the closet somehow reading my mind in that uncanny way of his.

The party is winding down. The living room is only half as full as it was before, and the music Anya's playing has a slower, groovier feel.

"I just want to make sure they can wrap this up without me."

"If you take too long, I'll be asleep," I warn.

His lips crook into a faint smile. "You won't be." He gives a tender kiss, and I lean into him, not wanting to separate my body from his.

He tugs the hem of my dress down like he wants to be sure no one will see my bare ass and kisses my neck. "Go up there and take off your dress. Then pick the position you want to be fucked in and keep that pussy wet, *malyshka*."

I nearly orgasm right there on the dance floor at his words.

He must see it because he kisses me again. "Good girl." He gently guides me toward the staircase where Feliks stands in front of the velvet rope cordoning off the stairs. "I'll be up to reward you in a few minutes." He gives my ass another squeeze, which jostles the plug and turns my knees weak.

I walk up the stairs. Every step I take jostles the plug in my ass, which feels—I'm embarrassed to say because it seems so wrong—*incredible*. My natural lubricant drips between my inner thighs. There's a sense of fullness inside me, heightened by my smarting ass and the feel of my anus being held open by the plug.

When I get to the bedroom, I remove my dress and flats, then brush my teeth and wash my face.

I debate Baron's directive. *Pick the position you want to be fucked in.*

I can't decide. As it turns out, Baron doesn't take long at

all. He opens the door to find me standing in front of the bed.

He closes and locks the door then cocks his head to the side and arches a brow. "Having trouble picking a position?"

I nod.

He starts quickly shucking his clothes. I watch, admiring the flexing muscles of his arms. "Is that pussy nice and wet?"

My fingers slide down my belly to dip into my juices. I nod. I'm beyond wet.

"Climb onto the bed, *printsessa*. Let me see if you're wet enough."

I gingerly climb up, careful to keep my anus clamped around the plug. Baron follows me up. "Let me taste this pussy." He pushes me onto my back and spreads my knees.

I cry out when he simultaneously pumps the plug in my ass and licks into my pussy. His tongue swirls *everywhere*, lapping up my juices, stroking between my folds, sucking all my lady bits.

I'm going to come. My knees clamp down around his shoulders, butt lifting from the bedcovers, inner thighs trembling.

"Come for me, *malysh*." Baron thrusts two fingers inside me and strokes my inner wall. "You deserve it. You took your punishment so well."

I shriek and orgasm, my internal muscles gripping and rolling. I'm light-headed, trembly.

Baron pulls his fingers out and rolls onto his back. "Climb on and ride my dick, love."

I'm still dazed from coming, but I do as he instructs, straddling his waist. He grips my hips and lifts me up to lower down on his erection. It occurs to me that I haven't sucked his dick yet, despite the number of times he's gone down on me.

Our relationship has a one-sidedness, born of the

arranged marriage and my resentment at being imprisoned by it. Baron holds the keys to my cage. Baron also offers me great pleasure, but it comes with the flavor of his particular brand of control. He asks very little of me in return, other than staying away from other guys, which admittedly, is a reasonable request. I can't fault him for that, and even when I've pushed that line, he's been remarkably gentle with me.

His punishments are sexual. Pleasure-based. Thrilling. They only make me want to disobey more, although, more and more, I also find myself wanting to win his approval.

Maybe wanting to give something in return.

I groan as I take his long, thick member inside. With the butt plug also in me, it feels like there's no room. The sensation is heightened. He feels even bigger. Stretches me wider. I gasp when I reach the hilt, the head of his cock deep inside me. He holds my hips, without moving, letting me get used to his intrusion.

Then he reaches around and pumps the plug. I gasp, instantly rocking my hips over his. I grind my clit down on his loins, finding the place where the head of his cock rubs an inner ridge. My breath quickens. Baron uses the plug to propel me over his cock, and I ride him faster, my hands braced on his shoulders, my long hair falling around his face.

He looks up at me like I'm the most beautiful thing he's ever seen. Like he's utterly fascinated by me.

My heart flip-flops in my chest. Something lets go. Everything spills open.

I realize Benjamin Baranov is nothing like what I expected. He's dangerous, certainly. Definitely controlling. But he's generous. Not just with me, but with his bratva cell. He's giving of his attention. His strategy. Even his violence. It's all for a purpose that seems to revolve around the people he considers his own.

For the first time, I'm actually honored to be included in

that group. To belong to Baron. To be someone he would kill for.

I now crave hearing him call me his wife in that possessive, proud way of his.

I replay the stunned look he wore when I first came downstairs tonight. The way he claimed me during the party, announcing to everyone that I was his wife. Beaming at me when I played the game of churning their rumor mill with him.

I feel another orgasm build, and I whimper, resisting it.

Baron flips me to my back without separating our hips and plows into me, his need for control clearly taking over.

I'm glad for the change because I can't even see straight. The room spins. My breath is coming in short, quick pants. Baron pounds into me, bracing one hand against the wall above my head and lifting one of my legs to get even deeper.

"Reach back and push that plug, *malyshka*," he orders.

I obey because I've come to trust that his directions result in crazy pleasure for me. My eyes roll back in my head at the dual sensations in my ass and pussy.

"Baron...Ben."

His brown eyes crinkle, and his lips curve into a wicked smile when I say his name. "That's it, Lara. Who owns this gorgeous body?"

I shake my head, wanting to deny it. He doesn't own me. At least, I don't want him to.

He chuckles, like he's conceding defeat. "Who makes you scream when you come, *printsessa*?"

"You do," I gasp, already out of my mind with pleasure. Ready to go off again like a rocket ship.

"I own this body." He slams into me, harder and faster.

I cry out, my pleasure tinged with fear at how rough he's being. How forceful. How hard he's fucking me.

"I make you come. Look at me, Lara."

I didn't realize my eyes were closed, but I pry them open now. I can barely focus, but Baron holds my gaze. "Come for me now." He rubs my clit with the pad of his thumb.

I let out a cry, but can't quite crest the peak. "You come," I pant, breathless.

Baron groans, and I watch in fascination as his face contorts. Control slips away. A muscle jumps in his cheek as he pumps with brutal force, his rhythm turning erratic. With a shout, he shoves in deep and comes.

The moment he does, I wrap my legs around his back and hook my ankles to hold him inside me. I come with him, my internal muscles squeezing and pulsing around his cock, milking it for the last of his essence.

Baron releases a hoarse laugh and nuzzles into my neck. "Damn. That was so hot. You make me crazy, Lara."

The pleasure of his appreciation mingles with the high from my multiple orgasms.

I hate to admit it, but I might be falling for my husband.

I'm addicted to being touched by him. Fascinated by watching him.

A knock sounds at the door, and Baron stiffens and pulls out. "Yeah?" He hurls himself off the bed and picks up the side of the bedspread to sweep it in a swift arc over my naked body.

Leo's voice sounds from the other side. "Baron, the cops are here. They don't have a warrant, but they're asking for you."

CHAPTER SEVENTEEN

Baron

Fuck.

I yank on a pair of jeans and shove my phone with my ID in the back pocket. "Let them in," I call through the closed door. "We've got nothing to hide. Everything was on the up and up." I tug a T-shirt over my head and throw the door open.

"Okay," Leo answers. "You coming down?"

"Right behind you." I shut the door again, remembering the state I left my wife in.

I climb back on the bed and kiss her temple. "I'm sorry. I'll be back as soon as I can. Do you need help removing the plug?"

Lara sits up, looking deliciously mussed. Her eyes are glassy and bright, her face is flushed, and her bedhead is spectacular. Her eyes are wide. "I've got it. You go."

I kiss her swollen lips and jam my feet into a pair of flip flops to run downstairs. Eight cops are scattered through the downstairs, walking around like they're looking for something.

I jog down the stairs. It's just past two in the morning. I heard the music go off about ten minutes ago. Any party-goers who remained are now streaming out the doors as fast as they can. My house members are all gathered, my soldiers standing at attention.

Except they all look worried. I don't want any of them to worry about this—whatever it is. I can handle it.

"I'm Benjamin Baranov," I say to the first cop I see, trying to project calm authority. "How can I help you?"

"Mr. Baranov, do you mind if we have a look around the premises?"

"No warrant," Leo mutters as a reminder to me. His dad, Maxim, is my dad's fixer. He knows the laws and how to avoid getting caught or how to get out of any situation.

"May I ask what you're looking for?" I ask.

"We're doing a wellness check on the party-goers in the house."

My brows fly up. "Wellness check?"

Does that mean they're checking for drug use?

The police officer doesn't respond. He and his partner walk through the rooms of the house, looking into the faces of the guests rushing out, stopping the more inebriated ones to ask questions.

I trail along. "May I ask what this is about?"

They ignore me, and one of them attempts to open one of the first-floor bedroom doors. "What's in here?" He knocks on the door.

"That's a bedroom." I raise my brows. Someone could be sleeping in there, for all he knows. There's someone beautifully naked behind my bedroom door.

The thought of them knocking on that door makes me grind my teeth. I need to warn Lara if they make their way upstairs.

"Can you unlock it for me?" the cop asks.

It's Alex's room. My thumbprint will open the door, but I look around for Alex.

"I'm right here." Alex steps up to my side.

"They want to look in your room."

He gives me an oblique look and shrugs, then unlocks the door and pushes it open. One cop goes inside and another asks for the next door to be opened.

"You're Benjamin Baranov?" A detective asks, entering the living room. He shows me his detective badge.

"I am."

"Come with me, please."

Anya and Zoe stand together, hovering. Glaring at the cops. Clearly worried.

I show them I have this under control. "Am I under arrest?"

"Not yet. We'd just like to ask you some questions down at the station."

Fuck. Fine. The sooner I find out what they're looking for, the better.

"All right. Let's go." I spread my hands.

"I'll call Lucy," Zoe says, meaning my mom.

"No one calls Chicago," I order.

My mom is the best criminal defense attorney in the state, but the last thing I want is to wake her in the middle of the night with the news that the police took her son to the station for questioning. All my life, she's tried to keep me out of the bratva business. When Lili and I got dragged into the violence as children, it rocked her marriage to my dad. They recovered, but it was part of me getting sent away to Swiss boarding school. I showed too much interest in the business.

Calling my mom will be a last resort.

I've got this covered. They have nothing on me; otherwise, I'd be in handcuffs with my rights being read to me.

Still, I don't like it.

Some more of my confidence slips away when I catch sight of Lara at the top of the stairs, watching me being ushered out the door.

I stop and look up at her, heaviness descending around me like an iron prison.

Her seeing me this way feels even worse than my mom knowing. My wife should be able to trust in me to keep this kind of shit away from her. I should be able to control every situation to avoid this kind of embarrassing scene. I somehow missed something tonight, but I have no idea what.

"Let's go," the cop says, pulling my arm to urge me through the front door.

I glance back as I walk out, but someone shuts the door behind us, blocking the view of my wife.

At the station, I'm ushered into an interrogation room. I swear I glimpse Chancellor Ogden talking with a man in a black t-shirt and jeans in the doorway of the room next door, but they disappear before I can be sure.

I sit down at the table in the seat the detective indicates and lace my tattooed fingers. There's a mirror positioned on the wall opposite me that must be a two-way. Which means Chancellor Ogden is watching this interview.

My stomach turns sour. Whatever this is about is important enough that the chancellor of Thornecroft University was brought in. Does this go beyond Titan House's vendetta against us? Is it bratva related? Does it have something to do with the Rostovs?

Fuck, I need more information to problem-solve.

The detective sits on the opposite side, opens a file folder and produces a photo, which he pushes across the table. "Do you know this woman?"

I glance at the photo and adrenaline crashes through my system. The warrior in me surfaces, ready to kill or die. To battle for her safety.

Now I understand why the Chancellor would be involved.

I lift my gaze with my eyes blazing. *"What happened to Melinda Tracy?"*

"So you are acquainted."

My brain tumbles down a cliff. Was she kidnapped? Murdered? I need to know so I can fix it.

I look at the two-way mirror and lift my chin in its direction. "So he's secret service? Or secret ops?"

I hear the bang of a door, and the guy stalks in. He's the type who wears his t-shirt two sizes too small, so it shows off the muscles on his torso. He yanks a chair up and turns it around to sit backward, like a cowboy. I imagine he thinks he's a bad-ass.

"When was the last time you saw Ms. Tracy?" he demands.

My mom would tell me not to answer questions without an attorney present. I should call her. Or at least call the young law professor who occasionally purchases drugs from me. I'm being stupid by answering their questions, but I need to know what happened to Melinda. "Two hours ago at Baranov House. Is she missing?"

She may still be there. Maybe Anders took her to his room after they played in the dungeon. Is this just about her not returning to her dorm last night? I try to slow my pounding heart.

She might not be dead. Not murdered and lying in a pool of her own blood. I might not have to live with the anguish of failing to protect someone else I care about.

"Was she in your company at Baranov House?" the detective asks.

"No. I didn't even talk to her. I just saw her toward the end of the party." I scrub a hand across the stubble on my face. "Is she hurt? Dead? Can you tell me what's going on?"

"How would you define your relationship with Ms. Tracy?" Black Shirt asks.

I wouldn't care to.

"We're friends." That's as accurate as any definition gets.

"Did you leave Baranov House at any point during the night?" the detective asks.

"No."

"Did you give Ms. Tracy a drink tonight?"

"Me personally? No."

"Did you have sex with Ms. Tracy tonight?"

"No. I'm married."

This seems to surprise both men.

Well, yeah, it was a surprise to all of us.

My eyes narrow. Why would they ask that question?

"Would you be willing to give a DNA sample to clear you as a suspect in this case?"

I sit and stare at both men, showing nothing on my face as I process the magnitude of what's going on here. It sounds like Melinda was raped or murdered.

What if I could have prevented what happened? I'm the one who left the party unsupervised in favor of playing in the dungeon with my wife. What if in neglecting my duties, something slipped by the rest of the team? Some danger that resulted in something terrible happening to arguably the most important young woman—at least politically—on campus?

I try not to picture Melinda crumpled in a pool of blood.

Not like Valentina. That's over.

We're not there anymore, as Lili would say.

Would my mom advise me to give a sample? No. She would tell me not to answer any questions without a lawyer present. She would tell me I'm being set up.

This definitely could be a setup.

I blow out my breath. "Sure."

Black Shirt nods at the detective, who goes to the door and says something to the people outside.

"Is she alive?" I try to sound cool, but my voice cracks.

Black Shirt studies me. After a long, agonizing moment, he nods. "She's in the hospital. She was drugged and sexually assaulted at your party."

CHAPTER EIGHTEEN

Lara

I huddle with the members of Baranov House in the kitchen. It's five in the morning, and no one has slept. I made espresso and steamed milk for everyone with the Italian espresso machine they have. The police searched every room in the house, possibly looking for drugs or drug paraphernalia, but they also seemed to be doing wellness checks on anyone who seemed inebriated. Leo, Alex, and Feliks followed them around like silent guard dogs waiting to be sprung. Except their owner wasn't here to command any action.

The house feels completely different without Baron's quiet authority. I didn't realize until his absence how much his control brings a sense of safety. Without him, everything feels unsteady. Adrift.

Scary.

I don't like the idea of Baron being down at the police station. Not one bit. Once again, it seems like he sacrificed his own comfort, safety, and pleasure in exchange for taking any pressure or stress off everyone else.

Except I do feel the strain.

I want him out. I want him safe. I want to know why they're harassing him when he worked so hard to keep everything above-board for this party.

"Should someone tell Lili?" I ask. She left the party at some point and went home. She knows nothing about her older brother being taken into the police station.

"Let her sleep," Leo says immediately, like he's already thought it through.

It seems like Baron's not the only one with protective instincts when it comes to Lili Baranov.

"Explain the American laws to me again," I say to Leo.

"He wasn't arrested when they left. They just took him in for questioning. If they don't have enough on him to charge him with a crime, they can't hold him for more than forty-eight hours without bringing him before a judge for probable cause."

I shake my head, still not understanding what it all means.

"I'm going down there," I declare, standing. "To break him out or bail him out or whatever."

Anders' phone beeps. "It's Baron."

We all crowd around.

Did you take Melinda home last night??

Ander's face turns pale. "Shit. Something happened to Melinda? Oh God." He quickly types back:

No, you said you needed me tc shut the party down, so I called security to escort her to her dorm.

They want you to come to the station for a statement and DNA swab as soon as possible.

Anders rises to his feet, looking wobbly.

"I'm going with you," I say firmly. "I don't care if I have to wait at the police station for forty-eight hours. It's better than sitting here not knowing what's going on with him."

Leo also stands. "Me too. I can pull security footage of her leaving, in case it helps."

Fifteen minutes later, the three of us walk into the small Whisper police station, where the cop at the front desk immediately leads Anders back, ignoring me and Leo.

Leo starts working on his phone, pulling up camera footage from the front porch of the house. His face is grim. "I hope nothing happened to Melinda," he says tightly.

"Are you friends with her?"

Leo shakes his head. "No. But I would feel terrible if anything happened to her leaving our party. I'd feel responsible, and Baron–"

He stops.

I try unsuccessfully to swallow. "What about Baron?"

Leo catches the intensity in my voice and looks up from his phone, where he's still working while we speak. "There's nothing between them," he says dismissively. "I don't mean that. But Baron has a hard time with people getting hurt on his watch."

There it is again—another reference to this protective aspect of Baron and a hint to an underlying trauma that caused it.

"What happened to him?" I ask quietly.

Leo sends me a quick look, then shakes his head. "Not my story to tell."

My pulse quickens simply at hearing I'm right—there is a story. But I respect Leo's boundary. He's right—Baron should share it with me. I hope he can.

Leo's phone buzzes, and he responds to something.

"Fuuuuuuck." He runs a hand through his hair.

"What is it?"

He hands me the phone, which is open to the *New York Times* app, with "Breaking News" at the top.

The headline reads "Daughter of Vice Presidential Candidate Gabe Tracy Drugged and Assaulted at Thornecroft Party."

I suck in a sharp breath, ice sluicing through my veins. "But... that didn't happen. Did it?"

Leo shakes his head. "Definitely not. This is Titan House fucking with us."

I see doubt on his face, though. "Would another society house go to such lengths just because your parties are better?" I ask doubtfully. "They wouldn't *assault* a woman, would they?"

A muscle jumps in Leo's jaw. "Well, she'd be the one to pick if they wanted to be sure we get permanently closed down and prosecuted."

He muses some more. "Or it could be her father's political opponents trying to make him look weak." He shakes his head. "No, that doesn't make sense. It has to be a set-up to get at Baron and our house."

He returns to his phone, scrolling through video footage. "Here, look." He shows me the video of Anders escorting Lara out to a security cart—one of the open-air electric carts the campus security patrol in. He gives her a kiss before helping her into the back seat then stands and watches as the cart drives away. "Did she look drugged to you?" Leo asks.

I shake my head, drawing in a much-needed breath.

Leo has evidence. Everything is going to be okay.

He stands and walks up to the counter. "I'd like to speak to the person in charge of the Melinda Tracy case," he says, showing the screen of his phone. "I have time-stamped video evidence of her leaving our party."

———

Baron

They grill me for what feels like hours. I don't second-guess not calling my mom. If I get formally charged, she'll probably kill me for not bringing her in immediately, but for now, I'm cooperating. For Melinda's sake.

Finally, they tell me I'm free to go. "Your wife is here to pick you up," the detective says.

Surprise pours like warm liquid into my chest. "She is?" I ask stupidly.

Lara came.

It's early morning, which means she probably didn't sleep.

Which means she cares.

My wife is here to pick me up.

No words have ever meant more to me.

"Don't leave town," the officer warns me.

I nod and walk out to the lobby of the small police station.

Another dose of warm liquid floods my limbs when I see her. Lara surges up from a waiting chair to meet me. She's in a pair of teal sweatpants with branding down one leg and a pale cropped pink t-shirt, fitted tight around her braless tits.

"*Malyshka*," my voice sounds rough. I stumble toward her. "You came."

She meets me halfway, throwing her arms around me. I catch her waist, lifting her off the floor for a long, tight embrace.

My eyes smart.

Leo stands nearby, and Anders emerges from the interrogation room, looking haggard.

"Let's get out of here," I say, and the four of us walk out.

When we're safely in Leo's SUV, I say, "I don't know what the fuck just happened. They said Melinda was drugged and sexually assaulted at our party."

Anders looks like he's going to be sick. "Can you take me to the hospital, Leo? I need to see her."

I nod. "Yeah, me too." I reach for and squeeze Lara's hand. "Is that okay with you?"

Her brows lift in surprise, but she nods.

"I showed them the video of her leaving the party, clearly *not drugged*," Leo fills us in. "And I verified that I personally saw you and Anders in the house the entire time after she left."

"Thank you," I say quietly.

"I told them I'd comb through all the footage from the party to find everything with Melinda in it. I can find footage inside the house of Anders after she left, and Lara was your alibi."

I turn to look at Lara, suddenly sick.

She nods. "They questioned me, and I told them we were together during the last hour of the party."

I grind my teeth. One thing I would never wish for is my wife being interrogated to corroborate my story.

"They questioned you? I'm so sorry, Lara."

She lifts her chin. "I volunteered."

Another wave of warmth washes over me. I bring her hand to my lips and kiss the back of it. "I'm sorry," I murmur again.

"Not everything is under your control, Baron." She holds my gaze steadily with her blue one, and it feels like I'm somersaulting. "You're not responsible for all the bad things that happen in the world."

"I'm a prime suspect," Anders says tightly from the front seat. "They're going to find my DNA all over her. But it was consensual."

"Of course it was," I say. "She'll tell them that when she wakes."

He turns to look at me. "Dude, what if she doesn't remember? She was covered in marks—everyone's going to think I'm some kind of heinous sexual predator."

That's when it becomes crystal clear.

"This *was* all a setup," I say, working it out in my mind as I speak. "Everyone knows or thinks they know that we have a dungeon. It might also be known that Melinda Tracy frequented it last year. Maybe that she frequented it with me." I dart an apologetic glance at my wife, but her face remains sympathetic.

"So someone roofies Melinda at the party and maybe calls for help, and the police find her drugged and covered in bruises with someone's DNA all over her," Leo finishes.

"Exactly. It has to be a setup, or they wouldn't have shown up at our party looking for me. I never said one word to her the whole night," I say.

"What if it was that guy I thought roofied Lili?" Leo asks.

I shake my head. "He had a flask of vodka. That was a coincidence. Or your gut telling you something bad was going to go down."

"Who found her and called for help?" Lara asks.

"I don't know. The newspaper article didn't say anything about how she was found," Leo says.

"*Newspaper* article?" I shove my fingers through my hair. "This went nuclear fast. Fuck."

"Yeah," Leo says. "I got a *New York Times* breaking news alert on my phone. That's how I knew to look for the security footage."

"So now the attention of the entire country will be on this case. Even if they can't bring charges, the Chancellor would probably do anything to make it go away, including expel me and shut down our house," I groan.

"Or me," Anders says miserably. "If that dude who works for her dad doesn't kill me first."

"Did you tell him the truth?" I ask. "About what you and Melinda did?"

Leo pulls up in front of the hospital, but none of us get out. This conversation needs to be finished in the privacy of our vehicle.

"I... said we had sex," Anders says. "But I didn't want to out her about the pain-play. I mean, the whole world could find out. Her dad could find out. He's probably going to have me killed."

"No one's getting killed on my watch," I growl. I can probably take that Black Shirt guy. He looks well trained, but so am I.

"What if Melinda doesn't remember that we had sex? Does the memory loss and confusion go back farther than when she took the drug?"

A chill fills the vehicle as we all consider that question.

"I don't know," I say quietly. "But I think Melinda is smart enough to put together the truth if we present the facts to her."

I hope. But Anders was probably right not to "out" her, and depending on how important it is to her to keep that part of her life a secret, there is a possibility she throws Anders under a bus to do it.

But I won't let that happen.

"Best-case scenario, we find the fuckers who did this and make them pay."

"Bring them to justice," Lara corrects. "Otherwise, you won't clear your name."

———

The hospital is swarming with press, and when I ask at the front desk for Melinda's room, the receptionist tells us they aren't releasing information about Ms. Tracy to anyone.

"Fuck. I'm going to send her a text. Christ, what do I even say?" Anders asks.

"Tell her you heard what happened and ask if you can see her," I advise.

A familiar figure in a tight black t-shirt cuts through the crowd and heads down the hall.

"Look." I lift my chin. "I'll bet he knows where Melinda's room is."

The four of us take off down the hall, following the government agent. He takes the stairwell, and I follow, hanging back in the doorway of the first floor and listen to how many flights he goes up. When the door on the third floor closes, I motion to my friends to follow.

On the third floor, I crack the door and peer out.

Gabe Tracy stands in the open doorway to a hospital room, flanked by two secret service members. He's listening to Black Shirt. His henchman spots me, and they both look our way.

Fuck it. I push the door from the stairwell open and stride out holding Lara's hand. Anders and Leo flank us.

"Benjamin Baranov and Anders Hansen," Melinda's dad

says. His expression is a dark glower. Who could blame him when his only daughter was attacked?

I'm guessing he knows our names from Black Shirt. I can only hope he already filled him in on our presumed innocence.

My mom worked to get him elected, but now is probably not the time to mention that. He probably knows.

"Senator Tracy." I can't decide whether I should stick out my hand to shake or not. I decide not to because he doesn't look like he's in the hand-shaking mood. "This is my wife, Lara Baranov, and my housemate, Leo Popov."

Black Shirt watches me with an assessing look. I don't imagine he misses much.

"Why are you here?" Senator Tracy looks as tired as I feel. No one slept last night.

"To support Melinda." I peer past him into the room, but the bed is empty.

"She's resting." The senator gives us all a hard look. I realize the secret service members flank the door next to this one. That must be the one she's in.

I gaze back without flinching. I need him to know I'm not guilty, and I have nothing to hide. At least not about this case. I have a lot to hide in other areas.

"Step inside this room." Senator Tracy tips his head toward the empty room beyond him, and we file in. Black Shirt follows and shuts the door behind us.

The senator shifts his glower to Anders. "Am I to understand you're...*dating* my daughter?"

Anders shifts on his feet. "I'm not sure she would define it that way, but honestly, Senator, I'd give my left nut to have that be true."

Gabe Tracy's eyebrows pop.

Anders has a way of disarming people, and it seems his

graphic confession worked because Melinda's dad's shoulders sag, and he scrubs a hand across his face.

"I just want you to know, Senator, that we're going to find whoever did this to Melinda and make them pay," I offer.

"He means *bring them to justice*," Lara corrects me again, squeezing my hand.

I crack my neck. The perpetrator will experience my violence. *Then* I will bring them to justice.

"Do you know who did this?" Senator Tracy asks.

"I have ideas. And I have resources. We'll find them."

Black Shirt watches me steadily. I expect him to say something like, "Leave the detective work to me," but he says nothing, so I plow forward.

"Who brought her to the hospital? Her roommate?"

"Campus security." Black Shirt throws us an unexpected bone.

Leo and I exchange a glance. The security guard. It had to be him.

"The same guy who picked her up intact from Baranov House?" Leo asks.

Neither man answers.

"We'll start there," I say.

"You want to tell me your ideas?" the senator asks.

I hesitate. I don't want to make accusations without proof, but guilt over what happened to Melinda eats at me. It happened because of me. Like Valentina, Melinda was an innocent caught in bratva crossfire. I scrub a hand across my face.

"Senator...it's possible this was an elaborate set-up to get our house shut down. Choosing a high-profile target like your daughter ensured heads would roll. Not to mention, it brought an avalanche of pressure and negative press to the University. Do you happen to know who called the *New York Times?*"

"We're looking into it," Senator Tracy says. He frowns at me. "So your theory is this was all about you and your house?" Derision laces his voice. Like I'm some narcissist making his daughter's tragedy about me.

I abandon sharing my thoughts and shake my head. "You're right. I'm probably just being paranoid."

"No, talk me through your theory," Black Shirt demands. His back is against the wall, hands caged loosely at his lap. Whoever he is, it's not some ordinary secret service. He's definitely some kind of special ops guy who has the complete trust of the senator.

I draw in a breath. "My hope is that no one assaulted Melinda—just drugged her. People knew she frequented our house, and it may have been rumored that she and I had a physical relationship in the past. Drugging her during or just after our party would guarantee a shitstorm for me. The fact that it was Anders she hooked up with isn't any better. If Melinda doesn't remember what they did together at the party before she was drugged, Anders is in a world of trouble, and our house will probably be shut down—at least from having parties if not closed altogether."

Gabe Tracy looks angry. "You're telling me this might be some kind of house hazing situation?"

I look straight back at him. "I'm telling you I will destroy whoever was behind this. No one hurts my friends."

The corners of Black Shirt's lips turn up for a moment, and then his face goes blank again.

"And Melinda is your friend." It's a question, but his voice doesn't rise at the end.

"Yes, sir."

"Okay. Here's what's going to happen. You find who did this to my daughter and bring them to me."

"Yes, sir."

"And you'd better pray your stories match Melinda's when she wakes up, or you're right—I will annihilate all of you." He gives all four of us the stink eye before waving his hand toward the door. "Now get out."

CHAPTER NINETEEN

Lara

I wake at one in the afternoon. I'm hungry, and the bed is cold. I climb out and look for Baron. I hear his phone buzzing with a text and see it's still on the nightstand. He must still be up here.

A cool breeze wafts through the room, and I realize the window is half open. When I walk over to shut it, I see Baron sitting outside on the roof in his tank top and a pair of jeans, his arms loosely draped over his drawn-up knees.

I push the window open, and he turns. "Lara." His gaze appears haunted.

I climb out onto the gently-pitched tile roof, and he instantly reaches his hand out to steady me. "Are you okay?" he asks when I sink down beside him.

"Yeah. Are you?"

For once, he doesn't give me his slick, in-control, closed-off act. He draws a long breath and sighs it out. Then he nods. "I'm okay." His words sound heavy, though.

"What are you doing out here?" I instantly regret the

dumb question. He obviously wanted to be alone, and I'm interrupting.

He gives me a faint smile. "Working on my tan."

"Your shirt's on," I point out.

"I can remedy that." He reaches between his shoulder blades and smoothly pulls his shirt off over his head in a move so sexy I swear my ovaries drop three eggs.

"Are you worried?"

The strong leader returns, and I kick myself for asking the wrong question. I want him to open up and be vulnerable, not reassure me.

He shakes his head. "No. I'm going to find the fuckers who did this and fix it." He speaks with total confidence, and I have zero doubt he will do it.

I look out at the view. I can see why Baron likes to come out here. We're on the third floor—the height of treetops. Our window faces away from campus toward the neighborhood houses.

"Is this where you come to think?" I try again.

He interlaces his fingers with mine and brings my knuckles to his lips. "Yeah."

"Am I interrupting?" I try to tell myself not to be hurt if he says yes, but my heart feels ripe and vulnerable. Like it would pop with a single pin-prick.

"Fuck, no." He looks over at me. "You're the best thing that's happened to me."

My chest squeezes like he just tied a tight ribbon around the center. I want to believe him. It freaks me out how much I care. I find it hard to breathe.

"When they let me out of jail this morning and told me my wife was waiting for me, I—" Baron breaks off, his gaze roving over my face. "I can't tell you what it meant to me. I couldn't believe you came for me."

"Of course, I came for you." I don't know why my eyes are getting hot. My throat feels clogged. "You're my husband."

Baron drops his head between his knees for a moment then leans his shoulder against mine. "I'm humbled," he mumbles. "I want–" He breaks off again.

He's usually so slick and confident. As *pakhan* of his bratva cell, he's strong, dominant, the leader, but right now, he's all mine.

I didn't realize how much I needed this. Not that I wanted him humbled–well, maybe I did–but that I craved prying him open like an oyster. Seeing the softer parts under the hard shell. I wanted to find out what makes him tick. What makes him sacrifice his own happiness for the sake of everyone around him? What makes him so fierce a protector?

I touch his face. "What do you want?" I murmur.

He lets out a humorless chuff of laughter. "I want you to care." His voice breaks.

My heart follows suit.

I throw my leg over his waist to straddle his lap. "I care, Baron," I whisper.

He holds my waist and leans his forehead against mine. "I'm crazy about you, Lara. I agreed to marry you out of duty, but the moment I met you, that changed. You felt like... someone I'd been waiting for my entire life."

Tears prick my eyes.

"I didn't want this. I still don't. But...you got past my defenses. I want to know you, Baron. The real you."

He stares back at me, his brown eyes dark. I see a faint alarm in them. Like he knows I'm storming the castle, coming for his deepest, darkest secret.

"Tell me," I murmur.

Genuine alarm flares, but he covers it. "Tell you what?"

"What happened that made you this way. Who did you lose?"

He sucks in a startled breath and holds it.

I cradle his stubbled jaw in my hands and stroke my thumbs back toward his ears, tracing the soft hairs that make up his sideburns.

"Our housekeeper. Valentina. And...Lili could have died."

I stay very still, hardly breathing. Waiting for him to go on.

"It was my fault. We never left our building without protection. My dad drove us to school in an armored car. Our building was a fortress—no one could breach it." Baron's breath comes in short, shallow pants.

The trauma of whatever he's about to tell me still rules his nervous system. He still relives it like it's happening in the present.

"I wanted ice cream." His voice is rusty. "There was this ice cream cart out on the beach—I could see it from our living room window. I was ten—old enough to go buy it myself, but we weren't allowed out alone, which I hated. I hassled Valentina to let me go, and when she wouldn't, I asked her to take us down there. I got Lili in on it, and she begged and pleaded and whined until Valentina agreed to take us."

I keep my mouth shut and continue to brush my thumbs over his temples, around his ears, trying to soothe the agitated state from his body while he tells the story.

"We got the ice cream, and we were walking back—almost in front of our building—when this white van drove up on the sidewalk, and three guys jump out. Valentina screams and picks Lili up. She tells me to run to the building, but I—" he shakes his head, looking confused. Like he's still that ten-year-old boy in shock on the sidewalk.

"I just stood there. I froze."

"That's a normal human response," I murmur softly, not wanting to interrupt his flow but also not wanting him to go on with some belief that he did the wrong thing.

He swallowed. "One of them shot Valentina in the head. She went down on the sidewalk with half her head blown off. He grabbed Lili's arm and pulled it out of the socket, yanking her out of Valentina's death grip.

"Two guys grabbed me. I finally woke up and tried to get away, but it was too late. They wrestled me to the van. Maykl—Alexei and Feliks' dad—rushed out of the building with guns drawn, but he didn't fire."

Baron's brows furrow. "I screamed at him to shoot. At the time, I couldn't figure out why he didn't, but, of course, he was afraid of accidentally hitting me or Lili."

Baron stops and doesn't go on. His gaze is unfocused, like he's still reliving the moment.

"Then what happened?" I whisper.

"They threw us both in the back of the van and took off. Maykl shot out one of the tires as they took off, but they kept driving, speeding away. There was a chase. The van flipped—a bunch of times. I got knocked out for a while."

"*Bozhe moi,*" I breathe.

For a moment, Baron's eyes focus on my face like I just reminded him I'm still here. That we're in the present. A future where he's all grown up. Where he escaped from that event with his life.

He swallows. "I heard gunfire in the front. The back of the van is blocked off from the driver's compartment, so I don't know what's happening. We're in the dark—upside down. There's a guy on top of me. Lili is screaming and crying because she's in pain. My head and neck hurt.

"One of the guys throws open the back doors. He has Lili in a chokehold, a gun to her head, and he's shouting for everyone to get back.

My dad and his men are there, but they drop their weapons, and I can't figure that out, either. I realize the guy on top of me is knocked out, so I get his gun. I knew how to fire it. My dad had been taking me hunting for a few years as an excuse to teach me how to handle weapons.

"Lili's crying, and the guy is shaking her, telling her to shut up, or she dies. I walk up behind him. My dad is saying *don't shoot*. It doesn't occur to me that he means me. I point the gun at the back of the guy's head and pull the trigger.

I remember the look of terror on my dad's face as he rushed forward to catch Lili. The other man groaned behind me and started to get up, so I turned around and shot him, too."

I try to hide the shock ricocheting through my soul. Baron's voice has taken on a deadened quality now. Like he went numb in the moment, and he's numb telling me about it, too.

"I missed, so I got closer and kept shooting. I emptied the chamber into the guy and still kept firing until Maykl took the gun out of my hand and pulled me into a hug."

Tears form in the corners of my eyes.

Gospodi, he was just a kid. He watched his housekeeper die and still believes it was his fault. He had to kill two men to save his sister's life. No wonder he tries to control every aspect of his life now to keep everyone he loves safe.

I wrap my arms around him and press my face into his neck. "I'm so sorry, Ben. That shouldn't have happened to you."

He pulls me tight, nearly squeezing the breath out of me.

"It wasn't your fault." I pull my face away to catch his eye. "If you're thinking you got Valentina killed, you didn't."

A muscle jumps in Baron's cheek. "I'm the one—"

"*Nyet*." I interrupt. "You didn't tell those men to come and shoot her. You had nothing to do with that. If your father wasn't a bratva boss, then going to the beach to get ice cream would've been a normal activity. You were denied that normalcy by his actions, not yours. None of it was your fault."

"I could've killed Lili." Baron's voice sounds tight.

"What? How?"

"When I shot the guy holding her, the gun could've gone off and killed her. That's why my dad was saying *don't shoot*."

Anger flushes through me. "Fuck your dad! Did he tell you that you could've killed Lili? You *saved* Lili. You saved Lili, Ben." I use his real name, trying to make sure his younger self hears me. "It was your dad's fault, not yours."

Agony washes over Ben's face, but he nods. "No, he took the blame. It's the only time I've ever seen my dad cry."

My eyes flood with tears again. Me telling him to blame his dad is useless. They all suffered. It was a shared family trauma. I hug him again. "I'm so glad you lived, Benjamin Baranov."

Baron lets out a chuff of air. "Yeah?"

I nod, considering. So much has happened in the last weeks. A seeming lifetime has passed. I was packed off from Paris to marry a stranger, started at a new university, was thrown into a cell made up of bratva heirs, experienced the wildest sex of my life, and...fell in love.

And if my dad hadn't arranged my marriage to Baron, I would've missed all of it. I wouldn't know this incredible young man, who is brilliant and strong and flawed in the most beautiful way. I wouldn't know what it's like to be the focus of a man like him. A man who commands attention from everyone around him and moves mountains to orchestrate the fate he desires. A dangerous, violent man who hasn't shown a shred of anger toward me, even when I provoke him. A man who might be morally grey but definitely operates under a code.

I kiss him. "Yeah. I'm falling in love with my husband." Saying the words out loud feels like pushing off the top of a double black diamond ski slope without poles.

Baron catches the back of my head. His eyes blaze. The

intensely focused bratva prince is back with me now—all trauma erased. "I fell in love with you the moment you walked off that plane, *malyshka*," he says. He kisses me fiercely, his lips slamming into mine, his tongue lashing into my mouth. His cock lengthens, pressing against my core.

"Inside," he rasps against my lips, lifting my waist to help me stand. "I need you on a bed. Under me. Naked."

I laugh as he follows me up. "Not a roof?"

He takes my hand and ushers me to the window, steadying me as I climb in. "Too risky." He suddenly sobers. "I'm not losing you."

My heart flops in my chest. My tragedy-tainted husband will probably always worry about keeping me safe.

The truth is, I feel completely safe with him. I was afraid at first because I don't understand why I'm here, and I'm still mad at him for not telling me, but I believe Baron will keep me safe, whatever comes.

"I'm always safe with you," I murmur.

———

Baron

She's falling in love with me.

My heart stretches and sings. It's sooner than I hoped. More than I expected. As soon as we get inside, I pick her up and pin her against the wall, kissing the hell out of her.

She bites my lower lip and tugs. "I thought you said on the bed."

I press the bulge of my cock against the notch between her legs. "Is it too vanilla? I don't want you to think I'm boring."

She laughs with her head thrown back. "Impossible." She pronounces the word in French instead of English.

"Oh, that's hot, *malyshka*. Speak to me in French."

She lets out a string of French as I lower her to her feet and peel her shirt off.

"Take your pants off," I say as I unbutton my own. I left my tank top out on the roof, but I don't care.

She reaches for my jeans. "I'm going to take *your* pants off."

My dick, already straining at the zipper, gets even harder. I thought my wife submitting to my domination was hot, but there's nothing hotter than her initiating sex.

She sucks in her lower lip and holds my gaze as she drags my zipper down.

I let out a rough breath when she frees my erection. She hooks her thumbs into the waistband of both my jeans and boxers and slides them down my legs.

My cock stands at full attention, already dripping pre-cum from the tip.

Lara grips the base of my cock and squeezes, lengthening my erection. She holds it up and licks my balls, gently sucking first one into her mouth then the other.

I groan, and the sound has a pained rasp to it. "That's so good, *malysh*. You're killing me."

She trails her tongue along the underside of my cock and swirls it around the rim. Then, in one smooth motion, she engulfs the entire head and slides my cock into the pocket of her cheek.

"Fuck, baby. That's so good," I praise her, my fingers sliding into her hair. I alternate massaging her scalp and closing my fingers into a fist and tugging gently, and she starts to hum around my cock.

The leash on my control starts to slip. She's more than killing me. I'm already dead. I've had a lot of sex for a guy my age—I started young, and I've experimented a lot—but nothing compares to this moment.

It's not her technique although that's great. It's Lara. Her willingness. Her beautiful, generous heart. Her capacity to forgive me for forcing her into this marriage. The tears she cried for me out on the roof.

It's knowing we're going to last. We're going to make it. She's wearing my ring, and I'm winning her heart.

I've accomplished a lot at Thornecroft, but I'd throw it all away for this. My beautiful wife on her knees at my feet, giving me pleasure.

I control her movements, pulling her mouth over my cock faster, making her take me deeper. Her eyes widen, but she doesn't protest. She holds onto my hips, her nails scoring my ass.

"Naked," I manage to grunt. I'm on the edge of coming down her throat, but I want her to come with me. "I need you naked right now." I try to make my voice stern, but it only sounds desperate.

Hell, I *am* desperate.

I need to fuck my wife so badly I'm going to explode.

She pops off my cock and licks the saliva from her lower lip.

"You are so fucking hot." It's a wonder I even know how to speak. I'm pretty sure all my brain cells are in my dick right now. "Come here, printsessa." I grip her elbows and pull her up to standing then shove her sweatpants down her legs. She isn't wearing panties, which drives me out of my mind. I pick her up and carry her to the bed, my fingers splayed across her bare ass cheeks.

"My turn to taste you," I say. I roll her to her side and pull one knee up over my shoulder to lick into her. I caress the inner thigh of her other leg as my tongue parts her pleats. She's dripping already, and the taste of her honey drives me insane.

I lick my thumb and bring it to her clit while I tongue and suck and *devour* her delicious pussy.

"Roll over," I command, my hand already turning her hips, so she faces the bed. "Do you like it from behind?" I keep her flat on her belly, but push her legs wide and enter her.

She moans her yes.

I glide in easily; she's more than ready to take me. As I rock my hips against the soft pillows of her ass, I nuzzle my face into her neck, breathing in the butterscotch scent of her hair.

"I love having you in my bed," I murmur although my brain is already scrambling from being inside her. "*Our* bed."

"Mmmm," she moans in response.

"I love having you in my house. In my life." The most vulnerable admission slips from my mouth in my sex-haze. "I want you to stay."

My fear exposed: I've been scrambling to seduce Lara into staying with me. Maybe because I never saw this as a permanent thing. Or maybe because I still think she's going to end up with Brash Rostov. But from the beginning, it's felt like there's a ticking clock, and I only have a certain amount of time with Lara before it's over.

"I'm here," Lara says.

She's right. She's here now. I can't control the future, as much as I'd like to. All I can do is enjoy the fuck out of my wife in this moment.

I pull out and roll her to her back and slow my heart rate by sucking and pinching her nipples.

"I want to see your beautiful face when you come," I say as I push back inside of her. "Squeeze my dick with your pussy."

Lara's internal muscles squeeze, and I groan. "Good girl. Just like that. Show me how fucking tight you can make it."

She squeezes in a pulsing rhythm, tightening when I stroke in, releasing when I go out.

I know from my research into the female orgasm that

tightening the internal muscles can help a woman come. She definitely seems to get excited, her eyes rolling back in her head, her breath coming out in little sobs, especially when I increase my speed.

I'm barely hanging by a thread. My balls have drawn up tight. I'm ready to explode.

"Hold your breath now," I tell her.

She tries to focus on my face, her brow wrinkled.

"Hold your breath until you come."

She sucks in a breath, but immediately lets it out on a sob of pleasure.

I chuckle. "Hold your breath until you come, *malyshka*." I put my hand around the column of her neck. I would *never* squeeze her throat to cut off her air. Not even with consent. I won't fuck with her life like that. But I know it turns women on to know I have the power to do it.

She stops her breath. Her gaze locks with mine and turns intense. I plow into her harder, jack hammering in with fast thrusts. Her face takes on a pink blush, and her eyes grow wide. Panic flashes over her expression the moment before she shrieks and convulses into orgasm. Her muscles grip my dick, and I lose control. I pump twice more and bury myself deep to come. I fill her with my seed, then ease back and push in, which sets off another wave of her contractions around my cock.

Her arms twine around my neck, and she holds me tight, her breath coming in sobs.

"I love you," I murmur against her ear, nipping the shell with my teeth.

She goes still, her heart beating against mine. "I love you, too," she whispers.

That's when I know it's all over for me. This woman walked in and flipped my entire life in one week's time. She makes me feel whole in a way I haven't felt since Valentina died. I don't ever want her to walk back out

If Abrasha Rostov tries to take her from me again, I will end him.

CHAPTER TWENTY

Baron

After Lara and I shower, we make it downstairs to find Melinda curled up on the couch with Anders.

Her face is pale, and her eyes are red. She somehow looks even skinnier than usual. Frail breakable. It makes me want to pop someone's head off their neck for hurting her.

She sends me a teary glare. "You can't ban me from your house after what happened."

Christ. I feel terrible for hurting her like that.

"Of course not." I walk over and lean down to give her a tight hug. "I'm so sorry this happened to you."

"I guess you were right," she said, her voice clogged with tears. "I did bring unwanted attention to your house."

"No. I had it backward. We already had the attention, and they used you to get to us. Instead of keeping you away, I should've brought you closer in."

Anders clears his throat. "That's good because she doesn't want to be alone right now, and I said she could stay in my room." He looks like he has a litany of arguments prepared to throw at me when I refuse, but it's a good idea.

I need her closer, so I can protect her. If her dad becomes Vice President of the United States, and they put Secret Service on her, I'll deal with that problem then. After this morning, I suspect they already know who I am and what I might be up to. I doubt much gets past Black Shirt.

"Good," I say. "I want you here where we can protect you."

Relief sweeps over Ander's face, and Melinda settles back into the crook of his arm.

"Melinda, this is my wife, Lara."

Lara gives her a hug as well. "I'm so sorry you got attacked."

The sound of my voice has pulled various house members into the living room. Alex and Leo show up, and the twins.

"She wasn't raped," Anders says quietly. "The DNA tests came back, and she was just drugged."

Thank fuck. I don't have to figure out how to dispose of a body today.

Leo speaks up. "I pulled every recording with Melinda in the frame from the party, and no one appears to have come close to her, at least not that we caught with cameras."

Melinda shakes her head. "No, I didn't even get a drink while I was here, so there would be no opportunity. I brought my own water bottle. And I was only with Anders."

Anders has one arm around the back of the sofa behind her shoulders, and he strokes the back of her head.

"So we're thinking the security guard, right?" I say.

"Yeah. I've got a name on him," Anya says. "Gregory Smith. He's not a member of Titan house, but he is on the football team."

"He's a sophomore," Alex says. "Not that bright. Football scholarship."

"Do you think you can hack his bank records?" I ask. "Maybe they paid him to do it."

"I already did." Anya looks smug. "There are no large deposits recently made to his account. But they could've paid him cash."

"True," I muse.

"I also have his address, found out he lives alone, and he's working right now."

"Did you now?" I roll my shoulders. "Who is up for a little recon?" I glance at Leo.

"I'll get my lock picks."

Melinda gets up from the sofa, and Anders follows. "I'm going."

"Me too," Lara says.

I wince. "We'll be breaking the law, *malyshka*. I don't want you involved."

Lara's mouth takes on a stubborn set. "I'm *going*."

Everyone else politely looks away.

Fuck. If there's one thing I learned from my dad it was not to involve family in the business. Keep things clean at home. Lara is my wife and shouldn't be tainted with anything illegal.

But she's ready to throw down with me over this, and I don't want to be the bad guy anymore. It feels too good to have her on my side for a change.

I draw in a breath and let it out. "Fine."

Suddenly everyone is up and moving.

"Hold up. Not you guys." I wave my hand at the rest of them.

Alex, Feliks, and Phoenix look disappointed as they sink back to the couch.

"What?" Anya asks with mock innocence. "I thought the sexism had ended. Lara and Melinda are going."

"I don't need your dad kicking my ass for getting his precious daughters in trouble. Anders, you should stay, too. If you get caught, you could lose your student visa."

Anders snorts in annoyance. "When has that ever stopped me? He attacked Melinda. I'm in this until the end."

"We all are," I say.

Leo nods. "That's right."

"Damn straight," Alex says.

"No one screws with friends of Baranov House," Zoe says.

———

Lara

Now that Baron and I are on the same page, I *love* watching him in action. Before, his prowess as the leader of a young bratva cell freaked me out. He was the enemy, and it proved I had a formidable opponent. Now it means I have a badass partner.

I mean, we still have things to work out. I don't like being a pawn in a game I don't understand, and I hate that Baron won't tell me what my purpose here is. I don't like thinking my family is in danger. Knowing Baron's father has us all in a vise-grip.

But holding my heart back from Baron was so much harder than letting it go. It's like now that he's opened up to me—said he loved me—the gates barring him from entering my care zone have swung wide open. The feelings I caught for him are big.

Really big. In fact, I seem to be catching more by the minute. I never knew love could simultaneously feel so wonderful and terrifying. It's like I'm free falling down a cliff side, trusting Baron will erect the net to catch me at the bottom.

I sit beside Baron in the vehicle, sneaking side glances at the corded muscles of his forearms as he drives. His jaw is firm, and there's determination in his gaze. He's already thinking through the next five steps, I'm guessing.

He already grabbed baseball caps for all of us and a box of latex gloves before we left.

I know he didn't want me to come–for my own protection–but there's no way I'm missing out.

I didn't like feeling left out of his operation before, and I'm not going to let him pigeon-hole me back into the sheltered wife category. Besides, I'm heavily invested in Melinda getting her justice. And I want to watch Baron in action–it's hot.

A thrill of adrenaline runs through me at being part of their caper. Baron pulls up in front of a student apartment building and studies it. We watch a student walk up and enter using a keycard. "Front door uses a keycard like a dorm," he mutters.

"I've got this." Leo pushes open the door, pulling a ball cap low over his face. "Wait for me to get in." We watch from the tinted windows as he walks confidently up to the building door. He pauses near a post and pretends to check his phone, and then when someone comes out of the building, catches the door and slips inside. He props a shoulder against the glass window of the atrium, pretending to look at his phone.

"Okay, now you two." Baron twists to look at Anders and Melinda.

They slide out of the car and walk across the street. The automatic door swings open for them, as if Leo hit the wheelchair button.

"Let's go, *malysh*." Baron hands me a baseball cap, and I pull my hair up in a twist and put it on.

The door swings open for us, too. Baron rubs a hand over his face strategically, murmuring in Russian that there's a camera straight ahead.

Anders and Melinda have disappeared.

"You take the elevator; we'll take the stairs," Baron tells Leo.

"See you there." Leo seems to vanish behind us as Baron leads me to the stairwell. We walk up one flight of stairs to the second floor hallway where we find Anders with Melinda boosted on his shoulders putting a stretched piece of chewing gum across the camera in the corner.

Leo faces a door, both hands working the knob with his tools. A moment later, he disappears inside the apartment. Baron and I follow, with Melinda and Anders right behind.

Baron produces two pairs of latex gloves from his pocket and hands me a pair.

"Right. No fingerprints." I take the gloves and slide them over my hands. They're too big, leaving gaps at the ends of the rubber fingers.

"Don't touch anything unless you have to," he tells me.

I nod, walking through the messy studio apartment. It smells like stinky socks and jockstraps. The school year just started but there appears to be a years' worth of crumbs on the floor. A bowl of half-eaten macaroni and cheese sits in the sink.

"Well, that was easy." Leo is on his hands and knees looking under the bed. "I found the cash." He pulls out a paper bag and turns the open mouth to show us stacks of money inside.

"How much was drugging me worth?" Melinda demands, taking the bag in her oversized gloves and opening it. She dumps bundles of money on the kitchen counter to count.

Baron picks up the trashcan in the bathroom and peers inside, then shows it to me. Inside is packaging from a syringe and some kind of medicine.

"Is that rohypnol?" I ask.

"Yes. Well, a generic brand," Baron confirms. He plucks out the used syringe and holds it up for the rest to see. To Melinda, he says, "You didn't ingest it. The fucker injected you, so it would act faster to seem as if you'd been roofied at the party."

Melinda looks horrified, her hand flying to her neck.

"Let me see." Anders quickly starts scanning her body, turning her around. When he gets to her thighs, he asks, "What's this?"

We all rush over to examine a tiny circular bruise on her thigh.

"I didn't leave that," Anders says.

Melinda blushes, making me wonder which bruises he *did* leave.

"If your dad can get a warrant, the police could find all this. It's probably enough to convict him." Baron's expression holds total neutrality. "Do you want to go the legal route, or can we take care of him?"

"What are you going to do to him?" Melinda asks.

"Take the money and torture him until he gives up who paid him to do this to you. Then break his leg." Baron considers and shrugs. "Or his arm. Something that will fuck up his football season, so he loses his scholarship, and you won't have to see him around here again."

"I'll take door number two," she says. Some life has come back to her now that revenge is in sight. Like the power this guy took from her when he drugged her has returned.

Baron flashes a grin, and there's a momentary boyishness to him that melts my heart.

Melinda hands the bag of money to Baron. "Six thousand dollars is what assaulting me and framing you was worth to him."

Baron glances in the bag but doesn't move to take it. "It's yours. You're the one who was hurt by this."

She thrusts the bag back. "Consider it my rent money. I'm living in Baranov House now."

Baron crosses his arms over his muscled chest and

considers her. "Okay," he says after a moment. "You're one of us now. But we'll have to tattoo one of your fingers."

Melinda sends a startled look Anders' way.

He shakes his head. "He's fucking with you."

"Oh." She laughs.

"Only if you commit a crime," Leo amends.

Melinda smiles. "Does this one count?"

"Do you want it to?" Anders teases.

Baron wraps me up in his arms. "You're definitely getting a tattoo." His voice is a low growl meant only for me.

"Yeah?" I pick up on the seductive vibe and purr back. "What is the tattoo for breaking and entering?"

He lifts my left hand between us and peels the glove off. He twists the wedding ring over my ring finger. "It's my name, right across here." He brushes his lips over the knuckle of my fourth finger.

I give him a husky laugh. "Your name, huh?"

"Mmm hmm. It can be in Cyrillic if you want."

"Oh, because it's much better to display the declaration of ownership in my native language?"

Baron laughs and bites my knuckle, holding it between his teeth for a moment before he lets go. "At least you understand you're owned."

One piece of me is still offended because it's literally true, but my body responds as Baron intends, heating for him, my nipples getting hard, my pussy clenching on air. My body adores being owned by him, as much as I half-rebel.

"Keep telling yourself that, husband. We will see who ends up owning whom."

CHAPTER TWENTY-ONE

Baron

We wait until Gregory Smith's shift is over and haul him into an alleyway on his way home. The irony of a member of campus security getting jumped in a back alley is a cherry on top of my revenge sundae.

I brought Alex, Feliks, Leo, Anders, and Anya.

Phoenix, Zoe, Lara, and Melinda opted out, which was good because I don't want Lara to ever see that side of me. I tried to talk Anya out of it, but she called me sexist again and then said my rules don't apply because she's gay, so rather than argue, I let her come. There's no harm in it—she'll be perfectly safe with us.

Feliks has Gregory in an arm lock while Alex and Leo take turns punching him.

I make a show out of putting on a pair of brass knuckles. "So, we found the cash, the syringe, and the Rohypnol in your apartment. Do you get off on date-raping women?"

The guy sags in Feliks' hold, like he's trying to drop to his knees. "I don't." His voice shakes with fear. "I don't rape women. I swear. I-I-I didn't rape Melinda Tracy. I just gave her the shot and took her to the hospital. She was totally safe the whole time."

"You have a different definition of *safe* than I do." Anders isn't usually into violence the way we bratva heirs are, but this time is different. He punches Gregory in the jaw with a solid right hook. "She's feeling anything but safe after the guy who gets paid to protect her actually assaulted her." Anders throws an uppercut and Gregory's head flies back.

His head lolls for a moment before he recovers.

I'd better step in before Anders gets carried away. "Who paid you? I want names."

He sobs. "It was the Titans. They said they'd let me in the house if I did it."

This *svoloch* didn't even do it for the money. He did it to get into a goddamn house. This is the reason I had to make my own. Thornecroft is a fucking cesspool of old money influence and elitism.

"*Names*," I snarl, wrapping my fingers around his meaty throat and punching his ribs with the brass knuckles.

He wheezes in pain. "I'll tell you. I'll tell you everything. It was... it was Ashton Basen and Charlie Daggert," he says quickly. "Those are the two who approached me."

"What did they tell you to do?"

"Just to inject her and take her to the hospital and tell them where I picked her up." Gregory is panting. Blood trickles from the side of his mouth. "That was it...that was it! That was all. Nothing else." He's babbling now.

"Who called the *New York Times*?"

His expression is blank, eyes wide with fear. When he shakes his head, blood flies from the corner of his mouth. "No idea."

I punch him again, and he groans. "What else?"

"The money!" he exclaims like he's grasping onto a life-line. "I got paid at the hospital. Charlie was there with another guy—a new pledge. He was the money guy. Short ugly guy. From another country." His eyes light up. "Russian! Russian like you."

This guy isn't too bright considering he just now put together that we're both Russian.

I glance at my friends.

"Denis Penkin." Anya's upper lip curls.

Denis Penkin, Rostov's spy. How in the fuck is he involved in all this?

The hair prickling at the back of my neck makes me look around. Black Shirt, the government ghost lurks in a shadow at the end of the alley.

Well, he'll stop us if he wants to. I figure if he doesn't interfere, it's still my show.

Anya saunters forward in her short shorts and a pair of Doc Martens. "My turn."

I step back and wave my hand. "Be my guest."

"Listen to me, Gregory Smith. If you ever roofie a woman again, I will personally cut your dick off and shove it up your ass. Understand?"

He looks at her blankly, obviously not afraid of a hundred and fifteen pound redheaded computer geek.

She brings her knee up sharply between his legs, and he doubles over. His grunt is so pained I think all the guys there instinctively flinch.

Then she steps back. "You can break his leg now," she says casually.

"Hold up." The ghost steps forward. He's dressed in black, holding a piece of black fabric in his hands. "Somebody else wants a piece of him before you're done." He slams a black hood over Gregory's head and zipties his hands behind his back.

"Would you boys mind putting him in my trunk for me?"

Feliks and Alex look at me, and I nod. "Go ahead."

He quickly backs his car into the alley and pops the lid of the trunk. Feliks and Alex dump Gregory unceremoniously in the back, and Black Shirt slams the door closed.

"The senator appreciates your concern for his daughter," he says to me, offering me his hand to shake.

I clasp it, and he squeezes firmly.

"If you need a job after graduation, reach out through Melinda. We have a use for people with your particular skills." He glances at the rest of my friends. "All of you."

As he drives off, Anya asks, "What do you think they're going to do to him?"

"No idea," I say. "But I'm sure he'll get what he deserves."

CHAPTER TWENTY-TWO

Lara

Tuesday afternoon I head to the Thornecroft bookstore to pick up one of the texts I need for a class when I hear the low tones of men speaking in Russian. Naturally, I turn to look.

Is it one of my friends?

No, it's an older man—a man who looks like a professor. He must be Baron and Lili's math professor—Vasiliev. The one Baron said hates him because he knows he's bratva. He's talking to Denis.

I haven't seen Denis since he left Whisper's End bloodied by my husband. His nose is taped, like it's been recently broken. My husband's handiwork, I presume.

Guilt twists in my gut.

At least it was just his nose. I wasn't sure what the blood had come from.

Not that it excuses Baron's violence.

Both of them look over at me, and Denis mutters something to the professor as he waves at me.

I wave back with an apologetic look, and he takes it as an invitation and leaves the professor to walk over to me.

"Hi, Denis." I greet him in Russian. "Did my husband do that?" I wince and point to my own nose. "I'm sorry."

Denis' expression is dark. Gone is the friendly puppy. "Yes. I did not report him as a favor to you." He takes my elbow and pulls me to the side, lowering his head.

I try to shake his touch off. The last thing I need is for Baron to see and get violent again. "Do you need help? Are you in danger? I think he is bratva. Did you know that?"

I have to forcibly pull my elbow from his hand and take a step back. "Yes, I'm a bratva princess, Denis," I tell him.

I look for shock in his gaze, but it doesn't come. Instead, he leans his face close again, speaking quietly. "I have connections. I can help you out of this marriage. You don't have to stay with him."

Gospodi, he sounds just like Brash. This is how it's going to be for the rest of my life.

That thought is too much of a downer to even contemplate, so I push it away.

I'm happy with Baron. Mostly. But that's between the two of us and maybe our families. It's no one else's business.

"I don't need your help," I say firmly. "But thank you for the offer."

"Take my number. Call me if you do need help," he insists.

Right. Like having another man's number in my phone would go well for me if Baron found out.

"No *thank you.*" I move away, holding my breath until I sense him leave the bookstore.

It takes me a few minutes to shake off the tense feeling in my gut.

As I check out, I glance out the windows and see Baron walking by. He sees me at the same time and comes to a stop, a smile cracking his normally serious face.

I hold up one finger to tell him I'll be right out, and he walks toward the doors.

A low voice speaks behind me in Russian. "Stay away from that boy—he's dangerous."

I whirl to find Professor Vasiliev standing behind me in line.

Bozhe moi, I'm getting sick of everyone trying to rescue me. I give him a condemning look as I pick up my new book and the receipt. "Yes, I know you hate Baron." I lift my chin. "He's my husband, so you'll probably hate me too."

"No, not Baron," he says. He darts a glance in the direction where I was standing with Denis. "The other one."

Before I can ask more, the door opens. Vasiliev abruptly turns and walks away just before Baron appears through the door.

I swallow, my heart beating a little too fast.

What in the hell was that?

Why would he say Denis is dangerous? That doesn't make sense. He must have the two of them mixed up.

"*Privet*." I lift my face to give Baron a smile and kiss.

He kisses me. "*Privet, malyshka*."

I swear, I sense at least a third of the students in the bookstore watching us.

"That's his wife," someone murmurs. I hear other snippets of gossip around us.

"...arranged marriage...Russian *mafiya*..."

Baron truly is famous on this campus.

And now, so am I.

I don't mind the attention.

He takes the new book from my hand and the book bag from my shoulder and puts an arm around me as we walk out to the murmurs around us.

"OMG, so jealous...they're so cute..."

"Yeah, but do you think it'll last?"

CHAPTER TWENTY-THREE

Lara

Wednesday night, Baron takes me out to a fancy dinner and gets me tipsy on a hundred dollar bottle of wine and lobster.

He pulls me close as we leave the restaurant. "I loved our first date."

"Is that what we're calling this?" I tease. Having a first date after I've already done everything else with this man—married him, had wild and crazy sex, broken the law, played in a dungeon—seems laughable.

But he's right. It felt like a first. I had the fizz of excitement in my belly when he told me he was taking me out, and I have it now going home with him.

This is the first date I *wanted* to go on with him. Even though he came on strong before, now that I care whether he loves me or not, his attention puts a glow of happiness around me.

We get to the SUV, and he opens my door and helps me in.

He leans his arm against the doorframe like he did that

first day he picked me up from the airport. He looks like he's going to say something, then seems to change his mind and shuts my door and gets into the driver's seat.

As we drive back toward campus, the sound of sirens grows louder.

I crane my neck, peering out the window. "What do you think is going on?" I ask. "Is that smoke?"

"I think it's possible there was a fire at Titan House while no one was there."

I suck in a sharp breath as I realize our date was also a public alibi for Baron. I consider it for a moment. Do I hate that he took down the organization that tried to pin a rape charge on my husband and assaulted a young woman to do so?

No. No, I don't.

I also appreciate that he said no one was there. So he didn't harm anyone. He just got retribution. The Titan House parties suffering as a result of Baranov House activities will no longer be an issue this year.

"Well," I say, "That sounds like karma to me."

Baron looks over with a flicker of relief, and I realize he was bracing for my reaction. The flutters start up again.

We pull up and park in front of Baranov House, but Baron doesn't move to get out.

He shuts off the engine. "Lara...I want to answer your question. The one you asked the other night that I dodged. About why you're really here."

I brace myself as my pulse picks up speed. What could it be? What use could they have for me? Or what trouble is my dad in?

What in the hell is going on, and why am I their pawn?

"My dad asked me to marry you to keep you safe."

I blink at him. That doesn't make sense. His dad is the threat. The one whose threats made us unsafe.

"I don't understand."

Baron opens his mouth but then looks past me through the window. His face transforms into a look of dark rage.

"*Blyad'*," he swears and throws open the door.

I twist to look out the window. It takes me a breath for my brain to catch up to what my eyes see. Or at least to process it.

Brash Rostov is here. He's here, reaching to open my door.

I freeze for a moment. Is he here for me? I remember Baron saying he knew Brash from boarding school. Is this about something between the two of them?

My door swings open, and I hear Baron snarl, "Get away from my wife."

Brash reaches in and unbuckles my seatbelt, dropping a light kiss on my cheek when he leans in.

I jerk away, confused. "Brash, what are you doing here? I told you not to come."

Baron grabs Brash's shoulder and yanks him back.

Brash whirls and punches Baron, who ducks and delivers a left jab to Brash's gut.

"Don't move!" several voices boom in Russian at the same time a flood of men carrying automatic rifles swarm around the two men.

"*Bozhe moi!* Stop!" I jump out of the car.

My fear is all for Baron, but I'm annoyed with him too. Why does he have to be so damn possessive?

Brash's upper lip lifts in a snarl, but he ignores Baron and turns to look at me. "Lara, you can forget this marriage entirely. You don't have to give up your studies and your apartment and everything you loved in Paris and let these thugs orchestrate your life."

My chest tightens. "Brash, I told you not to come." I try to look past him at Baron. Brash keeps his body between mine and Baron's. I suppose he thinks he's protecting me.

They both do. It would be sweet if it weren't so stupid. I don't need rescuing.

"Do you know why you had to marry him?" Brash jerks his thumb derisively at Baron.

I try to seek Baron's eye again, but he doesn't look at me; he's just glaring murderously at Brash.

I shouldn't have to explain this to Brash. He has greatly overstepped. "I told you, our parents arranged it when we were children. My life is with Baron now. I've accepted it."

Well, maybe not the life, but I've accepted Baron.

"It was because of me," Brash snarls.

I draw my brows together. Of all the arrogant, narcissistic things to say.

Except I finally catch Baron's gaze, and he looks furious. Like Brash just revealed a truth he didn't want told.

Like... it might be true.

What was he about to tell me before Brash arrived? The real reason I'm here.

"You had 'interest from another party'." Brash makes air quotes around *interest from another party* part. "*Me.*"

"Benji Baranov couldn't stand me moving in on his possession. He knew I have the power to stop this union. And so they whisked you off before you could tell me about the marriage and get my help."

I didn't know about the marriage, so there would've been nothing to tell.

It sounds absurd, but I see the truth crawl over Baron's face. He's not denying it. He's glancing at the guns around us, like he's wondering if he can fight his way out of this.

Icy prickles cover my skin. The same sense of betrayal I felt the day my father showed up at my apartment storms through my body.

"Baron?" I ask. "Is this true?"

His teeth clench, and he breathes through flared nostrils. He wears the same look he wore when Lili was trying to get him to stop killing the guy he thought had drugged her at the party. Like he's in warrior mode and will do anything to protect what's his.

"Baron!" I snap.

He doesn't look away from Brash when he answers me. "Not *exactly*."

Not exactly. Not. Exactly.

What the actual fuck?

Can this be true? That means this whole thing was orchestrated by my father and Baron together. My dad made me think his and my mother's lives were in danger when actually this is all because he feared the man I was dating could protect me from his machinations. From being a pawn and his stupid bratva games. From marrying Baron.

And Baron was either so competitive with Brash or so possessive of me—a woman he didn't even know—that he had to steal me away. Win me for his own.

I feel sick.

Furious tears flood my eyes. I need to get away—from all of them. But especially Baron. I turn and run down the sidewalk in my strappy heels.

"Lara," Brash calls after me.

Baron says nothing; he just stands there looking like he wants to murder Brash. I guess the guilt is too much for him. For some reason, that enrages me even further.

How dare he seduce me? Manipulate me? Knowing he was taking me out of the arms of another man. Knowing my father pulled the plug on my life in Paris on a whim and made me believe it was life or death to come here. He was a part of this entire game orchestrated by my father. All of them toying with my life, my affections, my reality.

Gospodi!

How dare he make me fall for him? Make me care about being loved by him?

How dare he stand there and say nothing? Say, *that's not exactly true.*

His is the biggest betrayal of all.

"Move and die," one of the Russian soldiers barks at him in Russian.

Good. He doesn't get to follow me. I'm not under his control anymore. I won't be controlled by him ever again. Not by him or my father.

"Lara." Brash's car pulls up beside me as I clomp down the sidewalk. The passenger door swings open as Brash drives slowly.

I don't want to be with Brash. I don't want to be with anyone. But I actually have nowhere to go if I don't accept Brash's help.

I stop walking, and he hits the brakes to match me. We look at each other through the open door.

He's a handsome man—a sharp dresser with a Rolex on his wrist. He can be charming and respectful. He's well moneyed and powerful. It's true. His father probably has the power to protect me from my own father.

Not that I should require protection.

The fact that I do makes me want to scream at the top of my lungs.

If I go with Brash now, he can get me out of here. I need space to figure out what I want to do.

Against my will, I look back over my shoulder at Baron standing on the grass in front of Baranov House, surrounded by gunmen pointing their weapons at him.

He's looking straight at me, and I know I'm right because he's no longer jealous or controlling. He looks gutted. His hands aren't in the air, but there's a look of shock in his frozen form. He knows he's wrong.

He knows he's lost me.

And that's the moment my heart splits open and falls in two pieces on the sidewalk. One half still wants Baron to pick it up and make things right. The other half never wants to speak to him again.

I pull the ring off my finger and fling it in his direction then climb into the front seat of the car and slam the door. As Brash peels out, a sick panic spreads through my body over the piece of my heart I left convulsing on the sidewalk.

I squeeze my eyes closed and will it to die along with all my memories of my time with Baron.

It's over. It never should have been.

I'm done with Benjamin Baranov.

———

Baron

I stand rooted to the lawn, staring after Brash's car.

I could not have fucked this up more.

My one job was to keep my wife out of Brash Rostov's clutches, and I failed.

She ran away from me and straight into his car. The image of her flushed face, eyes bright with tears, makes me want to drop to my knees. Her sense of betrayal couldn't have been more clear.

I don't get to complete my self-flagellation because someone knocks me to the ground with what must be the butt of an AK-47 aimed at the back of my head. I land on my hands and knees, my head ringing. The men descend on me. One of them kicks me in the ribs, and another catches me in the face with his steel-toed boot.

I don't try to fight back—I'm unarmed. I wouldn't survive. All I can do is curl up in a ball and protect my head with my arms. The bruising blows keep landing, and I can't help feeling like I deserve them.

This is what I get for hurting Lara.

Except she still needs me.

She may have run from me and willingly climbed in Rostov's car, but she's not safe with him. Not in the slightest bit. I need to get out of this, so I can get to her.

The blows keep falling, and my ears start to ring.

No, that's our fire alarm going off.

One of my friends must have turned it on. Probably Phoenix.

I chuckle through bloodied lips because the maneuver works. After a few more kicks, the men abandon beating me and jump in their cars, speeding off in the direction Brash drove.

I try to stagger to my feet, but instead, the grass comes rushing up to meet my face, and then everything goes black.

CHAPTER TWENTY-FOUR

Lara

I barely see the direction we're driving because tears blur my eyes. I can't stop the sense that I'm driving away from my very existence.

But Baron tricked me. He was in on some game with my dad, and I can't forgive him for that.

Brash is talking, but I'm not listening. I just keep replaying that look on Baron's face. The guilty knowledge. The regret.

I replay the conversation with my dad in my apartment. Brash's words, "you had interest from another party."

There are still parts of this story that don't add up. Like—why my marriage was arranged to Baron in the first place. What was so important to tie our families together when his dad and mine have worked together for years?

And if it was so important, why didn't he tell me about it from the time I was young? Why wait until I had interest from another party?

Well, I can demand answers to those questions when I get

back to Paris. I was giving my dad the silent treatment, but now I wish I'd pushed him more for answers.

Then again, he wasn't very forthright about any of it.

Was that because he was tricking me? Removing me from the supposed temptation of Brash Rostov? He never stopped me from dating men in the past.

He could've just told me if he didn't approve of Brash.

None of this makes sense.

I jerk back to the present when Brash pulls down the road to the airstrip I flew into just over a week ago.

"What are we doing here?" I don't know where I thought he was taking me, but this comes as a surprise.

"I need to get you away from the thugs who are trying to control you," Brash says, parking and getting out.

I don't get out. I may have wanted to get away from Baron, but Brash is being equally presumptuous with me and my life right now.

He opens my door and reaches out a hand. "Come. You want to get back to your life, no? I can protect you."

It feels wrong.

I wipe my eyes. "I don't have my things. I need to pack."

Am I really leaving Whisper? I'm pissed at Baron, but... my time with him was the best—and worst—in my life. I was furious and scared when I came here, but there was Baron. I guess I fell in love. I made friends. I became a part of something—willingly. I don't hate my classes, either.

Paris feels far away. Like the woman who lived that life is already gone. Changed into someone else. The internship and career possibilities for me there seem far less exciting than what goes on at Thornecroft.

I remember the thrill of breaking into Melinda's attacker's apartment yesterday. Watching my badass husband in motion.

But no. He's not a badass. He's a controlling bastard who

basically kidnapped me and then seduced me. He manipulated me just like my dad. I can't allow men to treat me like that.

"I will buy you new things, *milaya*."

I hesitate. That sounds like a nice offer, especially because I don't want to go back to Baranov House and pack my things. But something feels wrong.

Brash said he would return me to my life in Paris, but now he's going to buy me all new things? Is that a friendly offer because he's rich or is there something proprietary to it—like...I'm going to be *with him?*

Because I don't want to be with him.

Now that I've felt what it's like to have my heart set on fire, it's clear I feel absolutely nothing for this man.

"I don't even have my passport."

"You won't need it. Come, the jet is on the runway."

The jet is on the runway. Like...he had it waiting there for us? He knew he was going to whisk me away? Why don't I need my passport? Because he's paid someone off? This is getting weird.

My brain is slow to compute everything, probably because my heart is still hemorrhaging over Baron's betrayal.

But okay. Yes. Getting away from Whisper is the best thing. Once I'm back in Paris, I can take time to grieve the heartbreak and get some clarity. Maybe I'll give Baron a chance to explain.

I definitely will call my dad and have it out with him.

I allow Brash to escort me to the jet, and we buckle our seatbelts.

As the plane races down the runway, Brash pulls out his phone and makes a call.

"It's done." He glances over at me. "I have the Turgenev girl. Prepare the divorce papers. I want them ready to sign as soon as we touch down."

Everything in me stops. My heart forgets to beat. My breath goes completely still. Grief clears out of my system, replaced by adrenaline.

I unbuckle my seatbelt and surge to my feet, but it's too late. The plane is taking off.

"Ah ah." Brash snatches my wrist and yanks me down on his lap. He bites down on the side of my neck like he thinks he's a vampire.

"*Ou!*" I yelp. I don't know if he broke the skin, but there will definitely be a bruise.

"You're not going anywhere." His grip on my wrist hurts. There's a maniacal glee in his voice that chills me. "Your father shouldn't have refused our initial offer."

My brain stutters. What offer? What is he talking about? I struggle in his hold.

"As my wife, you'll soon learn I'm quick to punish and slow to forgive." He throws me off his lap. I career into the aisle, banging my hip on my chair before I catch it. "Now sit down and buckle up, or you'll earn your first punishment right here on the plane."

———

Baron

I drift in and out of consciousness. I hear my friends' voices as they struggle to pick me up and carry me inside.

She's gone.

I lost Lara.

I force my eyes open and find myself sprawled on the sofa. All of my friends gather around me. Some of their faces pinch with worry. Some scored with rage.

"Anya," I croak, trying to find her in the group.

"Right here." She lifts a hand, and I manage to focus on her.

"Where is she?" I croak.

Anya looks startled. For once, she didn't anticipate my next demand. "Lara?"

"Yes, Lara!" I struggle to my feet and throw my arms out when my vision blackens.

Phoenix shoves his slender shoulder under my arm to prop me up. "You're in no condition to rush after her."

"Where is she?" The sound of my own voice nearly splits my head in half. I wipe some blood from my mouth. One of my molars feels loose.

Anya unlocks and looks at the cracked screen of my phone. It must've fallen out of my pocket when Brash's army knocked me down. "Oh shit," she mutters.

"What?" I thunder.

"She's at the airstrip."

Whisper doesn't have a commercial airport, just the private airstrip used by the wealthy to ferry their private jets in and out of town.

"Take me there." I limp toward the door.

"Baron, in case you didn't notice, they had AK-47s," Zoe says. "We don't have those kinds of weapons. And even if we did, you can't start a war like that without calling your dad in first."

"She's right," Leo says quietly. "I'm all for going after that fucker, but we need to think this through."

I sag against the wall, the movement of my breath paining my cracked ribs. My eyes close. *Think, Ben. Think.*

They're right—we can't start a war. Not without my dad's backing.

Blyat'!

I should have thought of something to say to Lara to keep her from running. Why didn't I tell her sooner—at dinner? Or on the drive home? The fact that I'd planned to tell her everything tonight only makes losing her a million times worse. I could've prevented that terrible scene out there if I'd just had the nerve to come clean an hour earlier. Or days. Weeks. From the beginning.

Now she's in the clutches of Abrasha Rostov, and I really don't think he'll let her slip through his fingers a second time.

"Can you find out where they're going?" My lower lip swells more with each moment that passes.

"I can't just hack the FAA at the drop of a hat," Anya complains, her brow furrowed.

Zoe pulls out her phone. "Maybe I can get someone to tell me." She looks up the airstrip and hits the call button on speaker phone.

"Yes, this is Zoya Novikova," she says in a thick Russian accent that sounds exactly like Leo's mom, Sasha, when she's tipsy. "My friend Abrasha Rostov has plane there?"

The guy on the other end says, "Okay."

"*Da*. His girlfriend left ring at my house, and I'm checking to see if she's still there? Do I have time to bring it?"

"Ah…I don't know anything about that," the guy says.

Zoe rolls her eyes. "Has Rostov jet taken off yet?"

"Rostov? Uh…yeah, it's on the runway now."

"Ahhh, I'm too late. I'll have to mail it to him. Do you know, are they headed back to Paris? Or was it Moscow?"

"The Rostov jet? No, they're headed to Istanbul."

A chill settles over me.

He's not bringing her back to Paris. He's taking her to Turkey. The Rostovs probably have a palace there. He's bringing her somewhere he can lock her up tight and keep me away.

"Oh, Istanbul, that's right. Oh well. I will get address. *Spasibo*." Zoe ends the call.

"Good job, Zoe," I say.

The front door swings open, and Lili rushes in. "Oh my God, Baron. What happened? Leo texted me to come over."

I make a mental note to punch Leo later when it won't hurt so badly to move. As I give her the shortest recap possible, Leo makes a video call on his phone, and Phoenix brings an icepack for my face.

Leo's dad, Maxim, appears on Leo's screen. Sasha, his mom, leans into the screen with a big smile.

"Leonid! How are you?"

"Uh, okay, Mom, but can I talk to Papa in private for a minute?"

"If you promise to call me tomorrow."

"Promise."

"Okay, love you." Sasha blows kisses as Maxim walks away from her.

"Hey, Papa." He angles his phone to show my beat-up face for a second then turns it back to him. "Can we conference with you and Uncle Ravil?"

Maxim swears, and his camera jostles as he walks out the door of his penthouse and over to my parents'. "Was it Rostov?"

"Yeah." Leo props his phone up in the window sill, and the bratva heirs gather around. Phoenix and Anders hang back, out of the picture.

"Okay, give me a minute, so you only have to update us once." A moment later, he video calls us from my father's desk. Maxim, Dima, and my dad look back at us.

By now, I've had time to think it through. To run scenarios in my head. I have a half-baked idea for rescuing Lara.

"Are you all right, Ben?" my dad asks.

Am I? Not even fucking close. And it's not just because I had the shit beat out of me. It's because Lara's gone. I had one job—to protect her—and I failed at it.

Worse than that—I hurt her. All I wanted to do was win her love and trust.

I thought I was there, but my misstep demolished everything I'd worked so hard to build.

"Lara's gone," I say. Admitting my failure has a bitter taste. "Brash had a spy at Thornecroft who was involved in an assault on Gabe Tracy's daughter. It was meant to bring me and Baranov House down. They drugged her and brought her to a hospital where the spy must have had contact with her. I'm guessing while she was drugged, she told him something I shared with her in confidence about my arranged marriage, which was that it was made urgent because Lara had *interest from another party*."

My friends all stare at me in surprise. They weren't privy to the conversation I had on the lawn—they just witnessed it from the windows.

"Brash used those exact words—the ones I used with Melinda—when he showed up tonight. Oh, and in case you didn't know—Adrian didn't trust Lara with the truth, so she showed up here believing our marriage was actually arranged from birth, and I was the asshole. A heads' up on that would've been nice. So anyway, Lara was understandably upset about being manipulated, and she left with him."

"Also, they showed up with AK-47's, so Baron couldn't go after her," Anya interjects.

I continue, "He's got her on a flight to Turkey right now. I'm going to fly in solo, go in, and take her back. Could you arrange a plane for me?"

My father stares back at me impassively. We share the trait of keeping our expressions inscrutable while processing complicated situations. "Do you think she'll go with you?"

The pain of hurting her floods to the surface, raw and fresh. Will I find the words to make her forgive me?

No, wait. That's irrelevant. Her choice to love me or not is less important than her safety.

Like her father, I would choose her safety from Rostov over her forgiveness any day.

"I'll be persuasive," I say.

Zoe and Lili give me dubious looks. They must hear the resolution in my tone. The certainty that I'll take Lara back whether she wants rescuing or not.

"The Rostovs have a property in Istanbul. There'll be ten times as many guards there as came to pick her up. How will you get around them?" Maxim asks.

"I'll go in quietly. Like a secret ops mission. That way we can avoid a war."

My father's face still shows nothing. He considers me for what feels like an eternity. "Okay," he says at last. "She's your wife. You should be the one to go in."

Relief rushes through me. I was afraid he would try to protect me and hold back his assistance to dissuade me from going. "You will wait until Adrian and his team are in place as backup or for extraction in case things go wrong."

I nod. That makes sense. They can get there from Moscow faster than I can. "Don't let them go in without me."

My dad hesitates then nods. "I will give that order. But I can't guarantee Adrian will follow it. A father will do anything for his child, including disobeying his *pakhan*."

Right. This is why families are normally forbidden in the bratva. But my mother's pregnancy with me changed everything for the Chicago Bratva and later for the Moscow arm that Adrian runs now, too.

"But your plan may avoid a war. If it doesn't..." —my dad spreads his hands— "we go to war. The Rostov brat can't abduct my daughter-in-law and lay hands on my son without me fighting back."

I swallow, grateful for his full backing.

"Dima will work on getting through their security and providing you with whatever you need."

"I can help," Anya says.

Her dad nods at her. "We'll work as a team."

"I'm going with Baron," Leo says.

"No," I cut in. "I need you to stay here and protect the house. Especially after what happened with the Titans."

My dad raises an eyebrow, but when we don't explain, he lets it go.

Leo frowns but doesn't argue more.

"I'll see how fast I can get a plane to you," my dad says. "Maxim will prepare a list of things for Adrian to bring for you—weapons and kevlar—that kind of thing. We'll be in touch. Meanwhile, rest and eat. You'll need your strength."

I nod my agreement, but I don't need food or rest. Rage gives me all the strength I need.

My wife is in the clutches of a psychopath. I could burn down the entire world right now to get her back.

CHAPTER TWENTY-FIVE

Lara

I'm in deep trouble.

I pace in the large bedroom Brash brought me to. It's a master bedroom with a large king-sized bed and a huge window overlooking an orchard. We're not in Paris. We're at Brash's family's residence in Turkey.

The door is locked. If I had any doubts, it's confirmed. I'm his prisoner.

My head is muzzy because I didn't sleep at all on the way here, and it would be five in the morning back in Illinois.

It was just Brash and his henchmen on the flight over. There was no one I could appeal to for help. I waited until Brash dozed off to sleep and then tried to use my phone, but there was no service or wifi to send a message to anyone.

When we landed, he took my phone from my purse and tossed it out the window of the limo that picked us up.

"Deep breaths," I mutter to myself, trying to keep the panic at bay. I feel like I'm the heroine in a horror movie where she suddenly realizes that nothing was what it seemed.

I'm the heroine who is too stupid to live. Why did I leave with Brash?

What made me think he was safer than Baron?

Oh, Baron. Thinking of him still makes my chest feel like it's been cleaved in two.

I am trying to put this all together. I had the entire plane trip to think. To examine the puzzle pieces and try to fit them together.

Brash said my arranged marriage had to happen because I had interest from another party—him. Baron's expression had confirmed the truth of that statement. What had Brash said on the plane? *Your father shouldn't have refused my initial offer.*

Meaning he'd offered to marry me? After a few dates? Without even asking me?

I shake my head. This is so medieval. So it's not about Brash's desire for me. I'm the pawn. Maybe the plan is as obvious as it seems. An arranged marriage to make an alliance with my father. Except forcibly kidnapping me is not going to win my father's cooperation. Brash misplayed his hand if he thinks this ends the way he wants it to. Or maybe he doesn't care anymore, and this is just about getting even with my father for snubbing him.

Except he called me his wife.

He talked about punishing me.

A sick feeling washes through me. Somehow I know this isn't the seductive kind of punishment I experience at Baron's hand. The kind that includes a little pain and ends in pleasure for both of us. If I thought Baron had a sadistic streak, it's nothing compared to the real violence I sense in Brash.

I flop down on the bed. The pain of missing Baron makes tears sting my eyes. But damn him!

If our marriage was rushed or forced through to keep Brash from making a claim on me, why couldn't he just have told me that?

Better yet, why didn't my dad tell me? He was the one who put me in this horrible situation by not trusting me with the truth. If I get out of this, I don't know if I'll ever forgive him.

But those thoughts won't get me out of this. I need to keep a clear head. Figure out how to manage Brash. Find a phone to call Baron or my dad. My dad would be closer to Turkey, but it's Baron I want. It's Baron my body grieves for. Baron whose face I want to slap for conspiring with my dad without filling me in.

Knowing Baron, he could already be on his way.

Unless he really believed me—walking away was goodbye. Unless he thought I made my choice and was gentleman enough to let me make it. He does have that tendency to put everyone else's needs before his.

Would he let me go that easily?

That thought makes my heart seize up cold.

Please don't let me go, Baron. I send out the silent prayer up to whatever higher spirit will listen.

I hear the slide of the lock on the door, and Brash walks in. I sit up on the bed. There's a smug smile on his face that makes me want to throat punch him, but I try to hide it.

The trouble is, I'm not very good at masking my feelings.

"Have you settled in, darling?"

I bite back the angry retort on the tip of my tongue. Deep breaths. Pretend to be pleasant. Or at least don't antagonize him.

"It's hard to settle without my things."

There. That didn't sound too surly.

Brash waves a dismissive hand. "We will get you new things. What do you need now? A toothbrush? There are some under the sink. Shampoo and soap is in the shower." His eyes take on a dangerous glint. "You don't need clothes." He steps closer and reaches for me.

I want to knee him in the balls, but instead I sidestep and dart toward the window.

"I'd like to see that orchard." It's the first thing I can think to say, and I run with it. "Getting outside is helpful to adjust to the new time zone. The jet lag is already getting to me," I babble.

"You'll go outside when you earn it." He closes the distance between us, shoving me up against the glass with his fingers around my throat. "Now take off your clothes."

I clutch at his wrists, my nails scoring his skin. I can't breathe. The pain of my crushed windpipe is excruciating. Stars dance before my eyes, and I start to black out. He abruptly releases his grip on my throat, and I gasp and cough as my body desperately tries to re-oxygenate.

He fists the bodice of my blouse and yanks, tearing the fabric.

"You can't have sex with me!" I blurt. It's the only thing that popped in my head. "I'm on my period."

It's actually true. I don't know if it's going to save me from being assaulted right now, but it's worth a shot.

"And I need more tampons. Unless you have those under the sink, too?"

Oops. I might have put too much snark in my voice because his arm flies back, and he backhands me. Pain explodes in my face, and my body bounces off the window and crumples to the floor. Mercifully, I black out.

———

Baron

I check the ammunition in both pistols.

Adrian and his team met me at the private airstrip and bustled me into a passenger van outfitted with everything we needed for a siege.

Dima and Anya got the address for the Rostov property, along with the floor plan. They've hacked the security system.

I should wait until it's dark, but I'm going in now.

Lara's phone tracker went offline close to the airport, but the one in her purse and the one in her shoes both show her in the master bedroom.

That fact alone makes me violent. I know Abrasha Rostov. He tortures the weak for the fun of it. He's going to force himself on Lara—do terrible things to her. Maybe not tonight. Maybe he's still on his best behavior, trying to trick her into marriage.

But I doubt it. If that were the case, he would've taken her back to Paris. But he brought her here to his stronghold. She's a prisoner. I'm sure of it.

I have to get her out of here before he does unspeakable things to her.

I had my choice of weapons—the van has everything. I have two grenades tucked in the pockets of my cargo pants. An olive fitted shirt covers my Kevlar, and I have a camo skull cap on to hide my blond hair. Instead of an automatic weapon, I picked revolvers with silencers.

My plan is still to go in stealth to get her out. According to Dima's reconnaissance, we're outnumbered four to one.

"I'll go in with you." Adrian snaps his own Kevlar in place.

"No. I go in solo. You only come if I fail."

Adrian's upper lip curls in a snarl. I'm sure that look makes men piss themselves in fear when he's torturing them. He's got the tough guy air, for sure. There's more street in him. He's less refined than my dad and the rest of the Chicago Bratva. Despite having a wife and daughter, he seems hardened by running a crime ring in Russia. "This is not your operation."

"The fuck it's not." It's no way to talk to my father-in-law, but I don't care. "She's my wife. I'm going in to get her. Hopefully without starting a war."

Adrian glowers at me. I'm sure he's deciding whether to snatch the hair right off my balls.

One of his men hands me a comms unit, and I pop it in my ear. "Testing."

Dima's voice sounds in my ear. "You're all set. The security system is down. I have eyes on all the cameras and can talk you in."

I swing the van's back door open and drop softly to my feet. "I'm going now," I mutter.

"The back entrance is on the east side," Dima says.

I hug the block wall and head east, not waiting to see if Adrian will follow.

"I'm unlocking the gate there. There's one guard inside the guard booth scrolling on his phone."

The wrought-iron gate barring cars from entering softly unlatches as I walk up.

Thank you, Dima.

I palm the pistol in my right hand and push the gate open with my left just enough to slip through. I stay in the shadows, keeping my gun pointed at the guy in the booth, but he never looks up.

"Stay close to the shrubbery until you get to the house, then take a right to go through the gate there into the walled garden. There's a security guy just inside."

I slink into the garden and look around. A small orchard with walking paths and benches lies in front of me. There's a security guard patrolling at the opposite end.

"First door on your left. I'm opening the lock now."

I keep my gaze and gun pointed at the security guard as I slip through the open door, but he doesn't look over. Part of me is almost sorry. I wanted blood tonight.

But Lara's safety is all that matters. Until I have her secure, I need to be cautious.

"There aren't any cameras in the residence, so you're going blind now."

"I got it from here," I say. I memorized the floor plans. I know all the routes that lead to the master bedroom. There's a back staircase this way.

I round the corner and come face to face with an armed guard.

Fuck.

I shoot before he can react. He goes down in a silent heap. Thank fuck for silencers.

Now I have to move fast before someone discovers him.

"I heard a shot," Adrian says. "Report."

"I killed a guard," I mutter.

I find the stairs and take them two at a time. There's another guard at the top. A single bullet puts him down, too.

"Another guard," I report before Adrian asks.

The door to the master bedroom is at the end of the hall. There's a sliding lock on the outside, like Brash has imprisoned women here before, but it's not locked. Which means she's either not in there, or he's with her.

A scream sounds from inside.

Lara.

Adrenaline rushes to my limbs. My mouth washes in saliva, like an animal preparing to bite its foe.

"Where is she?" Adrian demands in the comms in my ear.

I ignore him and push the door open, gun pointed.

No. Fuck no. Not my Lara.

Goddammit!

I shouldn't be shocked by the scene in front of me. I fully expected something horrific. But seeing my wife strung up by her wrists from a hook in the ceiling ignites a rage in me so fierce I could tear him apart with my bare hands. I *will* tear him apart with my bare hands.

She's in nothing but her panties. There are bruises on her cheek and throat. Brash points a dagger at one of her nipples.

Her eyes meet mine and widen. "Baron!"

Brash whirls and takes in the gun in my hand.

One bullet. One bullet is all it would take to kill him. But not with Lara behind him. Besides, a swift shot would be too kind for this animal.

These thoughts happened in a split second because I'm already in motion.

Brash dives away, thinking I'm going to shoot. I follow his movement with the gun, and as soon as he's clear of Lara, I cap him in the thigh.

He yelps and drops behind the bed.

"Report!" Tension radiates in Adrian's bark.

I don't have time to give him the play-by-play. I leap onto the bed in a single stride. With the next step, I drop onto Brash's sprawled body, stomping into his solar plexus to knock the wind out of him. My next step is onto his throat, then I drop down and straddle him.

He fights back, but I punch the muzzle of the gun into his mouth, knocking out a tooth. I want him to look in my eyes when I kill him.

He reaches for the lamp by the bedside table and swings it at me. I angle my back to take the blow as I fire.

He gurgles blood.

Too fast, dammit.

I wanted to make him suffer for touching Lara. For all the pain he's caused in this world.

I holster the gun and punch his face, satisfied by the sound of his nose breaking. Then his cheekbone. I knock his teeth out.

"We're coming in," Adrian says.

Fuck.

"Taking all cameras offline," Dima says.

I hear the rat-a-tat-tat of machine gun fire out in the orchard, and it brings me back to reality.

Brash is dead. I shake myself and put two fingers against his throat to make sure.

I need to get Lara out of here. I whirl and rush over to her, pulling a knife out to cut her down. "Lara. *Malyshka.* Fuck."

I realize I've lost the right to call her *malyshka*, but she throws her arms around me, and I want to weep.

CHAPTER TWENTY-SIX

Lara

Baron squeezes me so tight I can't breathe, kissing my hair, my temple, my forehead.

"I'm so sorry," he rasps.

I cling to him, my legs not holding me yet. I don't mean to, but my gaze returns to Abrasha. If I were a better person, I would be horrified about what I just witnessed. My husband shooting then brutally beating a man to death. But I drank in every second of it.

I soaked up Baron, covered in bruises but looking every inch the badass. Dripping competency porn.

I never once doubted he would win the battle.

"He's dead," Baron says.

Shouts and gunfire sound from inside the house.

"Your dad is here." Baron whips his t-shirt off his head and pulls it down over mine. I shove my arms through the holes, and he hustles me into his bulletproof vest.

"Come on," he says. "We have to go." He takes my hand and leads me to the door. "Stay behind me."

"But you're not wearing Kevlar."

He turns, emotion blazing in his eyes, and kisses me fiercely.

I gasp when we come apart. What was that? A goodbye kiss in case he doesn't make it?

"You care," he murmurs.

My heart pinches painfully. Of course, I care. I never stopped caring. Baron's mine. I'm his. We belong together. I've never felt so certain of anything in my life.

I'm pissed at him, but my heart started to heal the moment Baron walked through the door. Even when I'd walked away, I didn't want us to be over. I was hurt and mad, but I hoped he'd follow. Hoped he'd figure out how to fix us.

We still have a huge problem to work out, but he's here. Sexy as hell with his muscled torso bare and the cargo pants with guns strapped to each leg.

He hands me one of the guns, and I slip off the safety. Baron nods when he sees I know my way around a gun and pushes my torso down, so we're moving at a crouch. We leave the bedroom, stepping over the body of a dead guard. Baron keeps his body angled protectively in front of mine.

Gunshots sound from multiple directions. I saw dozens of guards when we drove in. I pray my dad brought an army because this place was defended like a fortress. We get to the bottom of the stairs where another guard's body lies. I step square on his chest with my bare foot. I'm in nothing but Baron's t-shirt, Kevlar, and my panties, but I have a gun, and I'm with the most powerful man I know.

And I don't mean my father.

Every bit of fear Brash invoked in me has now turned to power. I raise the gun, ready to fire. I plan to protect Baron while he protects me.

He's my husband. We were made for each other.

I fell in love with you the moment you walked off that plane, malyshka.

He knew it from the start. I didn't know it until I thought we were over. Sometimes it takes the worst to bring things into crystal clear focus.

We round the corner, and Baron jerks back. Machine gun bullets hit the floor exactly where we were standing a moment before.

Baron presses me up against the wall, smashing his body in front of mine with his gun poised to shoot.

When the machine gun fire stops, two shots ring out, and I hear the sound of a body falling to the ground.

"Clear," my father shouts in Russian.

Baron releases me, and we both round the corner.

Two men lie dead at my father's feet. He beckons us forward, and we jog down the hall.

He wraps me in a quick one-armed embrace and lifts his chin in Baron's direction. "Get her out of here."

"Come on." Baron takes my hand and tugs me out a door into the orchard. I hear gunfire come from inside the house. Two guards lie dead in the garden.

We run out a gate, along a hedge, and out a larger gate where we leave the property.

Baron keeps running, leading me to a white van.

I recognize the driver who gets out as one of my father's men.

Baron pulls open the back door, and we climb inside. "Lara is secure," he says, and I realize he's wearing a comms device in his ear.

"Get her out of there," I hear my father's voice come back through.

"*Da*" The driver slams the door shut.

Gripping my hips, Baron directs me into a seat and

crouches in front of me, his worried gaze traveling faster than his fingertips as he inspects me, grimacing at the bruises on my face and neck. "Did he..." The hardset line of his mouth and the danger in his eyes speak murder.

"No. I told him he couldn't because I have my period."

I watch something crack apart in Baron before his face returns to that of the hardened knight.

The van takes off, but Baron easily balances on the balls of his feet. He pulls the comm device out of his ear and flicks a tiny button. The light on it goes off.

"Anatoli Rostov—Brash's father—called your dad after you started dating and proposed a union of your two families." Baron launches into the story without preamble. Like he's had time to think about all the things he should have told me, and he wants to make it right immediately.

He's still crouched in front of me, his hands lightly resting on my hips, his eyes locked on mine.

"Your dad feared for your safety and told him it was impossible because your marriage had been arranged since birth to me. Rostov figured your dad would not be as equipped to fight against my father and the American Bratva with just your father's cell."

I blink, taking in the rush of information. Reassembling the puzzle pieces with this new context.

"Your dad immediately called my father and asked if I'd be willing to marry you and bring you to the United States for your protection. I said *of course*."

I fight the sudden urge to weep. Of course, Baron agreed. He always puts the protection of the weaker as his first priority over his own needs.

"I knew Brash from prep school." Baron's face darkens to thunder clouds again. "I've seen his psychopathic tendencies. I got kicked out for avenging one of them.

"Your father was worried about his family, but I was

concerned about Brash and what he would do to you if he had control of your life."

Tears stab my eyes. Why didn't my dad just tell me?

"I thought you knew it was a farce, but when you arrived pissed off and thinking I was the enemy, I realized he hadn't told you the truth."

Oh God. Baron was the hero all along. And I'd treated him like the enemy. And he had taken it. All my anger and acting out. He had taken it without defending himself. Without acting wounded. He just accepted my lack of gratitude with complete stoicism. With total grace.

"I figured your dad hadn't told you for a reason. You're very transparent with your emotions. I don't know how good you are at lying, but I'm guessing not great."

As angry as I am at my dad, Baron is probably right. I'm a terrible liar, and I can't hide my feelings.

"He didn't want the Rostovs to figure out it was a farce. But they did. Brash sent a spy to Thornecroft—Denis.

I gape at him, my eyes widening. Denis? *Gospodi*! No wonder Baron didn't want him near me.

"He was a part of the attack on Melinda. He was at the hospital when she was brought in, and I think he must've spoken with her while she was drugged. I had told her we had an arranged marriage. I also said something I shouldn't have—that the timeline on our marriage had been moved up because you had interest from another party. That was all Brash needed to realize your departure was about him and to believe he had a chance to convince you to leave with him."

I have a dozen questions and certainly things I should care more about, but my brain snagged on Melinda, and the fact that he told her about us.

My lips tremble when I ask, "were you with Melinda?" I need to know. While he's here being so honest and telling me everything, I need to know if she's his girlfriend. Or if she *was*. I need to know what she meant to him.

Love storms Baron's expression. His eyes go soft. He grips my hips tighter, in a more possessive hold. "*Malyshka*, no. Melinda is a masochist who uses pain to help her cope with the stress of her type A personality. I used to deliver that pain. When she showed up asking for it this year, I told her I was married, and she was no longer welcome because of the scrutiny her father's elevated political position would bring to our house. Plus, I knew Anders had a thing for her."

I nod but my eyes swim with tears. Baron deceived me about something so huge. I guess I need to know what is real. If *we* are real.

"I'm sorry I hurt you. I never meant to do that. I will never lie to you again. I promise. I told you before that I fell in love with you the moment you walked off that plane. It's true. I agreed to marry you out of duty, but the moment I met you everything changed."

I stare at him. I want to believe. I want to believe so much. But I'm not sure.

"I had thought we would have a marriage in name only. For appearances only. We'd have separate bedrooms. I'd let you do your thing, and you'd let me do mine. But meeting you felt like destiny. And then I didn't care what method fate used to bring us together, I wasn't going to walk away from a gift like you."

Tears spill down my cheeks, and I suck in a sobbed breath. I clap a hand over my mouth to hold it in.

"I'm so fucking sorry I hurt you, Lara. Please forgive me."

There's a question in his gaze, but before I can answer, he says, "Brash is dead, but I'm not giving you up." A fierce expression settles on the hard lines of his face.

"I don't want you to give me up," I choke.

"Oh, baby. *Malyshka*." He rises a little to cup my face. "I love you so much."

"I love you, Baron." I throw my arms around him, knocking him down to the floor of the van. He takes me with him, pulling my body over his, so he can wrap his arms around me.

"Marry me, Lara," he murmurs.

I smile. "We're already married. Or was that a lie, too?"

Baron rolls us to our sides, so we're nose to nose. "Not a lie. We're married. You're mine. But I want a do-over. Call me a modern guy, but I want my bride willing. Consensual weddings are all the rage now."

"You want the wedding with the white dress?" I tease him, remembering what he said to me the day we married.

We'll have a do-over later. You get to have the ring you want. And the dress you pick out. Flowers. All your friends and family there to celebrate.

He kisses the bridge of my nose. "I want it all with you. A proper courtship. A wedding. Mad love. I want to know all your secrets. To be your best friend." He swallows. "To be the father of your children."

"You want kids?" I'm suddenly catapulted out into space. No earth is under my feet. No gravity. Just stars winking from every direction.

He nods, searching my face. Looking like he's holding his breath.

I see it—a future with Benjamin Baranov. The future I never imagined. A real marriage with true love and children. The kind of love my parents have. Ben would make an incredible father. He'd move mountains to make sure his children had everything they could ever need. He'd sacrifice his life to keep them safe and happy. Just like I know he'd do for me.

"Yes," I whisper.

A boyish grin splits Baron's face. "Yeah?"

I laugh. "Did you think I'd say no?"

Pain clouds his eyes. "I wasn't sure. I was afraid I'd lost you forever." His brows slam together. "Not to Brash—I wasn't going to ever let that man have you. But after I got you free..." He exhales. "I didn't know if you'd forgive me. You got jacked around hard by your dad and me. That's a lot to forgive and forget."

A tight band closes around my throat.

"Not to mention the fact that you had a life in Paris. If you want to go back to it, I will–" He swallows, and I can practically see the quick calculations taking place in that brilliant brain of his.

"I will figure it out. I'll move there to be with you. Leo can run Baranov House. You're what matters."

My chest gets tight. He would give everything up for me. Everything he's built—an entire kingdom. People he feels responsible to protect. His business enterprises.

"I don't want to leave Baranov House."

I realize it's true. Even when I ran from Baron, I knew I'd be back. Knew that was where I belonged. Baranov House with its lively occupants is home for me now.

I needed space in that moment, but I wanted him to fight for me. To make it right. To convince me to come back and rule by his side.

I love this man. In a miniscule amount of time, he's become my everything. My present and, yes, I can see it now—my future.

Joy ignites in Baron's expression, and he kisses me hard. "I love you, Lara."

His lips feel different.

When he breaks the kiss I touch them lightly with my fingertips. His lower lip is split and swollen. "How did you get this?"

Baron shakes his head dismissively, like he doesn't want me to worry about it. "Brash's men. After you left."

Anger thrusts up my throat. While Brash was whisking me to the airport, he left his men to beat my husband. I wish I could've killed him myself. Brash was pure evil. How did I not see it?

Baron sees my distress and strikes my hair back from my face. "It's over now."

"*He's* over," I say. "We're just beginning."

CHAPTER TWENTY-SEVEN

Lara

I wake in my childhood bedroom with my head resting on Baron's shoulder. We flew into Moscow last night—or maybe it was this morning. I have no idea how long I slept. I just know that everytime I woke with adrenaline running through my system, Baron's arms tightened around me, and he murmured softly into my ear until I relaxed and fell back to sleep. He murmured that it was over. That I was safe. That he'd never let anything happen to me.

You're mine, Lara Baranov, and I won't let anyone touch you, was the last thing he murmured a few hours ago.

He's still asleep, which is unusual for him. I guess we both needed the rest. I ease the blankets back to slip out of bed and gasp when I see the state of Baron's body. He's in his boxer shorts—we were way too wiped out when we arrived for any sexy times—and his ribs are covered in black, blue, and green bruises.

Gospodi, he probably has some cracked or broken ribs. And this was the state he was in when he came to rescue me!

The word *hero* doesn't fully express the magnitude of what Baron is. He's a knight. No, a prince. *My* prince.

I shower and dress in clothes that were still in my drawers from the last time I visited. Then I head to the living room to find my mom. I saw her when we came in, but I was delirious then. I need another hug.

My father owns three different properties in Russia. Our home in Moscow is an enormous penthouse with gleaming hardwood floors covered in plush rugs. The ceilings are vaulted, and the penthouse is filled with large windows and skylights because my mother likes bright spaces.

I find her in her clay studio, but she's not at the pottery wheel. She's standing looking out the full length window holding a cup of tea between her two hands. It's in a mug she made, and it smells like mint. My father stands behind her, his tattooed arms wrapped around her from behind. Her head rests back against his chest.

"Lara, *lyubimaya.*" My mom's face lights up when she sees me, and she sets down her mug of tea and spreads her arms wide.

"Mama. Papa." I choke up. Even though my kidnapping wasn't long, it still feels like a miracle to be home back with the people I love.

My parents sandwich me in a tight hug, and I soak in their love. The reason I became a strong, independent woman going to school in another country was because I knew they always had my back.

"I'm mad at you," I tell my dad, but my voice is teary.

"I have...regrets." My dad's voice is gruff, as always.

"You should have told me that Brash was the danger, not Baron. I never would've left with him."

"Yes, he should've told you," my mom says.

I draw a breath to continue to berate him, but my

husband walks in, torso bare, hair tousled, wearing the same cargo pants he was in when we arrived. He stops in the doorway, looking uncertain.

That's when I realize it doesn't matter.

My dad did what he thought he had to do to keep me safe. I could argue up and down that he should have made other choices, but if he had...I wouldn't have this gorgeous man in my life right now. If I'd thought he was just a nice guy doing me a favor, I might have insisted on separate bedrooms, knowing he'd honor that. I wouldn't have fallen head over heels in love with the guy I thought was the enemy.

I wouldn't be madly in love with my sexy prince.

So, I guess I have no regrets. And if *I* don't have regrets, I can't very well blame my dad.

"We're getting married," I announce.

My parents release me from the sandwich hug, and my mom claps her hands in delight. "You and Benjamin? Aren't you already married? Oh, I'm so happy!" She throws her arms around me again. "I always wanted him for you, *lyubimaya*. You were the best of friends when you were toddlers."

Huh. I imagine my mom planning our marriage from the sandbox. I can't help but wonder if her wish for me as a toddler found its way into the ether, pulling on quantum entanglements to years later manifest this way—with my father ordering me to marry him to keep me safe, and Baron feeling the pull of destiny the moment he met me. Meanwhile I was oblivious to all the magic conspiring around me until it was nearly too late.

My mom turns and gathers Baron up in a hug, too.

"Be careful, I think his ribs are broken," I warn.

"I see that," my mom says. "We can get them Xrayed right away."

"Not necessary," Baron grunts.

My dad clasps Baron's palm in a wordless, somber hand-shake. I take it he approves.

I shouldn't care—especially not after the machinations my dad made with my marriage, but I'm happy. My parents support my choice of a husband.

Still holding Baron's hand, my dad claps his other hand on Baron's shoulder. "Benjamin." It's a bratva bro moment. There's tremendous weight in my father's tone.

Baron meets his eye, waiting. Steady. My father has intimidated every guy I've dated, but that will never be possible with Baron.

"*Spasibo, moy brat.*" Thank you, my brother.

Baron bows his head. "My honor."

My mom beams up at him. "Now, what is this about you getting married?"

My dad releases Baron, and I slide under the protection of Baron's arm, nesting myself against his side. "Baron wants a real wedding." I look up at him, and he kisses the top of my head. "With a willing bride."

My mom's eyes dance in the mischievous way she has. "And now you're willing?"

"I am."

"I'm so happy. For both of you. I didn't like that you thought he was your enemy when he was the one trying to help you, but your father thought it was safest that way." She frowns up at my dad.

My dad remains silent.

"But it all worked out in the end," my mom waxes on. "Love is messy. It's uncomfortable. It brings up our deepest needs and our worst fears. But in the end it heals us."

"Wow. You should write that down for the wedding toast." I laugh. "Which reminds me. You're going to tell me about how you two fell in love." I point between her and my dad.

"*Nyet,*" my dad says.

"She can handle it," my mom says. "After what she's just been through, she will understand how circumstances can turn even the worst enemies into lovers." She sends Baron an impish look. "Your parents' marriage began as a kidnapping, too."

Baron is usually good at not showing any reaction, but I can feel his body go still as he absorbs that.

"I can't wait to call Lucy. We can plan the wedding together. Are you thinking it will be in Chicago?"

"*Da*," my father answers even though the question wasn't for him. "I want you to move back to Chicago. Things may be too hot here after what happened in Turkey."

My mom nods.

"I'm sorry." I hear the weight of responsibility in Baron's voice, and I want to erase it. "I tried to avoid a war, but...he had to die."

"He did," my father says simply. "And we cleaned up. Anatoli Rostov will never know for sure who did it. So I can't run, or it will make it obvious, but I need Kat to be safe, and she'll be safe at the Kremlin with your father."

"The Kremlin?" I ask blankly.

"That was the name the neighbors gave our building in Chicago," Baron explains. "Because so many Russians lived in it."

"Ah. Kind of how the students at Thornecroft call Baranov house, the Gulag."

"Exactly." I see the twitch of a smile on Baron's face, and his eyes heat, like he's planning another trip to the dungeon with me.

My nipples get hard.

"Perfect!" My mom claps her hands together. "I get to go plan a wedding. You two will go back to the Gulag." She looks up at my dad. "I won't like to be away from you, though," she says softly.

Regret and longing wash over his face, and I see that deep, always passionate love the two share.

The kind of love I found.

With the man I trust with my life.

And my heart.

And my soul.

CHAPTER TWENTY-EIGHT

Baron

Sunday afternoon, I stand by the grill in the backyard of Baranov house, flipping burgers and brats. Melinda is in Ander's lap on the outdoor sofa. Alex, Feliks, and Phoenix play frisbee with a few other house members.

Zoe's acting hostess-y and setting out all the side dishes, plates, and silverware. Anya's playing DJ.

Lara and I got back to Thornecroft a full week ago. We spent the past week recovering from our bruises and catching up on our studies, but today I decided it was time for a house party and invited everyone for an afternoon barbecue.

My beautiful wife hands me a beer from the cooler, and I give her a kiss. We've been on honeymoon all week, starting over with our relationship, falling more deeply in love. She's friends with everyone in the house, becoming more playful and spontaneous every day.

The atmosphere in the house is lighter than it's ever been. Or maybe that's just me. *I* feel lighter than ever. There's still a serious edge to me. I know I'm responsible for the safety, well-being, and financial abundance of everyone here, but that sense of having my very soul on lockdown—that fear of looking away for a moment and missing something—is gone.

Lara took the blade out of my heart—the one I inserted myself after watching Valentina die— and she patched it up. The wound is still there, it's still sore, but I no longer feel like I'm fighting to survive every night while I sleep.

"Hey bro." Lili walks outside with a guy and gives me a hug. "This is Carlos." She introduces the tall, lanky blond guy in soccer shorts and a T-shirt that reads Manchester United. They're holding hands.

"Carlos." I try to muster a menacing air to show this guy he better not fuck around with my little sister, but my heart isn't in it.

"Be nice," Lara tells me in Russian, coming up behind me and placing her hand in the center of my back. I fucking love it. Her casual touches, her giving me orders. The fact that she's really my wife.

Leo must think I'm slacking because he saunters over and looks the guy over with a frown.

"Is the food ready?" Lili asks.

"Ten minutes." I flip a burger in the air and catch it on my spatula then slide it onto the grill, showing off for Lara.

"Leo made Bloody Marys," Lara tells her. "And there are mimosas too."

"She's not twenty-one," Leo growls, still glowering at Carlos. "And I'm guessing he's not either."

Lara rolls her eyes.

Considering both the twins are drinking, and they're not of age yet, it seems odd that Leo's being an asshole about it, but I don't interfere.

"How are classes?" I ask, feeling guilty that I haven't checked in on her more. But losing Lara made me realize that despite all my micromanagement, I can't keep everyone safe all the time. Maybe I need to let Lili be free to make her own mistakes. "Is Vasiliev still giving you trouble?"

Lara gasps beside me. "Vasiliev!"

"What?"

"He warned me about Denis."

I turn to give her my full attention. "What? When?"

"The week Brash showed up. That Monday when I was in the bookstore. Remember you found me there?"

I'm ready to pull Denis' tongue out of his throat. I looked for him when we got back to school, but it seems he has vanished. According to Anya's research, he hasn't attended any classes in the last week.

I nod. "Yes." I'm wary, my entire body cn full alert.

"Well, Denis had tried to talk to me in the bookstore. He basically said the same thing Brash had offered on the phone—that he could help me get away from you if I needed it."

My upper lip lifts in a snarl. If I were a lion, I'd be showing my deadly canines. "And then what?" There's so much menace in my voice that Lara recoils slightly, then reaches out a hand to wrap around my forearm and reassure me she's still here. She's still mine.

"Then I walked away, and when I was checking out, Vasiliev came up behind me in the line. I had just waved at you in the window, and he told me to be careful because you were dangerous."

I snarl some more.

"And so I snapped at him and said, *yes, I know you hate Baron.* And then he said, *not Baron, the other one.*"

My brows pop. What does Vasiliev know about that oligarch *mudak*? "He warned you about him? Interesting. I had seen them talking and thought they might be working together. But it sounds like Vasiliev is under their thumb."

I file that away for future reference. It could become an

interesting lever to pull if I ever need it. Or it could be something I offer to get him out of for a fee.

The front doorbell chimes through Leo's phone, and he glances at the face of it. His eyes widen slightly, and he meets my gaze. It's Chancellor Ogden.

I roll my shoulders. I expected this after the Titan house burned. "Well, invite him in. The meat is ready."

A moment later, Leo leads the president of Thornecroft University back.

Zoe sees him and pours her Bloody Mary into a plant.

He's in his early sixties, but he carries himself with the same stealthy grace as Gabe Tracy's special ops guy. He's extremely fit—we often pass each other running in the morning, and he appears alert, like he's taking in everything around him.

"Benjamin." He offers his hand to shake without a smile.

I clasp his hand. "Chancellor Ogden." I don't smile either. We met before when I was petitioning to donate Baranov House to the university to make it an official society house. "You're just in time for our barbecue." I hand him a plate.

He accepts it, which surprises me. I slide a burger onto the bun he opens on the plate, and he helps himself to the simple but tasty side dishes Emma left for us—potato salad, watermelon, and chopped vegetables with hummus.

"This is my wife, Lara," I introduce him.

"Lara, this is Chancellor Ogden. He's the *pakhan* of Thornecroft." I give her a faint smile at my use of the Russian word for bratva boss.

I wait, but he doesn't broach any conversation at first, so I serve the house members then fix myself a plate.

"Have a seat. You probably didn't come for the burger."

We settle onto one of the plush outdoor sofas beside each other. He's giving off interrogation vibes—treating me to the same silence I got down at the police station where they seem to hope you'll fill in the space with chatter.

But I'm not that guy.

The chancellor finishes all the food on his plate before he says to me, "So, the Titan House was behind Ms. Tracy's assault."

"Were they?" I play dumb.

Melinda looks over at hearing her name, and her smile drops away. I want to punch the chancellor for reminding her of it. Anders says she's even more tightly-wound than ever although I think she looks better now that she has him in her court.

"I can understand wanting to exact revenge for that. Sending a message that your house isn't to be fucked with."

So this visit is definitely about the fire. I made sure everyone in the house has an alibi for that night. The bomb had a timer that Leo activated from the library where at least a dozen people saw him studying. He planned it when the entire house was out at a pledge event, and even activated the fire alarm before it went off, to make sure.

"The fire marshal said the alarm went off before the fire started, which is odd."

I take a bite of a pickle spear and give a polite but disinterested nod.

"I don't accept violence of any kind on this campus. I am committed to the safety of all students here. It's one of the reasons people like Gabe Tracy, Sultan Khalid al-Nasir, and members of the Russian *mafiya* alike trust sending their children here."

I tense. This feels like boarding school all over again. Is he about to expel me?

He sets his empty plate down on the wide square slate table in front of him and puts his hands on his knees. "So it ends here. I told the boys at Titan House that if I hear of any more house warfare, they lose their charter. Same goes for you. Understood?"

"Message received," I say easily, rising as he does. "Thank you for stopping by." I stick my palm out.

He squeezes my hand in a vise-like grip and locks eyes with me. His blue-grey gaze bores a hole in mine. "I know what goes on here, Benjamin."

My heart skips a beat.

"You're quiet and careful, which is why you get away with it. But the moment you bring negative attention to this school, it's over."

I greet that mild threat with silence, and he releases my hand. "Thank you for the burger. Enjoy your barbecue. I'll see myself out."

"Stop by anytime, Chancellor," I call after him.

CHAPTER TWENTY-NINE

Lara

I turn to look at myself in the full-length mirror in our walk-in closet.

Um...wow. This outfit is a lot. But I can pull this off.

This afternoon I borrowed Baron's Range Rover and Zoe, Anya, and I drove to the next town where there's a mall with a Victoria's Secret. I bought a wine-red bustier that laces up the back with a matching pair of G-string panties. I'm currently wearing it with a pair of black open-toed stilettos.

I've never worn anything like it before. I feel hot and naughty and ready to be spanked.

Now to find my husband.

As I reach for my bathrobe, the door to our bedroom opens with Baron in mid-sentence to someone on Facetime. "She's right here if you want to show her the optio—"

I freeze.

He freezes, his eyes popping wide. His mouth falls open.

My nipples harden from the way he looks at me.

"Uh, actually, she's busy right now, Mom. We'll call you

later, okay? Bye!" He ends the call without taking his eyes off me.

"Holy fuck." He tosses the phone onto the dresser and stalks toward me. "What is happening in here without me?"

A tingling starts up between my legs. A thrum of excitement at his nearness.

I smile. "Nothing is happening *without* you. This is happening *for* you. I was going to come down and lure you to the dungeon."

He picks me up with his forearm underneath my ass and carries me back into the depths of the closet. "Uh uh. No way you're going downstairs in that. Nobody sees my wife in this but me."

My back hits an inner closet wall, and he presses me against it, pulling my legs around to straddle his hips.

I laugh again. "I was going to wear a bathrobe."

"A *bathrobe?*" He drags his open mouth across my exposed collarbone to my shoulder. "Nope. No. Huh uh. Nobody sees you in a bathrobe, either." He takes the tiny ribboned strap in his teeth and pulls it down my shoulder. "They'll just imagine you naked beneath it. *I'm* the only guy who gets to imagine you naked."

"I'm not sure you have control over what other people imagine."

He grinds the bulge of his cock in the notch between my legs. "I have *all* the control. I'm the fucking *prince* of control," he claims.

Heat flushes my body. My clit pulses in a slow thrum. I love when he gets intense like this.

He boosts me a little higher to get his lips around my nipple, which he exposed when he dragged the shoulder ribbon down with his teeth. His tongue swirls around it first, then he sucks, hard.

I gasp at the corresponding tug in my core.

"So you like it?" I fish for a compliment even though he's obviously thrilled with the outfit.

"Like it," he growls, tearing the bodice down to my waist. "I fucking *love* it."

He suddenly drops me to my feet, spins me around, and presses my hands against the wall. "You look so hot, *malyshka*." He slips a finger under the edge of my panties at the top of my ass and traces it to the cleft of my ass. "I'm losing my mind." He lightly slaps my right buttcheek.

"I need to fuck you now," he says abruptly, kicking my feet wider. "Otherwise, I'm going to tear this pretty thing off you, and you'll be sad that I ruined your pretty new outfit."

He slaps my left butt cheek. "This is a *new* outfit, right?"

I love the tinge of jealous paranoia in his voice. "It's new," I gasp, as he grips my waist and pulls my ass backward. "I bought it for you."

"You're killing me." He tugs the G-string from between my cheeks and pulls it to the side with one hand, then uses the other to stroke between my legs.

I'm wet for him, my juices slick, my flesh plump and swollen with blood flow.

He buries his face in my hair with his lips pressed against my neck. "*Malyshka*, I love how wet your pussy gets for me." I hear the scrape of his zipper.

His narration about my juices makes me gush more arousal.

He rubs the head of his cock against my slit, and I moan.

"Arch that back for me," he orders.

I hollow my lower back, and he pushes in.

"That's right. Just like that, baby. Take it like a good girl." He eases in. As always, his dommy talk is tough, but he's paying attention, going slow. Making sure I'm ready to take him.

I love it. I feel sexy and beautiful and utterly claimed by

him. He makes me feel like the center of the Universe, and nothing could make me give up my position.

"You bought this sexy little outfit for me, *malyshka?*" He fills me and retreats, fills me again.

I'm beyond the capability of words now, so I just moan, "Uh huh."

"Did you know what it was going to do to me?" He grips my hips, thrusting in faster.

I'm moaning now.

"Hmm?"

"Mmm..."

He starts to pump harder, making me lock my elbows to keep from getting pushed into the wall. "You're such a good girl. I'm going to reward the fuck out of you tonight, baby."

He slows his strokes and wraps his forearm around my waist, bringing his hips in tight against mine to thrust up. I rise up on my toes with each thrust, then gravity brings me back down firmly on his cock.

I moan because it feels incredible.

"You like that, beautiful? You like riding my dick until you come?"

"Yes," I moan.

He bounces me faster, taking me on a celestial ride. I'm lightheaded with pleasure, unable to hold myself up, but it doesn't matter because Baron has me. He has control of my body, and he won't let me slip. Won't let me fall.

I believe that now, with my whole heart. I misunderstood and misjudged him before, but I'll never doubt him again. He's as solid as they come. More than a rock—a mountain.

"Baron," I moan. "Yes."

"You're so gorgeous. You're incredible." He continues to praise me as he fucks me into oblivion. "I'm going to come," he warns. "You'd better come all over my dick. Are you going to come with me?"

His dirty talk already has me orgasming. My internal muscles start to contract. He shoves in a few more times and then stays in while I squeeze and milk his dick with my orgasm.

"Good girl," he pants against my ear. "You're such a good fucking girl."

Another orgasm ripples through me, pulsing around his cock.

"I'm so in love with you," he murmurs, nipping the shell of my ear.

I blink back tears because this moment feels so perfect.

It's not how I imagined things would go when I put on the outfit—but it was honest and raw and utterly perfect.

"I love you, too," I say.

He pulls out and picks me up, carrying me to the bed. "Don't think I won't keep you up all night in this hot little outfit," he warns, tossing me in the center of the mattress.

I laugh and reach for him, pulling him down on top of me. "Let's see what you've got."

EPILOGUE

Lara

"This is it." Baron's voice clogs with emotion.

The silvery moonlight makes the water shimmer. We stand on the boardwalk of Lake Michigan, a half-block from the Kremlin. It's almost midnight on Christmas Eve. The icy wind off the lake hits our faces, but it doesn't bother me. I'm Russian—I'm warm in my woolen jacket. Warm from Baron's bed.

Baron clutches blood-red roses in his hand, strangling the stems with white knuckles.

We made love and were talking in bed when I asked him to show me where it happened. He froze up, like the idea made him go dead inside, so I suggested we do it right now. Tonight. We went to the corner drugstore to buy the roses, and now we're here.

I hope the more he talks about Valentina's death, the less of an impact it will have on him.

I wrap my arms around him from the side and squeeze.

"I honor Valentina for giving her life to protect yours," I say. My voice wavers, even though I didn't know the woman. I can sense how much she loved the children and how much they loved her.

"I honor Valentina for giving her life to protect ours," Baron repeats, the words barely making it out of his throat.

"It wasn't your fault." I'm going to keep saying this as many times as it takes until he believes me. "None of it was your fault. You were just a kid. Only terrible people gun down an innocent woman caring for innocent children."

I hate the haunted look in Barron's eyes. I want to hug it away. Kiss it away. Make him forget. But this moment isn't about forgetting. It's about remembering. Honoring. Memorializing.

I pry the roses from his fingers and set them in the middle of the sidewalk. Tomorrow, they'll make a sweet Christmas surprise for whoever is out here walking in the morning.

"Thank you, Valentina. We love you. We miss you." Of course, I don't even remember her, but I'm trying to voice what Baron may have left unsaid.

Baron makes a choking sound.

"It's okay to cry," I say. "Your tears are a tribute to her. And by letting them flow, you honor her and the child who suffered as a result of what happened here."

I don't even know where this wisdom is coming from, but I go with it. I figure the important thing isn't the words I speak, but that we are sharing this moment. But he is not alone in his grief and torment anymore. But he knows I'm here to talk about it anytime he needs to.

Baron wraps his strong arms around me and sobs. I hold him, imagining I'm also holding that child within him who took the world onto his shoulders.

It only lasts a few moments. He lets himself release the pent up grief from that traumatic moment years ago. And then he squeezes me tighter and tighter.

"I love you so much," he murmurs into my hair. "I love you more than the moon in the night sky. More than the sun on the coldest day. *You* are the sun who came into my life and warmed me up." He gives a rough laugh. "I'm a terrible poet, but I mean every fucking word."

I lift my face to his. "I love you more than the moon and the night sky and the sun on the coldest day. You are my warrior. My defender. My protector. My lover. My man. I'm so grateful we found each other. And I do believe in fate now. I do believe it was meant to happen. I do believe you were meant for me, and we were meant for each other."

We're getting married in a week, but these feel like our true vows. The words we speak into each other's hearts straight from our souls. The words that forever bind us—not into our legal marriage but our spiritual one.

Baron catches my hand and starts to run across the sand toward the water. I laugh, running with him. Every moment with him feels like a new beginning. This moment. The one we just had. And every moment going forward.

We run along the waterline, the icy air making my lungs contract. My laughter is an offering up to the gods:

Thank you for this gift of a man. Help him to heal. Bless this union, I pray.

———

Baron

I stand in a tux at the end of the aisle with my hands clasped in front of me. I'm not at an altar because we aren't getting married in a church, but a white satin strip of cloth covered in rose petals marks an aisle between the chairs set up for our guests. Leo stands beside me as my best man. Beside him stand Alex, Feliks, Phoenix, and Anders as my groomsmen. On the bride's side stand Zoe, Anya, and Lili, Melinda, and Lara's cousins Darya and Niko.

We decided to get married on New Year's Eve while we were in Chicago for winter break. Anders flew in from Norway right after Christmas. Lara's mom, Kat, moved into the Kremlin where my dad could keep her safe right after we saw her last. Adrian arrived two weeks ago, so Christmas was a festive affair this year. All of our bratva family from Los Angeles came—Lara's aunt Nadia and her famous uncle Flynn, of the band The Storytellers, and her two cousins who are in our wedding party. Oleg and Flynn's sister, Story, and their three kids came. Pavel, Kayla, and their daughter, Mila, who says she might transfer from USC to Thornecroft next semester.

We've had an incredible week here—the younger generation bonding as our parents do their thing.

My parents love Lara. She told me that even though there wasn't a marriage pact, her mom had secretly always wanted me for her. And it seems that my mom did too. They certainly planned the wedding of the century for us. It's not big—it's mostly bratva family with the exception of Gabe Tracy and a few other political guests my parents invited for their business purposes—but it's lavish and much care went into it.

My mom paid a fortune to rent a five-star "rooftop" restaurant downtown for the night. It's not actually on the roof because that would be too cold, but we're on the top floor of a downtown highrise. It has floor-to-ceiling windows along three walls with views of Lake Michigan and Chicago. Their usual American Nouveau cuisine is to die for, but they put together a Russian-inspired menu tonight.

Fresh pale pink and peach roses decorate the space and fairy lights twinkle everywhere.

The five-piece band my mom hired for the event strikes up "Bridal Chorus," and a lump rises in my throat.

Five months ago, marriage wasn't anywhere in my realm of possibilities. I wasn't even interested in having a girlfriend. I was totally dedicated to my mission of controlling everything in Baranov House to keep people safe.

I now realize that's not possible. Shit happens that's out of my control. And when it does, it's not necessarily my fault.

I'm still working on that one, but Lara reminds me of it every time she sees me go into emotional lockdown. Christmas Eve, she asked me to show her the site where Valentina was murdered, and we left roses there. Since then, I felt an unburdening. There was a pressure that was always in my chest that released.

My bride appears in the arched doorway, and my breath stops. Her hair is down in the back, curled into soft waves. A tiara initiates the veil that floats over her dark locks—sheer tulle that floats from her crown to her mid-back.

Her dress is incredible. Strapless and short in the front and tapering down to full length in the back. Her breasts peak out of the top of the crystal and pearled bodice, her waist is snatched, and her legs dazzle with each step she takes. She looks high-fashion and fairytale princess all at once. I didn't think it was possible, but I fall even more for her.

I swear, every day I fall deeper and deeper in love with this woman. Her softness and her strength. Her courage and her vulnerability. Her confidence and her insistence on being my partner—in all aspects of my life. There's no hiding.

I love how I've learned more about myself and grown, through and with her love. I love how she meets me toe to toe. I love the way I can see her micro-emotions, how she doesn't shrink from the myriad of her feelings. How she tries to get me to own mine.

I adore how I can read her body like a delicious map. How she surrenders to me and trusts me. Respects me. How we delight in each other's bodies, riding all the edges of pleasure and pain that I show her. I love how our life together is a great exploration where I can let down my guard sometimes.

She holds soft pink and peach roses in her hands as a bouquet.

The guests all stand to watch her float down the aisle, but her gaze locks on mine. Her love shines in her eyes—her choice is clear. A tiny smile, a knowing smile, plays on her lips. Whatever she sees on my face must confirm what she means to me. And she knows she undoes me.

My wife, my beautiful wife, is marrying me for real this time. She's more than willing.

My bratva uncle Nikolai officiates. I asked him because he's the kind of guy who can hold space. He has a calm, accepting quality that has always made him a favorite of mine. Since it's not a real wedding, it doesn't matter that he's not a pastor or a judge.

"We are gathered today to celebrate the union of two of our own—Benjamin Baranov and Lara Turgeneva," he says. "Like many of you here, I remember each of their births. I remember them playing together as tots. Their mothers laughingly plotting their future marriage. And now, years later, through many twists of fate, those lightly-spoken words have become a reality."

My throat closes.

I can't wait. I reach for Lara, taking the bouquet from her hand and tossing it behind me as I cradle the side of her face and kiss the hell out of her.

The guests erupt into laughter and cheers.

"Oh...okay." Nikolai plays it up, pretending to be taken aback. "Looks like we're skipping ahead. That's fine. That makes sense. You're already legally married. What do you need me for, anyway?"

"Sorry." I break the kiss and rub my lips together. "I'm good now."

Our guests laugh again.

I feel better having touched her. All that emotion building up as she walked down the aisle was too much for my body to hold.

"Okay, great. Let's go on." Nikolai retrieves the bouquet from Leo, who caught it. "For future reference, the bride is supposed to throw the bouquet, not the groom."

More laughter.

I take the flowers back and put them in Lara's hands. Her smile is brilliant. I grin back at her, absorbing the light that shines from her face.

"How about we do a little ring exchange, huh?" Nikolai suggests. "Can you wait for that, or do you need to kiss her again?"

Well, since he asked. I cup her face for another kiss. The bouquet gets crushed between us.

"Flowers!" Lili yelps.

Lara tosses the bouquet over her shoulder, and I hear the guests laugh and cheer some more while I kiss my beautiful bride.

This time when I come away, I feel *much* better.

"Okay, let's do the rings, shall we? Lili, hand that bouquet back. I'm going to rush ahead to see if we can get through this ceremony and get the party started. Or maybe these two are heading straight to their honeymoon—I'm not sure," Nikolai jokes.

It's turned into a comedy show, with everyone primed to laugh at every remark now.

The lightness tonight is markedly different from the serious tones of my entire existence. Of my later childhood.

My college experience. My heart feels like it grew wings to fly.

"Quick, repeat after me, Ben, I *give you this ring as a symbol of my love and commitment today, tomorrow, and forever.*"

More laughter.

I take the ring box from Leo and produce the ring that Lara and I picked out together. It's an emerald-cut morganite stone, framed in little diamonds. "Lara, my partner, my wife, my best friend—I give you this ring as a symbol of my love and commitment today, tomorrow, and forever."

Since we're doing things backwards, she's still wearing the simple band Lili bought for our first wedding, so I slide this engagement-style ring on in front of it.

Lara's eyes get bright with tears, and her lips tremble.

She repeats the line, slipping the band Lili bought for me to wear back on my finger. I felt too attached to it and what it symbolized—the beginning of what has become a beautiful marriage—to want anything different.

"Benjamin and Lara, here before your friends and family in an ancient rite that creates a bond and holds meaning deeper than any law, I now pronounce you husband and wife."

Our guests applaud.

"You may kiss the bride—*again!*"

I kiss Lara for the third time, then pick her up and carry her down the aisle as our guests roar into cheers and the band strikes up a celebratory tune. Our groomsmen and brides-maids dance down the aisle behind us.

Screw dinner—we're ready for the party to begin. And for once, I'm not in charge.

———

Thank you for reading *Prince of Control*! If you loved it, it would mean all the world to me if you left **a review and/or**

posted about it on social media. Your recommendations help indie authors reach new readers and keep marketing costs down.

To get news of the release of **the next Bratva Heirs book** and read a **Bonus Epilogue** of what happened the night Lara and Ben confronted their parents to hear how their marriages began, click here to join Renee's newsletter. If you're already a newsletter subscriber, just click the button at the bottom of any newsletter that takes you to bonus content.

To read Lucy and Ravil's story, check out *The Director*.

To read Kat and Adrian's story, check out *The Cleaner*.

WANT FREE RENEE ROSE BOOKS?

Go to http://subscribepage.com/alphastemp to sign up for Renee Rose's newsletter and receive a free copy of *Alpha's Temptation*, *Theirs to Protect*, *Owned by the Marine*, *Theirs to Punish*, *The Alpha's Punishment*, *Disobedience at the Dressmaker's* and *Her Billionaire Boss*. In addition to the free stories, you will also get bonus epilogues, special pricing, exclusive previews and news of new releases.

OTHER TITLES BY RENEE ROSE

Contemporary

Bratva Heirs

Prince of Control

Chicago Bratva

"Prelude" in Black Light: Roulette War

The Director

The Fixer

"Owned" in Black Light: Roulette Rematch

The Enforcer

The Soldier

The Hacker

The Bookie

The Cleaner

The Player

The Gatekeeper

Yacht Kings

Revenge

Chicago Sin

Den of Sins

Rooted in Sin

Taste of Sin

Made Men Series

Don't Tease Me

Don't Tempt Me

Don't Make Me

Alpha Mountain

Hero

Rebel

Warrior

Vegas Underground Mafia Romance

King of Diamonds

Mafia Daddy

Jack of Spades

Ace of Hearts

Joker's Wild

His Queen of Clubs

Dead Man's Hand

Wild Card

Master Me Series

Her Royal Master

Yes, Doctor

Her Russian Master

Her Marine Master

Her Fire Master

Her Hollywood Master

Her Stepbrother Master

Double Doms Series

Theirs to Punish

Theirs to Protect

Holiday Feel-Good

Scoring with Santa

Saved

Other Contemporary

Black Light: Valentine Roulette

Black Light: Roulette Redux

Black Light: Celebrity Roulette

Black Light: Roulette War

Black Light: Roulette Rematch

Punishing Portia (written as Darling Adams)

The Professor's Girl

Safe in his Arms

Paranormal

Wolf Ridge High Series

Alpha Bully

Alpha Knight

Step Alpha

Alpha King

Alpha Varsity

Bad Boy Alphas Series

Alpha's Temptation

Alpha's Danger

Alpha's Prize

Alpha's Challenge

Alpha's Obsession

Alpha's Desire

Alpha's War

Alpha's Mission

Alpha's Bane

Alpha's Secret

Alpha's Prey

Alpha's Sun

Shifter Ops

Alpha's Moon

Alpha's Vow

Alpha's Revenge

Alpha's Fire

Alpha's Rescue

Alpha's Command

Werewolves of Wall Street

Big Bad Boss: Midnight

Big Bad Boss: Moon Mad

Big Bad Boss: Marked

Big Bad Boss: Mated

Big Bad Bully

Alpha Doms Series

The Alpha's Hunger

The Alpha's Punishment

The Alpha's Promise

The Alpha's Protection

Two Marks Series

Untamed

Tempted

Desired

Enticed

Wolf Ranch Series

Rough

Wild

Feral

Savage

Fierce

Ruthless

Primal

Rugged

Ravenous

Sci-Fi

Zandian Masters Series

His Human Slave

His Human Prisoner

Training His Human

His Human Rebel

His Human Vessel

His Mate and Master

Zandian Pet

Their Zandian Mate

His Human Possession

Zandian Brides

Night of the Zandians

Bought by the Zandians

Mastered by the Zandians

ABOUT RENEE ROSE

USA TODAY BESTSELLING AUTHOR RENEE ROSE loves a dominant, dirty-talking alpha hero! She's sold over two million copies of steamy romance with varying levels of kink. Her books have been featured in USA Today's *Happily Ever After* and *Popsugar*. Named Eroticon USA's Next Top Erotic Author in 2013, she has also won *Spunky and Sassy's* Favorite Sci-Fi and Anthology author, *The Romance Reviews* Best Historical Romance, and *has* hit the *USA Today* list sixteen times with her Chicago Bratva, Bad Boy Alpha and Wolf Ranch series, as well as various anthologies.

Renee loves to connect with readers!
www.reneeroseromance.com
renee@reneeroseromance.com

facebook.com/reneeroseromance

instagram.com/reneeroseromance

amazon.com/Renee-Rose/e/Boo8ASoFTo

bookbub.com/authors/renee-rose

tiktok.com/@reneeroseromance